MW00938281

KING'S
MAN

Book 2 of *The Order of the White Boar*

Praise for Book 1

'A wonderful work of historical fiction . . . altogether a very
enjoyable book for both children and adults.'
Isabel Green, *Ricardian Bulletin* of the Richard III Society

'This engaging and exciting story has the power to captivate
readers of any age . . . extremely well researched and a
pleasure to read.'
Wendy Johnson, member of the Looking for Richard Project

'A really gripping historical novel . . . well written, vivid and
absorbing.'
E. Flanagan, author of *Eden Summer*

'Finally! A book written for a younger audience, which
brings to life the just and fair leader that Richard III truly
was.'
Richard III Loyal Supporters

Also by Alex Marchant

The Order of the White Boar

The
KING'S
MAN

Book 2 of *The Order of the White Boar*

Alex Marchant

First published 2018

ISBN-13: 978-1717276193
ISBN-10: 1717276199

Cover illustration: Oliver Bennett, morevisual.me

To

the families of the Hillsborough 96,
who know what it's like to have had history
rewritten in the present day…

and

to my friends of long centuries past,
Angela and Kate –
they know why

Contents

Cast of characters

The Order of the White Boar
Matthew Wansford, a page
Alys Langdown, ward of Queen Elizabeth
Roger de Kynton, a page
Edward, son of Richard, Duke of Gloucester*
Elen, companion to Alys

On the road to London
Edward V, King of England*
Richard, Duke of Gloucester, uncle to King Edward V, brother
	to King Edward IV, Protector of England*
Henry, Duke of Buckingham, a cousin, husband to Queen
	Elizabeth's sister *
Anthony Woodville, Earl Rivers, uncle to King Edward V, a
	brother to Queen Elizabeth*
Richard, Lord Grey, older half-brother to Edward V, Queen
Elizabeth's younger son by her first husband*
Francis, Lord Lovell, Duke Richard's friend and companion*
Sir Richard Ratcliffe, Duke Richard's companion*
Master John Kendall, Duke Richard's secretary*

At court
Anne, Duchess of Gloucester, wife to Duke Richard*
Elizabeth Woodville, Queen to late King Edward IV (later Dame
	Grey)*
Elizabeth, her daughter, elder sister to Edward V*
Richard, Duke of York, her son, younger brother to Edward V*
Marquess of Dorset, oldest half-brother to Edward V, Queen
	Elizabeth's elder son by her first husband*
Sir Edward Woodville, a brother to Queen Elizabeth*
John Howard, Duke of Norfolk*
Margaret, Duchess of Norfolk, his wife*
Lord William Hastings, King Edward IV's friend and
	Chamberlain of England*
Margaret Beaufort, Lady Stanley, mother to Henry Tudor*
Thomas, Lord Stanley, her third husband*
Sir William Stanley, his brother*
Lady Alice Tyrell, wife to Sir James*

Walter, Lord Soulsby, a knight
Ralph Soulsby, his son, betrothed to Alys Langdown
Hugh Soulsby, nephew to Lord Soulsby, a squire

In London
Master Ashley, a merchant
Mistress Ashley, his wife
Master Lyndsey, his steward
Master Hardyng, his secretary
Master de Vries, his print master
Simon, his apprentice
Friar Shaw (or Shaa), a preacher*

At Middleham Castle
Sir James Tyrell, Master of the Henchmen*
Doctor Frees, tutor to Edward and the pages
Master Fleete, the weapons master
Master Petyt, the dancing master
Master Reynold, the horsemaster
Master Gygges, the chief huntsman

In York
John Wansford, a merchant
John Wansford, his son
Frederick Wansford, his son*

Known to history...
Henry Percy, Earl of Northumberland*
John de la Pole, Earl of Lincoln, nephew to Duke Richard*
Henry Tudor, 'Earl of Richmond', Lancastrian claimant to the
        throne*
Lord Strange, son to Thomas, Lord Stanley*
Sir Robert Brackenbury, Constable of the Tower*

In the past...
Edward IV, late King of England*
Richard, Duke of York, father of Edward IV*
George, Duke of Clarence, brother to Edward IV*
Richard, Earl of Warwick, cousin to Edward IV, known as the
        Kingmaker*

* Historical figures

The Code of the Order of the White Boar

a b c d e f g h l j k l m n o p q r s t u v w x y z
u v w x y z a b c d e f g h l j k l m n o p q r s t Monday
r s t u v w x y z a b c d e f g h l j k l m n o p q Tuesday
o p q r s t u v w x y z a b c d e f g h l j k l m n Wednesday
l m n o p q r s t u v w x y z a b c d e f g h l j k Thursday
i j k l m n o p q r s t u v w x y z a b c d e f g h Friday
f g h l j k l m n o p q r s t u v w x y z a b c d e Saturday
c d e f g h l j k l m n o p q r s t u v w x y z a b Sunday

Where coded items in the text are marked with an asterisk (*), a translation can be found at the end of the book, after 'About the author'.

1

Broken Rendezvous

The first warning of their approach was the faintest rumble as of distant thunder on a summer's day. The sun shone still, though low in the sky, throwing long shadows across the cobbles of the square. Its last rays touched the tip of the ancient stone market cross to gold.

As the noise reached us, my master raised his head, turning it first one way then another, like a boar at bay hearing the winding of a huntsman's horn. At a word, his companions melted away behind, leaving him standing alone at the very edge of the inn yard. Clad simply in riding gear of deepest mourning, his slight figure moved not a muscle as we waited.

The far-off grumble grew into drumming, then on into hammering – the hubbub funnelling through the narrow street opposite, cannoning off the buildings crouching to either side. I could tell now it was the sound of hooves, of many dozens of horses, galloping along the highroad that cut through this town.

Deep within my chest, my heart beat harder, in echo of those thudding hooves. My breath was racing too. My hands, clammier by the second, gripped my hound's collar and I whispered to her to stay close. Surely even her sharp ears could not hear me above the rising tide of sound, but she lifted her shaggy red head as my grasp tightened, her deep brown eyes gazing imploringly up at me.

No other movement broke the stillness about us, save the flap, flap of my master's dark red and blue banner as it caught the wind, the shining white boar upon it rearing as though brought to life by the sparking tension in the air. The Duke and his gentlemen remained motionless, though each of his companions, I now saw, clasped the hilt of his still-sheathed sword.

The ground underfoot quivered at the coming squall. Murrey's ears pricked, her nose trembled, and perhaps only a minute after its first herald, the storm surge burst from the mouth of the main street out on to the wide market square.

I flinched at the shock of its arrival, but my master, feet firmly planted, did not stir as the company of horsemen flooded towards him across the cobbles. Two or three score, heavily armed, mail glinting, hooves thundering, scarlet and white standard streaming on high in the sharpening breeze. Galloping as though all the devils of hell were at their heels, heedless of the townsfolk who scattered out of their path, clutching at their children and possessions to keep them from harm.

The leading horses checked their headlong rush and clattered to a halt only feet in front of the Duke, blowing hard, their flanks heaving under their costly trappings. The fair-haired man on the foremost stared down for a moment after he reined back his mount, his blue eyes expressionless, before touching the end of his whip to his forehead in salute.

'Greetings, Your Grace,' he began, his breathing rapid after his swift approach. 'I beg you to forgive our late arrival. The King has gone on before to Stony Stratford, and will sleep there tonight. He bid me return to greet you most cordially and await your pleasure.'

This man who spoke so courteously to my master Duke Richard was unknown to me. But a murmur of recognition had rippled through our company as he and his party had swept across the square. Beside me, Master Kendall, the Duke's secretary, breathed the newcomer's name, incredulous.

'Earl Rivers! And he dare show his face here without the King?'

The Earl swung down from his fine-boned mount with the ease of a much younger man, and I recalled that this brother of the Queen was spoken of as once the finest jouster in the land. He bowed now to the Duke, a memory of his sister in his elegant features and light-coloured hair. It was perhaps no more than two months since I had come face to face with Her Grace – yet it seemed a lifetime ago. All was different now.

Duke Richard received the Earl with equal courtesy. But did I detect in his next words a trace of the anger that had surfaced only minutes before, when we had ridden at a leisurely pace through the streets of this evening-quiet town – and found no rendezvous with the new King and his escort as arranged?

'To Stony Stratford? Why so? We were to meet with him here in Northampton.'

The Earl's response was smooth, as though well rehearsed.

'So you and I had agreed, Your Grace. But it was in our nephew Edward's mind that there would not be lodgings enough here for all his men and Your Grace's. Therefore he thought it best to move his retinue on to make way for yours. Our manor at Stony Stratford is well provisioned for a large party, and he rests there now with his brother, Lord Grey, and other companions.'

A hiss issued through Master Kendall's teeth at this speech, heard only by those of us nearby. Several paces ahead of us, Duke Richard's expression did not change.

'It is late now for you to rejoin him tonight, my lord. Will you and your gentlemen take lodgings here in the town and dine with us at our inn?'

The Earl bowed once more, and soon grooms and serving men were scurrying this way and that, leading horses and carrying baggage, until only the two noblemen and their closest companions remained beneath the swinging tavern sign. The Duke stood aside with grave civility to allow the Earl to enter first. I brought up the rear, behind Lord Lovell, Master Ratcliffe and the other gentlemen, sticking close to Master Kendall, as had been my habit over recent days.

Since news of the death of old King Edward had reached us, I had dined at his brother Duke Richard's table often in such inns, on our journey south from Middleham to meet and escort the new King to his coronation in London. Now, though, I found a stool in a corner and my hound pup, Murrey, threaded her lithe body between its stubby legs before settling down, her pointed muzzle resting on her outstretched forepaws. From there I watched the tavernmaster and his womenfolk bustling about setting places with their best pewter and platters, and listened while the gentlemen exchanged pleasantries and seated themselves at the richly furnished oak table.

This evening I knew my place, knew that the talk around the high table would not be of a kind for mere boys like me to join in. Yet, as Duke Richard and the Earl raised a toast to the new King in the innkeeper's best wine, I was reminded that young King Edward himself was but a boy, a younger one even than I – and a boy I had once had the pleasure of riding alongside for a whole afternoon last Christmas-tide.

I cannot deny the pang of disappointment that had struck me on finding he was not in the town when we arrived. Had I been wrong to hope we could take up our friendship again as we had left it on Twelfth Night? Yet so much had changed since then. I had been dismissed from my knight's training at Middleham Castle and had to leave behind my friends, Alys, Roger, Elen, and of course, little Ed, the Duke's son. And he – he had lost his father, the old King. Perhaps that day of the ride had been their last together. And now he was about to take on the heavy burden of kingship.

The solemn oath that I had sworn at York Minster came back to me now. Reunited with my old comrades in the choir of that great cathedral of my home city – almost a year after my shameful expulsion – we had sung the requiem Mass for the dead King. The last notes of my solo rose into the heights of that holy space as though accompanying his soul to heaven.

Then the most important men of the city and country of York had knelt as one behind his brother, Duke Richard of Gloucester. Following his lead, all there swore fealty to the new King – the Duke's nephew, Edward, the fifth of that name. The raw emotion of their massed voices, resonant with loyal intent, dashed against me like a storm-wave as I stood near the altar, swamping the sound of my own words. And I had been, oh, so proud of my countrymen.

Another grey morning farewell, to my family and the other townsfolk, then we were journeying again, three hundred strong now with the men who had joined us from my home town.

Always southwards we travelled. To Pontefract's castle with its soaring tower, to Nottingham's crouching on its crag above the River Trent.

Hourly we were met by messengers from every corner of the realm. From Earl Rivers travelling with the new King towards London from his estates in the west. From the Earl of Northumberland with his vow to hold the northern marches. From Henry, Duke of Buckingham, journeying out of Wales to join us. And from Lord Hastings – from Lord Hastings in London, always with a warning.

For in the capital events were moving fast, events I didn't understand. But from the little I heard, and the dark shadows gathering on Duke Richard's face, it was clear the news was not good.

Queen Elizabeth's family, the Woodvilles, were gaining strength, becoming bolder in their claims to take the reins of power now that her husband was dead. And the old King's chamberlain and adviser, Lord Hastings – never the Queen's friend – feared for his position, and perhaps even for his life. The failure of our rendezvous with the young King and the Earl would hardly soothe those fears.

Yet here in this small midlands town, the company of gentlemen passed a pleasant meal. The tavernkeeper himself was busy about them, serving with his own hands the tastiest dishes his kitchen could provide. As the evening wore on, and more wine was poured and more toasts drunk, chatter and laughter spilled from the gentlemen. Duke Richard, however, barely even smiled. Between the toasts, he did not touch his wine, and from my vantage point, I watched him watching the Earl. His lordship's face was soon flushed in the heat of the room, but he also drank little.

No more than an hour after we sat down to our supper, another tumult of horses' hooves and jangling harness and men's voices erupted outside the shuttered windows. A serving man rushed in, bowing, to announce, 'His Grace, the Duke of Buckingham.'

Duke Richard and Earl Rivers were already on their feet as the burly, haughty man I had first encountered on Twelfth Night made his entrance, flanked by several companions, each as weary and mud-flecked as the other.

Duke Richard stepped forward to clasp the newcomer's hand.

'Welcome, Harry,' he said in greeting.

The warmth in his voice surprised me. There had seemed little liking between the two men at his brother's court at Yuletide. But then I remembered young Edward's words to me about his aunt's husband on that winter afternoon: 'I don't think my mother likes him very much.'

Had Duke Richard found an ally against the Queen and her family in these difficult times? One might be needed, if all that Lord Hastings reported was true. Indeed a certain coolness marked the embrace of the Earl and the new arrival, but my lord Buckingham readily joined the party. The inn servants brought in extra chairs and lighted candles, while the innkeeper was tasked with finding ever more plates of delicious food.

Despite the clamour of so many men, soon my head was nodding in the cramped, warm, smoky tavern room and I was wishing for my bed. Murrey had long ago curled up fast asleep beside my feet. Lord Rivers had perhaps also had a long day – how many extra miles had he ridden to Stony Stratford and back? – for less than an hour after the newcomers' arrival, he took his leave to retire. He bid farewell to his host and departed with his companions into the gathering dark.

The two royal Dukes seated themselves again, either side of the long table, and my lord Buckingham waved the tavernkeeper across to splash more wine in their cups. When the man left the room to replenish the jugs, Duke Henry quaffed another mouthful, slammed his cup down, making the candle on the table beside it jump, then asked abruptly,

'What news from London?'

'The same,' said Duke Richard. His voice was quiet, but with a little effort, blinking the sleep away, I could hear well enough. 'Hastings tells me the old Royal Council has reassembled and take decisions under the watchful eye of the Marquess of Dorset.'

'The old Council? That Woodville clique?'

Duke Richard nodded, but said nothing. Duke Henry blustered on, like the guttering flame of the candle by his fist.

'They have no right. Surely Hastings knows that – he should stand against it. No matter that Dorset is also the Queen's son. Only the new King can appoint his Council. And while he is here, with us —'

'I'm afraid the King is not here.'

'Not here?' exploded Buckingham. 'Then where?'

'He rode on with his escort to Stony Stratford this afternoon – fourteen miles hence.'

'Then they intend for him to reach London before us. To crown him before you arrive.' His fist clenched tighter on his cup. 'Why then is Rivers here?'

'To assure me all is well. But also to delay me, I imagine. He gave some poor excuse about too few lodgings here for both parties. How many ride with you?'

Buckingham snorted.

'Three hundred, no more, as you specified. Would now that I had brought four times as many.'

'We are here to escort the King, not as an invading army.'

'Yet Rivers brings two thousand? Hastings told me of it in his letter. That is not a simple escort.'

'He has no more than fifty with him tonight. The rest – if there are so many – are with Richard Grey and the King.'

'Stony Stratford is a Woodville manor. They will have ready access to even more men there. And assuredly there will be ambushes set. The road onwards will not be a safe one to ride in the morning.'

Duke Richard was silent for a moment.

'I doubt they will go so far. Rivers —'

'Is not the leader in this,' cut in Buckingham, his bulky frame leaning forwards over the platters of fruit and cheese still on the table. 'Dorset and the Queen – they sit in Westminster like a spider in her web. They will be directing all from there. And if the Duke of Gloucester suffers an accident in his haste to meet his King – who will question it, once they have the boy crowned and in their power?'

Lord Lovell, by Duke Richard's elbow, spoke softly.

'Lord Rivers showed some surprise when my lord of Buckingham appeared.'

Duke Henry threw a sharp glance at him.

'Maybe he was too focused on your progress to think much on mine. One advantage to so small a party – we were able to press on at speed to join you.'

'But now you are here, and they see our intent to do my brother's bidding with the will of Parliament, they will not obstruct us.'

At Duke Richard's words, Buckingham's features twisted into a scowl, thrown into flickering relief by the light of the many candles.

'With their prize so close to hand? A day's ride, maybe two, and the new King – crowned – is theirs to control. They will not stay their hands now. Do not be naïve, cousin.'

Duke Richard's face and voice remained calm.

'I well know how the Woodvilles scheme. I have no need of your warning. Parliament and the people of London will not allow such manoeuvres. Their loyalty to my brother was steadfast. And if his will is well known...'

Buckingham drank deeply, then placed his cup down on the table, with care this time, and gazed across at Duke Richard. His next words seemed chosen in a more deliberate fashion.

'And if the rumour I hear is true?'

'What rumour?'

'That your brother's death was – suspicious. That maybe – and, as I say, it is only a rumour – that maybe he was... poisoned.'

'Poisoned?

'They say it has become all the rage at the Italian courts.'

Without a second's hesitation, Duke Richard shook his head.

'Nay, cousin, rumours are dangerous beasts and should not be believed lightly. Hastings' messenger said apoplexy.'

Buckingham sat back again, revolving his wine-cup slowly with the fingers of one hand, while watching his fellow Duke.

'Apoplexy can take many forms, so too can poisoning. But how often does a man recover from apoplexy, only to die of it a week later.'

'Hastings did not report that.'

'They say the King fell ill, then rallied. But after several days, and an evening spent in the bosom of his wife's family... The first illness was a failed attempt – seven days later came success.'

A moment of quiet. The gentlemen from Yorkshire exchanged glances, the candlelight catching their eyes.

When Duke Richard remained silent, my lord of Buckingham ploughed on.

'It is perhaps no coincidence that Dorset was made Deputy Constable of the Tower only weeks before. In preparation for seizing power – and the royal treasure. They say Edward Woodville has shipped half of the treasury away to his fleet in the Channel.'

'I have heard that about my brother's treasure also, and perhaps it is true. But I cannot believe the Queen capable of such a crime as murder. She loved my brother... at least, once she did.'

'Yet now her charms have faded. You saw for yourself at Yuletide. Mistress Shore and others had become favourites. And they say Hastings himself has had a part to play in that. Elizabeth's hold over Edward was perhaps broken and her family feared their grip on power ending. When so threatened, it takes little to drive a pack of dogs to turn on the hand that feeds them.'

'But not to kill a king. That is a crime beyond all others. No, even the Woodvilles, for all their scheming, could not turn to that.'

'Careful, cousin.' One forefinger lifted from Duke Henry's grip on his cup, as though in warning. 'Do not forget the fate that has befallen other Protectors at the hands of kings' families. Think of Humphrey of Lancaster – he also a Duke of Gloucester.'

'Those were different days. Times have changed, I thank the Lord.'

'And yet you fear for the lives of your wife and child.'

All this time, sleepily watching the faces of both Dukes in the fluttering of candlelight, I had not taken in the full import of their words. But now I learned – what? That the old King had perhaps been murdered – and that the same fate could befall my little friend Ed and his mother.

The very idea shook me awake. Until that moment I had not grasped how serious the situation was.

Duke Richard's expression did not change, however.

'They will be safe at home in Middleham.'

'And you are willing to stake their lives on that?'

'The Woodvilles can't touch them there.'

'Perhaps not. But we must do our job here well to make sure they remain safe.'

'Not just for them, cousin. For my brother's son and his kingdom.'

'Aye, for the kingdom too,' growled Duke Henry, draining the last of his wine before placing his cup back on the table with deliberation. 'Though, the Lord knows, sometimes I wonder whether it deserves such care.'

Duke Richard rose. All the gentlemen stood with him, my lord of Buckingham last of all, pushing himself up with his ham-like hands flat upon the table. Dog-tired though I was, I had dragged myself to my feet with the rest of the company.

'The care of the kingdom is a sacred trust, cousin. And we neglect it at our peril.' My master's words had a firm finality about them, despite his quiet tones. 'But now is the time for rest. We shall be ready to leave at daybreak.'

My lord Buckingham said quickly, 'And you will send outriders before – to check for ambushes?'

Duke Richard's fingers played with his red-stoned signet ring in that habit I now knew so well, but he didn't speak. After a moment, Buckingham said,

'And Rivers?'

'I will sleep on it.'

'You must deal with him.'

'I said, I will sleep on it.'

'If he manages to get a message to Dorset and the Queen —'

'To say what?'

'That...' Buckingham hesitated, uncertain.

'That I am performing my role as Protector? Perhaps it's a message I would wish them to receive. If the Queen is loyal to my brother's memory, she will act correctly. If not...'

'We will know what action to take.'

'Indeed I will know.'

I caught the slight stress that the Duke laid upon the word 'I', and glancing at my lord Buckingham could tell he had too. His eyes narrowed, but he fought to keep a scowl from darkening his face.

'Then I bid you goodnight, cousin. May the morning bring less trouble than I foresee.'

Duke Richard bowed his head and his fellow Duke swept out of the room past the grovelling innkeeper, his companions close behind.

The sound of their many feet retreated along the street towards the lodgings that had been found for them and I discovered that I had been holding my breath. As I released it, a sigh whispered around the room as though the gentlemen remaining there had done the same.

Lord Lovell was the first to speak.

'He's right, Richard. You should beware Rivers.'

The Duke dropped back into his seat. Taking up his goblet, he at last downed a great draught.

'I'm sure that is wise counsel, Francis. But now I am too weary to think on it. All this talk of murder...'

He swallowed another gulp, then his eyes slid towards me at the moment I was ambushed by a yawn. The ghost of a smile flitted across his face.

'And I see I am not the only one. We must all to bed. It will be an early start, and a long ride to London with our King. I wish you all a good rest, gentlemen.'

He stood and, as his companions stepped back to allow him passage to the stairs, he said quietly aside to Lord Lovell,

'Join me, Francis, we must talk.'

I bowed low as he passed, then scooping up the sleeping Murrey, followed up the steps, a pace behind Lord Lovell. My palliasse had been laid across the Duke's threshold by an inn servant, ready for me to do my page's duty and sleep on guard outside his door. Stepping over it, Duke Richard turned back and placed a hand on my shoulder.

'I have no need of you tonight, Matt. Take as much rest as you can. I saw you fighting sleep – and we'll likely have a long day of it tomorrow.'

I was grateful for his permission to lie down and arrange my blanket. Lord Lovell stifled a laugh as his long legs strode across me, but I was too exhausted to care whether I was the cause. With Murrey a comforting weight upon my chest, my eyelids drooped and I drifted towards sleep. What seemed only a minute or two later there came a muffled apology from his lordship as, stepping back over me, his boot grazed my arm, but then, sinking down, down, into deep, warm darkness, I knew nothing more...

2

Ambush

Until... until... something hard and pointed prodding my ribs. A greyish glimmer from somewhere. The murmur of men and animals at a distance – no, nearer now, just beyond the walls. A whimper from Murrey as I moved. A quiet voice.

'Matt, you've slept long. It is time to rise. Get what food you may before we ride.'

I struggled to my feet, rubbing my eyes.

'But Your Grace, I must help you dress.'

Duke Richard laughed.

'No need, boy, as you see.'

I did indeed. Even the dim half-light could not disguise that he already wore his sober black riding clothes. On his feet were the boots that had nudged me awake, and in one hand a sheaf of papers. Even his sword belt was already buckled on.

'While you lay dreaming, I have already performed half a day's work. Now up with you and run downstairs – you'll find the tavern long awake.'

Ashamed, I gathered my things together and slunk downstairs after him, Murrey stealing along behind. How had I overslept? How had the Duke risen without waking me? What if his enemies had come to attack him during the night?

In the large room below sat Masters Kendall and Ratcliffe among several other gentlemen, all breakfasting already amid a murmur of conversation. Their faces serious, they stood to greet the Duke, who seated himself in their midst and bid them continue their meal.

I found a spare stool at a table alongside Master Kendall, not far from the cheering warmth of the banked fire. The innkeeper's daughter bustled up with a plate of bread and cheese and a cup of ale.

'There you go, sir. Better late than never.'

Was that a wink as she set them before me?

In the pre-dawn flickering of embers and candles I could not be sure – except of the sudden glow of my cheeks. But, taking no notice, the girl turned away to stir up the fire.

As I sat there chewing and dropping morsels down to Murrey, a great clamour of hooves arose in the street outside. As one, the gentlemen jumped up, clapping hands to sword hilts, before Lord Lovell and several others burst through the doorway, their riding gear freshly bespattered with mud and dust.

The Duke sat still at his table as Lord Lovell strode forward. The men nearby made way for the newcomers, resheathing their part-drawn weapons, some seating themselves again, all remaining watchful.

'Well, Francis?'

'We found more after I sent word to you, Richard. No livery again, but undoubtedly Woodville men. We...' he paused, his eyes scanning the gathered faces, 'We questioned the leaders of each band. They all admitted their purpose was to stop you reaching Stony Stratford – by any means. Though none would name who gave their orders.'

Duke Richard rose to his feet. The candlelight played across a strange expression on his face. Sadness I could see. Perhaps also apprehension, determination?

'Thank you, Francis. Sadly it seems my lord of Buckingham was correct – at least in one way. We cannot be sure who is behind these attempted ambushes, but we cannot afford to take any chances. Arrest my lord Rivers!'

The Duke's words were spoken almost in an undertone, but they rang in my ears like a clarion.

Lord Lovell and his men left the inn in an instant, followed by others, until only Duke Richard and a handful of gentlemen remained. To one of these, the Duke turned.

'Go raise my lord of Buckingham, and tell him what has occurred – if he is not already aware. We will leave for Stony Stratford by sun-up.'

To Master Kendall he passed the papers that had lain untouched on the table since we had come down.

'They are signed and sealed, John. See that they are sent. Now that the road towards London is clear, let the messenger also give word to Lord Hastings that we meet with the King this morning.'

Master Kendall nodded and hurried out, but I waited, quiet in the corner, watching.

The Duke stood for a few seconds in complete stillness, no expression now on his face. His eyes were fixed on the fire flaring again on the hearth and one hand rested on the pommel of his sword. I was reminded of when the message had come that his elder brother, the King, was dead – the utter quiet of that moment, the tension in his lean frame, like a bow-string before release. Then he reached out for his cup of ale and drained it, and all was in motion again.

'Come, gentlemen. We must be on our way.'

Outside the inn all the horses – including my pony, Bess – were waiting in the morning twilight, ready saddled by the inn servants. Gathering also from the surrounding dusky streets were the men who had ridden with us from York. The innkeeper himself was directing matters and as we emerged, came over to hold the bridle of the Duke's pale grey stallion, Storm, while his most illustrious guest mounted. He bowed deeply at the Duke's words of thanks for his hospitality and in a few moments the party was on its way.

The hooves rang loud at this early hour, the echoes bouncing off the buildings overhanging the road. Local people who were already up and about their business ducked into the shadows or dragged their beasts or wagons to the side to let us pass.

The Earl's inn was at no great distance. As we approached, rosy-tinged clouds could be seen above the grey road stretching off to the east.

Several dozen horsemen surrounded the inn, silent but for the occasional stamp of a hoof or jingle of bit or buckle. The nearest riders parted to allow the foremost members of the Duke's party through. I urged Bess forwards to ensure I was among them. As we entered the circle, a commotion exploded through the doorway opening on to the inn yard.

Voices raised in anger, a sharp rebuke, scuffling, and men spilling out on to the cobbles. Earl Rivers and Lord Lovell walked calmly side by side, but beyond them, a number of the Earl's companions struggled and cursed in the firm hold of Lord Lovell's men. Their sword belts had been taken from them, carried now by squires in the rear, but the Earl's was still strapped to his waist, the hilt of his weapon gleaming in the mellow early light. His face in shadow, Lord Rivers turned his head to view the ring of silent horsemen.

Duke Richard had reined Storm to a halt just within the encirclement, forcing the Earl to step across the muddy courtyard to reach him. To my surprise, the Duke did not offer him the courtesy of dismounting as he approached, but gazed down at him unspeaking. His face was unreadable, though I sat astride Bess only three or four horses away.

Lord Rivers bowed.

'Your Grace. To what do I owe this early awakening?'

His lordship's manner was calm, but his voice was strained, and made me long to clear my throat. But now that his gentlemen's curses had ceased, the yard was hushed and I dared not.

The Duke lengthened the silence before he spoke.

'Lord Rivers, it has come to our attention that the road towards Stony Stratford is not safe. Bands of men have been waiting to waylay unwary travellers, particularly it seems those who seek to join the King. They admit no allegiance, but they are well drilled and well equipped. I can afford to take no chances on who may have given them their orders. Therefore I require that you and your men remain here for the time being.'

'Lord Lovell informed me I was under arrest.'

The Duke paused again, as though weighing every word.

'I regret using the word, but I must ask you to stay within your lodgings and to send no messages.'

Earl Rivers moved as though to speak again, but he was interrupted by a cacophony of hooves approaching along the narrow main street. A large company of riders cantered around the final bend, then slowed to a walk, only a few of its leaders advancing through the encirclement of the inn.

At their head was my lord of Buckingham. He hauled back on the reins of his enormous jet-black charger as it drew alongside Storm, wrenching its neck into a tight arch and causing it to toss its head against the pain. The first rays of the sun breaking through the clouds on the horizon lit up the sneer upon his face. He also did not dismount, throwing a glance down at the Earl standing before him. Then, with no word of greeting, he turned to Duke Richard.

'Now do you see the truth of what I said last night? Never trust a Woodville.'

Duke Richard's face was impassive.

'I hope you are well rested after yesterday's journey, Harry. As to events overnight, we have no proof of who is responsible. I have requested my Lord Rivers keep to his inn while we ride on to the King.'

'Keep to his inn? Surely it would be best to slap him in chains and drag him to Westminster in a wagon!'

There was now light enough on Lord Rivers' upturned face to show upon it only scorn for the younger man above him. But he remained silent while Duke Richard replied.

'There is no need of that, cousin. If you wish, you may leave a detachment of men here to ensure he keeps his word. For myself, I am in haste to meet my nephew with his escort. I want no more misunderstandings about what is to happen over the coming days.' Now, directing his words more to Lord Rivers, he continued, 'My brother made me Protector of his realm and I intend to fulfil that trust to the best of my ability, come what may.'

Earl Rivers bowed his head and drew back. After leaning down to speak to Lord Lovell, who passed instructions to his own men before hurrying to mount his horse, the Duke turned Storm back towards the road. He raised his voice to ensure that all gathered there could hear.

'And now it is time to be off to Stony Stratford. We must reach the King before he departs.'

And as we all spurred our horses on, the Duke of Buckingham's words from last night came into my mind – about young Edward being soon crowned and in the Woodvilles' power.

3

Stony Stratford

The speed of our progress afforded little chance to enjoy the countryside through which we passed on this fine spring morning. The rolling fields with their bright green shoots and orchards full of apple and pear blossom caressed by the rosy fingers of the early sun were very different from what we had left behind in the north.

Spring had seemed to be racing ahead of us as we rode down from Middleham. Here the hawthorn was already in full flower although it was not yet May. We had left tiny lambs sheltering from the biting wind behind high stone walls, watching their mothers grazing the sparse late winter grass, while here boys and their dogs stood guard over flocks of sheep almost half-grown. All raised their heads at the thunder of so many hooves upon the ancient roadway, wondering perhaps at the fluttering standards of the two Dukes, the glinting harness, the whipping of horses into a lather, and the need for such a cavalcade. Yesterday, had they gazed at the passing of the King, then the later return of Earl Rivers, with similar curiosity?

Stony Stratford, as we entered, appeared no more than a village, its main buildings strung out along the road towards distant London. Glancing around, I understood why Duke Richard had disbelieved the Earl's reason for moving the King's retinue from far-larger Northampton to this place. Men at arms were streaming in from every direction, having no doubt been forced to find what billets they could in the surrounding countryside. Seeing our banners and our hurry, they made way before our party, saluting the two Dukes at its head. Before long we had clattered out of the village and were crossing open pastureland towards an imposing stone manor house, set among barns, fishponds and pleasure grounds. In fields beyond, men were busy collapsing myriad tents, pitched perhaps overnight to house more of the King's numerous escort.

Our swift approach caused a flurry among the scores of men and riders already assembled on the manor's wide cobbled courtyard. Cries of alarm, startled horses dancing around their handlers. One, a gleaming chestnut bearing a rich red saddlecloth, tore its lead rein from the groom's hands and would have dashed away. But Lord Lovell kicked his horse forward and stretched out a hand to grasp its silver-buckled bridle as he had for Alys all those months ago in Middleham. He led it back to where the rest of us had slowed to a halt, just as the huge oaken door of the manor house was flung open.

Through the doorway lunged four or five young men in bright travelling clothes of blue, green, russet, their long cloaks swinging about their striding legs. The face of the leader blanched as he caught sight of us, and his hand flew to draw his sword, which flashed in the sunlight as he brandished it. His fellows likewise unsheathed their weapons and stood with him amidst the general melee, a tight knot of dazzling steel before the manor's threshold.

Duke Richard's nearest companions closed ranks in front of him and the Duke of Buckingham, their mounts' hindquarters bunching together protectively before anyone else could react. I could barely glimpse their adversaries through the thicket of their upraised blades.

But Duke Richard was quick too. Just as I spied another person in the shadows of the doorway, so it seemed did he, for he cried out,

'Put up your swords, gentlemen, in the presence of your King.'

His men instantly obeyed, lowering their weapons, but those about the boy King hesitated, until he himself stepped forward and placed a hand on the shoulder of the man in russet.

'Brother, see, it is my uncle Gloucester. Our uncle Rivers said he was riding to join us. Remember?'

This speech told me that the russet-clad man grasping the costly, jewel-hilted sword was the King's younger half-brother, Richard, Lord Grey. He was still reluctant to obey, and his fellows glanced at him for guidance, their razor-sharp blades poised to strike at a word.

In their moment of indecision, Duke Richard swung down from Storm and slipped through the defensive shield of horses to stand alone before them. As Lord Grey and his men stared at him amazed, their swords still raised, he knelt on one knee on the ground, a small, dark figure against the pale cobbles.

'My liege, I come to bring you my allegiance. Your noble father, my beloved and lamented brother, willed that I should govern the kingdom for you until you are of age. That I will gladly do. And my men and those of our cousin the Duke of Buckingham will here also do you homage.'

All around, our companions dismounted and knelt in their turn. I followed their lead, the cobbles chill and hard through the thin fabric of my hose. As I removed my cap, I watched the unfolding scene out of the corner of my eye.

My lord Buckingham was the last to dismount, swinging his leg stiffly down from the saddle and never taking his eyes away from Grey and his men.

Edward's brother himself appeared confused by the turn of events, transfixed by the sight of Duke Richard kneeling only feet away from him. Tension crackled in the air like a coming thunderstorm, but then, at another word from the new King, he lowered his sword and motioned to his companions to do likewise.

Then Edward stepped past them and I could see him clearly for the first time.

His face was thinner than when I had met him at court, and pale, no longer flushed by our ride through the crisp winter air, or by the music and dancing of the Twelfth Night revels. Though taller than me, of course, to my eyes he also appeared far younger than his twelve years. Duke Richard's question to me at Middleham stole into my mind – it seemed so long ago now: how would I feel to have the job of ruling England thrust upon me at that age?

He stood now in front of his uncle, clad in his sober mourning suit of darkest blue, the colour reflected in his shadowed eyes. Despite these family members nearby, he struck me as very alone. Then he spoke. Though his words were formal, his voice was high and my ears detected a slight tremor in it.

'My thanks, uncle, for your allegiance, and for that of your men. Also to my uncle Buckingham. I know that the loyalty of the foremost nobles of my kingdom is vital to me as it was to my father.'

He put out his hand on which glistened a large-stoned ring and Duke Richard bent his head to kiss it. Then Edward's eyes swept across all those gathered before him.

'But tell me, uncle, where is my uncle Rivers? They tell me he rode back to meet you last evening, yet I do not see him here with you.'

The Duke rose to his feet, and Lord Lovell, who had moved forward to his side, signalled to the rest of us to do the same. Despite the scraping of boots on stone as scores of men obeyed, the Duke's measured reply reached my ears.

'Your Grace – Edward – we have reason to think Earl Rivers attempted to delay us.'

'Delay you?' It was Edward's turn to be confused. 'Why so?'

'To prevent us reaching you before you can enter London. Not only did he miss the rendezvous we arranged at Northampton yesterday, but it seems ambushes were set along the road.'

'Ambushes? I don't understand.' Edward turned to his brother, still standing beside him. 'Richard? Do you know anything of this?'

The young man flushed scarlet and his knuckles whitened on his sword hilt.

'He lies, Edward,' he hissed. 'Do not trust him. Our mother told uncle Rivers that —'

The Duke of Buckingham thrust himself forward at this.

'Your mother, boy? She has nothing to do with this. It is the business of men, not of women, to govern kingdoms. Place not your confidence in anything she says!'

Duke Richard laid a hand on his arm.

'Calm yourself, Harry. Let Lord Grey talk. If he knows anything of the ambushes, I would rather hear him out. And the King asked to know the truth. Although now Earl Rivers is in our custody, he perhaps will explain —'

At these words the blood drained from Lord Grey's face. Before the Duke could finish, the younger man had lunged towards him, his sword arcing through the air. But the Duke's own blade, unsheathed in a flash, parried the blow, and with a twist my eyes barely caught, flicked the sword out of his assailant's hand. His sword point was at Lord Grey's throat and Lord Lovell and his gentlemen had disarmed his companions before they'd even managed to step forward or lift their own weapons.

I was stunned by the speed of what happened. I heard Lord Lovell bark orders at his men. Saw Lord Grey's mouth twist into a soundless snarl as he glared first at Duke Richard, then at Lord Lovell. Then he glanced at his younger brother.

Edward was staring at him, his face white with shock.

Lord Grey's expression changed. His eyes dropped, and a few stuttered words fell from his lips.

'Edward, I'm – I'm sorry – I – we...'

His voice faltered and died away. When Master Ratcliffe stepped up with cord to bind his wrists, he offered them up without a murmur, then followed his companions as all five were led away.

Edward watched until they disappeared into the huge gathering of men and horses in the manor's courtyard. None of the soldiers of the escort had made a move to assist Lord Grey and many now turned away to busy themselves with their mounts or their gear.

Calm restored, the Duke of Buckingham came out from behind Lord Lovell, brushing down his doublet with an air of unconcern.

Duke Richard resheathed his sword and said to the boy King,

'I'm sorry, Edward. I would have spared you that if I could. But now we must talk. Are your chamberlain and tutor within?'

Edward, a look of misery having driven the shock from his face, nodded, then led the two dukes into the manor house. Pausing briefly to speak to his men, Lord Lovell followed them in, closing the oaken door behind him.

Before long I stood almost alone in the courtyard, bar Bess and a few grooms and horses, including the flighty chestnut with its costly harness. I had overheard Lord Lovell's orders to his men, which were to disperse most of the King's escort back to their homes in Wales or the Marches. They would not be needed now Duke Richard had arrived. Despite the scene outside the manor house, or perhaps because of it, the escort didn't need to be told twice. The enormous company that had been assembling melted away again in a matter of minutes.

I was not as sure what to do with myself. So, taking from my saddle bag the precious book that the Duke's son Ed had given me at our parting, I settled down on a mounting block outside a barn, with Murrey at my feet, to read. Yet it was some time before any of the words on the page sank in. My thoughts wandered back unbidden to the scene that had just passed.

I had never before seen the Duke with a weapon in his hand, nor had I ever witnessed anyone wield a sword with such calm precision. Duke Richard was spoken of by everyone as a great knight and a famous general, but I had not placed that alongside the reality of the man I knew best at home – with his family, reading romances or enjoying music, or riding with my friends and me and seemingly few cares across the heather on the moors around Middleham. Here now was another side to him.

Time passed, however, and I ceased to ponder what was happening inside the manor house. My attention was at last captured by the book on my lap, the ominously titled 'Death of Arthur'. So engrossed did I become in that verse tale of an ancient king and his knights that I noticed neither that the Duke's gentlemen were gathering again in the yard nor that anyone had quit the manor house. It was only a shadow falling across the page and Lord Lovell's voice saying, 'Come, Matthew, the Duke wishes to speak with you,' that drove me to my feet again and back into the courtyard, Murrey trotting at my heels.

Duke Richard stood in the doorway of the house, pulling on his riding gauntlets. His face was shadowed, the expression suggesting he was barely aware of the bustle of men and beasts around him. Seeing me, however, he motioned me closer.

'Matt, though you are soon to leave us, it seems I may have a further use for you after all.'

'I'm ever at your service, Your Grace,' I said, bowing.

'So I have found,' he replied. 'And I am grateful for it. But today it is not just me but your new King whom you will serve.'

'I'm honoured, sir.'

He looked down at me and a small smile curved his lips. But he continued in the rather official manner I had seen in him all morning.

'I find that our plans have changed and we must return to Northampton. I would that you would ride with the King.'

'Of course, my lord. It will be a pleasure.'

I truly believed what I said, but his face was darkened by a faint frown.

'I hope so. It will not be like your ride together at Christmas, Matt. It has been a difficult day for the poor lad – one in very many such days since his father died. And it will not be the last for him. Or for us.'

He paused. But before I could think how to respond, he continued quietly,

'He hardly knows me, Matt. I see him shrink from me as though he fears me. He has been shut away with Lord Rivers for so long – and perhaps I have been shut away too long in the north, away from the court. Our paths have hardly crossed, and who knows what he may have been told about me. And now his father...'

A spasm passed across his face and he set off striding across the courtyard towards the pleasure grounds. I had to trot to keep pace, as did Murrey alongside us both.

As we left behind the last of the crowds, finding ourselves amidst the bright-blossoming trees and shrubs, he spoke again.

'If you go to Edward, and speak with him, boy to boy, it may make things easier for him. For all his training to be king one day, now he is just a frightened lad. And my lord Buckingham does not help.'

He halted, causing Murrey and I to skitter to a stop beside him. His frown had deepened.

'Although in one thing Buckingham may be right. Perhaps young Edward has been too softly brought up among his mother's family. When I was his age, his father had set me to work raising troops for his wars. At only a few years older, he had lost his own father and brother and fought to win his crown at St Albans and Towton. I wonder whether this boy would be able to face such troubles as those.'

He fell silent, his shadowed eyes watching the activity back in the courtyard. For some minutes he seemed unwilling to return to his men or to speak again.

Waiting there for him to continue, a question that had been welling up in me since the previous evening at last broke out.

'Your Grace, forgive me asking, but why does the Duke of Buckingham hate the Queen's family so much?'

He stared at me for several moments. Had I perhaps been too impertinent? But then he spoke again.

'Perhaps he has reason enough. He was the Queen's ward as a boy and when he was younger even than you, Matt, she chose to marry him – and his fortune – to her sister Catherine. I fear they have never been happy together. My lord is too mindful of his proud ancestry – and of her family's lowly origins. No matter that he thereby became brother to the Queen, and King... My brother's marriage to Elizabeth has caused much trouble over the years. But perhaps... perhaps now things will change.'

A shout came from among the gentlemen in the courtyard and Lord Lovell raised his arm to signal to us.

The Duke placed his gloved hand on my shoulder.

'Come, Matt, we must be on our way again. And I am relying on you to put young Edward at his ease.'

As we walked back, Edward emerged from the house, flanked by the Duke of Buckingham and several soberly dressed older men, presumably the chamberlain and tutor the Duke had mentioned, and other members of the new King's household. Soon they and we were all mounted – Edward on the fine-boned chestnut Lord Lovell had seized earlier – and back on the main road, travelling away from the morning sun towards Northampton. This time our party, now numbering several hundred men, rode at a more sedate pace, under not just the Dukes' but also the King's colourful banners. Rearing lion, white boar, leopards, silver rose and golden suns fluttered all together in the stiffening breeze.

After a few minutes I pushed Bess into a trot and wound a way through the King's gentlemen until I was riding next to Edward himself. Several of the older men glanced askance at my impudence, but as the King showed no surprise at my approach, and even raised his riding whip to salute me, they voiced no complaint.

'Matthew, isn't it? I remember you from my father's court at Westminster. And your little hound.'

'I'm honoured, Your Grace.'

As ever, I was recollected as much for Murrey, slung across my saddle bow as usual now except on the shortest of journeys.

Edward reached across with his riding crop to tickle her behind her ear. Waking, she lifted her head and gnawed gently at its leather tip.

A smile touched the King's pale lips.

'Does she still dance?'

'Aye, Your Grace. Since you taught her so well at Twelfth Night.'

His expression changed and he pulled his crop away.

'That was the last day I spent with my father,' he said.

I told him I was sad at his loss and we rode together side by side in silence for a mile or two. The Duke had asked me to speak with him, but my training as a page had drilled into me that it was not my place to start a conversation.

It wasn't long, though, before Edward spoke again.

'You were with my uncle Gloucester when I met you at Twelfth Night, were you not, Matthew?'

'Yes, Your Grace.'

'Edward was good enough for you on our ride then, Matthew. I wish that you would call me that again.'

'Aye, Your Gr – I mean, Edward.'

'And you were among his gentlemen this morning. Do you know my uncle well?'

'A little.' Recalling the past day or two – and how different the Duke had been – I could claim no more.

'My uncle Rivers says he is angry at my family. That he hates us because of something that happened long ago – and that he may seek revenge on us.'

'Your family?' How strange that he spoke this way. And did he mean what Roger had told me months before – about the execution of the Duke's brother George, which some blamed on the Queen and her family? 'But Duke Richard is your family – he's your father's brother.'

'Well, yes. I suppose I mean my mother's family. Uncle Rivers is my mother's brother. I know him better than my other uncles. I've lived with him for as long as I can remember. But no one now will tell me where he is, or even – even if he is alive.'

'I saw him this morning and he was safe then,' I said. 'The Duke of Buckingham was angry with him, but he and Duke Richard spoke courteously to one another. I believe the Earl agreed to stay in Northampton while the Duke rode to meet you.'

'And yet he is under arrest? Like my brother Richard?'

'I believe so.' I searched my memory. 'To be honest, I'm not sure I know exactly what happened. It was all so quick, and so early in the morning. But the Earl was well when we left him. And I do know Duke Richard is a good man – and I believe that your father trusted him and wouldn't have made him Lord Protector if he didn't.'

'I suppose you are right.'

We fell into a companionable silence again as we jogged along behind the Dukes and the banners, the great bulk of the soldiers formed up in lines behind us. As my thoughts drifted back over the morning's events, I hoped fervently that I was right.

Within a few more miles, Edward was talking once more. His words spilled out like water from a cracked jug. Was I the first person he had been able to speak to like this since he'd been told of his father's death?

'It scares me, Matt, no matter who is to be Protector. I shall have to be King, I know that. I have trained for it ever since I was small. My uncle Rivers tells me I will be a good King, maybe even a great one. He's been telling me so for months, and I had begun to believe him. But now my uncle Gloucester tells me I still have so much to learn. And my uncle Buckingham says I have been badly taught before now and must have better advisers. He even says that my mother should not help me, even though she is Queen.'

He paused. I had no response ready for him, but he needed no prompting to carry on after a moment.

'I want to be a good King, Matt. I will do all I can to become one. But I had not expected to be King so soon, not for years. Not – not until my father was an old man and I had been in battles like him and uncle Gloucester. And now my father is gone, and perhaps my uncle Rivers and brother too. I'm not sure I know how to go on, or who I should trust.'

He fell quiet once more.

My heart went out to him – this boy who had so much before him, but to whom too much had come so soon. All that Duke Richard and his wife had spoken of that last night at Middleham came back to me – the intrigues among the young King's family, the difficulty and responsibility of kingship, and the horrors of the civil war in our country's so-recent past.

I also thought of my own close-knit family back home in York.

And I knew I would not change places with this King for all his riches, his palaces, his wonderful prospects, his title, his power – not for a single instant.

4

The Road to London

Our entry into the city of London four days later far
outshone the Duke's arrival before Christmas. That,
though a spectacle in my eyes, had been just the start of a
family visit. This by contrast was the first entry of a new
King into his loyal capital.

He came flanked by two royal Dukes and
accompanied by an escort of five hundred retainers. The
procession approaching Aldersgate must have been
impressive indeed – so many men clad in ashy black, the
only specks of colour being the royal and ducal banners.
Duke Richard had even ensured that Edward's gaudy
saddlecloth was exchanged for one of midnight blue velvet
stitched with silver to match the young King's own outfit.

Townsfolk lined the city walls to watch our
coming. A single dolorous note was tolled by the bells in
each of those more than four score churches that I knew
were in the city, and had thought perhaps I might never see
again. Before we reached the vast gatehouse, we were met
by the mayor and aldermen resplendent in fur-trimmed
scarlet robes, followed by such hordes of important men
arrayed in vivid violet that I lost count.

The numbers and finery of the citizens, and the
size and clamour of the crowds as we passed under the
portcullis, and the din of their cheering, and the sudden
outpouring of bell peals from the churches as we wound
through the narrow streets, put our reception at York two
months before in the shade – though I would never have
confessed it out loud.

I fear that Master Kendall, had he not himself been
overwhelmed by the display, would have told me to close
my gawping mouth as he did on my first entry into
London. He and I rode close enough behind the King and

his two uncles that the city folk's joy and affection for their new sovereign were clear. Flowers of many hues were strewn before him on the cobbles, swept clean today in his honour, and colourful tapestries and bannerettes draped and fluttered from windows at every turn. On occasion someone would dart forward – a woman carrying an infant, an old man – to beg a favour from the King. To each of these Lord Lovell's men, forming Edward's personal bodyguard, slipped a shiny coin before pressing them back into the throng.

One jarring note alone marred that joyous morning. Far ahead of the river of black-clad soldiers trundled four gigantic wagons piled high with weapons and harness. Seized from the ambushers on the road from Northampton, among the haul was equipment that had been found to bear the emblems of Earl Rivers and his family. My lord of Buckingham claimed this proved they were to blame for the plot. He had wished the weapons to be carried immediately in front of the King, as though the spoils of war of some victorious general on his triumphal entry to the city of Rome. Duke Richard had refused, preferring to send the wagons some way before us. Accompanying them, heralds on every street corner announced the King's approach, bringing the cheering crowds flooding into the streets.

In this way the procession wended its way towards Ludgate Hill and the tall spire of St Paul's Cathedral. In after days, onlookers said it took more than an hour to pass by.

Skirting the massive buttresses of the ancient church, the cavalcade came to a halt at the ornate carved door of the palace of the Bishop of London. Here Edward was to stay and to receive oaths of fealty from all the lords and churchmen and great citizens there gathered. I watched as his small figure, flanked by the dukes, mounted the wide flight of steps to be greeted by the Bishop in his full regalia. Then I turned Bess's head to follow Master Kendall away from the palace, my thoughts full of all that had happened. Would I and the King ever meet again – let alone as friends?

For I believed we had become friends in the days after that tumultuous morning in Stony Stratford. We were often thrown together when he was not needed by his uncles for official business, and he seemed to enjoy the company of someone outside his usual circle. He had asked that I attend him as page, though he already had pages and squires of the body aplenty in his retinue. Duke Richard had agreed, ordering that my mattress be laid outside the King's chamber in the inn that night.

I was proud of my new privilege, but sad no longer to do the same for Duke Richard. For that day a letter had at last reached us from the Duke's friend Master Ashley in London, agreeing to take me as apprentice in his merchant's business, and I knew my brief spell as the Duke's page was over. My unhappiness was doubled when I realized that my last ever night of that service was one when the Duke had had to nudge me awake – knowing that I had failed in my duty on the very night when it might have been most needed.

Much business was undertaken during those days before our entry into London. Master Kendall and several other secretaries were almost constantly employed in sending letters and messages both for Duke Richard and in the King's name. News of the Duke's actions was sent to the capital, and we received word of events there in return.

Everything the Duke had done was approved both by Lord Hastings and by other lords who had been assembling for the coronation. For it was discovered that the Marquess of Dorset had persuaded the Royal Council to set a date to crown his younger brother that was only three days ahead. The Duke of Buckingham insisted this confirmed what he had said – that Dorset and Rivers had planned to rush young Edward ahead of us to the capital – and that it was more proof that the Marquess himself was determined to rule England through the new King.

Master Kendall was my chief informant throughout this time. Not directly, of course. He would often speak of such matters to the other gentlemen over dinner. They were not confidential, he said. But I was not sure how happy my lord of Buckingham would have been knowing his words were overheard by a mere page.

'So, yes, Lord Hastings says Sir Edward Woodville has launched his own fleet and is busy menacing English ships in the Channel. And, yes, it seems he did ransack the royal treasury before he left – half of it went with him on his fleet. And most worrying of all, the Marquess of Dorset did boast in Council that he could rule without Duke Richard.'

Gasps and grumbles rumbled around the supper table as the gentlemen digested these snippets along with their meal.

Master Ratcliffe's wine-cup stopped halfway to his mouth.

'And what of the citizenry? And the lords? How have they taken these outrages?'

Master Kendall stabbed another piece of mutton with his knife and chewed on it for a moment before continuing.

'Well, it seems that separate factions had been forming in the city – those who support Duke Richard and Lord Hastings, and those who openly favoured the Woodvilles.' Several gentlemen hissed in disapproval. 'But Lord Hastings says, now it's widely known that old King Edward appointed the Duke as Protector in his will, and people have heard what he's done here – well, most people believe he's in the right.'

'And the Woodvilles?' asked another gentleman.

'Ah, well, there's a story. And one I wouldn't have believed if it hadn't come from Bishop Russell as well as our esteemed Lord Chamberlain himself.'

Master Kendall laid down his knife and looked around the table at his listeners. When certain he had their full attention, he said,

'When they finally realized that the people weren't with them, and that they wouldn't be able to raise troops to challenge the Duke, the Queen and the Marquess took themselves off to sanctuary at Westminster.'

'Sanctuary?' gasped one gentleman.

'At the Abbey?' asked another.

The rest sat in silence, stunned by the news.

Even to a lowly boy such as myself, listening in with no knowledge of politics, this revelation was shocking. Everyone knew that fleeing to sanctuary was usually only the last resort of someone, criminal or otherwise, who believed they were about to be arrested or even executed. They could throw themselves on the mercy of the church and they would be safe from their enemy – but only for as long as they remained on that church's premises. It was not a route chosen lightly or by those who had nothing to fear.

'Not only that,' resumed Master Kendall, 'but the Queen took all her other children – and what was left in the treasury.'

Master Ratcliffe snorted.

'No more evidence of their guilt is needed if you ask me. If they weren't plotting to seize power, and if they were innocent of those ambushes, why would they flee like that – and take all young Edward's treasure with them?' He shook his head as though struggling to believe what he'd heard. 'If I were His Grace, I'd break down the Abbey walls and drag them out by force. They say King Edward did that to the Duke of Somerset when he claimed sanctuary after the battle at Tewkesbury. But we all know Richard won't.'

The other gentlemen around the table nodded in agreement.

'He's not so like his brother as that,' said Master Kendall. 'He'll probably try to talk them out and offer them a pardon for their crimes. My Lord Buckingham said he should rather leave them there to rot, bricked up like rats in a drain.'

But far from heeding his gentlemen's views or those of the Duke of Buckingham, Duke Richard's calm response had been to write to tell London's mayor and aldermen to expect the new King's entry on the following Sunday, and to request that the great royal seal be kept safe so it did not fall into the hands of the Queen or Marquess.

That night I was woken from my sleep by the noise of men and horses outside the inn.

Squinting out into the darkness, I spied Master Ratcliffe leading a detachment of soldiers setting off away from the London road. In their midst rode the cowed figures of Earl Rivers, Lord Grey and several of Edward's household gentlemen, their hands bound.

The following day we had left the inn at Northampton to travel to St Albans, the final stop before London. Once more I rode alongside Edward. This time he requested that Murrey lie across the front of his fine leather saddle when she wasn't scampering at our horses' hooves. I was happy to say yes, to give him some small pleasure in the midst of all his difficulties. He hadn't talked so openly to me again as he had on the road to Northampton and I could hardly imagine how he felt about what was awaiting him in London – or how his confidence in his mother and her family must have been badly shaken by their actions.

Instead, on our rides, and when he had time to spare from signing documents and letters with his uncles, we chatted on much the same topics as I would with Alys, Roger or Ed – hawking, horses, hounds, archery, romances, music and the foibles of our tutors – subjects favoured by boys our age the world over I imagined. On the morning that we rode to St Albans, he told me of an incident the evening before. Duke Richard had been urging him to practise his new royal signature, and to encourage him, had neatly signed his own name on a scrap of parchment, topping it with his motto.

'*Loyaulté me lie*,' I said promptly. 'Loyalty binds me.'

'I know,' said Edward. 'He wants me to choose a motto too, though I haven't any idea for one yet. He says every nobleman should have one, and especially the King. So he asked my uncle Buckingham to sign too.'

'What's his?'

He fished a piece of parchment from his pouch and squinted at it.

'*Souvente me souvene*, I think.'

He handed it to me. Beneath Duke Richard's neat signature and the words 'Edwardus Quintus' in a boyish hand was an unfamiliar ink scrawl.

'Remember me often,' I translated roughly. 'That's rather strange.'

'Not so strange as his translation,' returned Edward. 'He said it was "Often I recall" – but couldn't recall why, or what he meant by it!'

As I laughed along with him, this talk of mottoes brought to mind my very first meeting with Roger and his idea for an emblem for our fellow page, Hugh Soulsby: a dumb ox, or 'vache noir on a muck brun champ'. Roger and I had no love for Hugh – even less now after the part he'd played in my dismissal.

Edward winced as I repeated the tortured French, but laughed again. He reminded me then, not for the first time, of his little cousin Ed. A spark of recognition had also kindled in Duke Richard's eye after supper the evening before when the new King had shaken off his usual melancholy at some quip of Lord Lovell's. Did the Duke see in his new sovereign some likeness to his son too – or was it to his dead brother?

Lord Lovell's men were eyeing us with curiosity. Hastily I tucked the parchment scrap into my pouch. Edward sobered up.

'Don't tell my uncle Buckingham of that. He'd be shocked at someone mocking a member of the nobility.'

I wouldn't dare, I thought, casting my mind back to Duke Henry's haughty words to me at Twelfth Night, when I had encountered him outside Duke Richard's bedchamber in the palace of Westminster. A mere merchant's son, riding with the King, let alone mocking a nobleman? Bricking me up like a rat would be too good for me.

Late that evening, Duke Richard summoned me to his chamber in the Abbey guesthouse at St Albans. Lord Lovell and Master Kendall, passing me, bid me goodnight as I approached the door. The Duke was alone when I entered – the first time I had seen him so since we had left Middleham.

He was sitting staring into the fire that was crackling in the hearth though it had been a warm May day. A flagon of wine and cups were untouched upon a table near his elbow. The guards who were always posted now outside his rooms had announced me, but he did not look up.

'Your Grace?' I said after a moment.

He roused himself and waved me forward. The deep lines and shadows about his eyes, accentuated by the light of the flickering flames, startled me as I straightened up from my bow.

'Your Grace, would you like me to sing? I have brought my lute.'

'Please, Matthew. We have not had enough music in these past days.'

I hadn't sung to him since the night in the castle at Nottingham on our way south. Every evening since he had spent immersed in business which left little time for relaxation. Now, as I sang – the sad French *chanson* that was the first to come to mind – he tipped wine into a cup and sat nursing it for some time, before taking a sip. As the final notes faded away, he poured a second cup and pushed it towards me, with a tiny tray of sweetmeats.

'No more, Matt,' he said, to my surprise. He was rarely content with just one song. Had I made the wrong choice? 'I would rather remember the cheerful songs of our last night at Middleham. For this will be your last evening as part of my household.'

'Yes, Your Grace.'

I needed no reminding. Through all the busy times of the past few days, that thought had never left me – excited though I should be at entering the service of a great London merchant.

I propped my lute against the table and took up the cup he offered, gulping the strong wine. I was glad it burned as it went down, giving a reason for the smarting of my eyes.

'And I wished to speak with you before you leave us.'

He gestured to a stool nearby and I sat, Murrey wrapping herself around my booted feet. As I nibbled on a sweetmeat from the salver, I hoped the Duke would be talking rather than me. Now that I was no longer singing, I wasn't sure I could trust my voice.

'Master Ashley has agreed to take you as apprentice on my recommendation. I know I do not need to tell you this, but serve him well and he will look after you well. It is an opportunity such as few young men have.'

I nodded mutely. I knew full well how lucky I was – even though luck such as this could never make up for what I had lost.

'Though much has changed, Matt, since first I told you that you must leave my service, one thing has not. Though he is my nephew now, no longer my brother, our King will still need the loyalty and support of men such as Lord Soulsby. We must give him no further cause for complaint.'

He paused to toss a tidbit from the salver to Murrey. Leaning forward, he cannot have seen the flame that touched my cheek at mention of the name. At the memory of Hugh's uncle's suspicions about me and Alys –

his son Ralph's intended wife, if Alys's guardian Queen Elizabeth had her way.

Sitting back again, the Duke took another sip of his wine, then continued.

'However, it is likely that Alys will accompany my wife to Westminster for the coronation. Your fortunate move to Master Ashley's household in London may allow you to meet with her from time to time while I am Protector. As I said before, you also have my permission still to write.' He broke off, uncertainty upon his face, as though he were about to ask a favour. 'And I hope also that you will continue to write to my son. His health I believe will keep him at home in Middleham.'

'Of course, my lord. And thank you.' I hesitated in my turn before saying more, but knowing it was my last evening drove me on. 'Ed has become almost like a brother to me. I would not want to let him down.'

His features relaxed into a smile.

'I thank you for your loyalty. I know how good a friend you have been to him. To us all. And there is one more thing.'

He took something from a purse lying on the table and handed it to me. It was a small badge, less than the length of my thumb, fashioned from silver in the shape of a boar.

'Here is my token in remembrance of your valued service to us. If ever you have need of me, you may call on me and I will do my best to help.'

Gratitude washed through me, carrying with it fond memories like flotsam on the tide. Before I could stop myself, I replied, 'Thank you, Your Grace. And if you are ever in need, call on me.'

'If I'm in need?'

'Yes, Your Grace. We...'

I almost wished I'd not started, but the amused interest on his face spurred me on.

'We – that is, Ed, Alys, Roger and me – we've founded our own order – the Order of the White Boar – to be loyal to each other and to you. If ever you have need of us...'

Now I said it out loud, to an adult, it sounded foolish to me. But the Duke showed more real pleasure than I had seen for days.

'Then, yes, I thank you, Matthew – I shall call on you and your friends when I am in direst need. In these days, who knows when that shall be?'

And he raised his cup to me, and I to him, and we drank a toast to seal the bargain.

The wine flowed down and into my veins. Warming me throughout, it gave me the courage to ask a question that had been lurking for some time.

'Your Grace, what has happened to Lord Rivers and Lord Grey? The King has asked me and I've been unable to tell him.'

The Duke's hand checked as he lifted his cup to take another draught.

'The King has asked you?'

'Yes, Your Grace. I think he trusts me. That was what you wanted, wasn't it?'

'Yes, Matt, it was.' He was thoughtful for a moment. 'It's a shame you are leaving us. Young Edward might have done better with you as a companion than his tutor, old Alcock. If he ask again, you must tell him the truth. That they have been taken to Sheriff Hutton and Middleham for safekeeping until they can be brought to trial. If they are innocent of any wrongdoing, they will be released. If not, then being uncle and brother to a King will not save them.'

My face must have betrayed me as, with a slight frown, he asked,

'Does that seem harsh to you?'

Not expecting the question, I nodded without thinking.

He laughed, but with little humour.

'Perhaps it is true. Perhaps I seem a different man in these days to the one you've known before? But, Matt, I was bred in war. Before I was eight, my father and brother were killed and I was exiled from my mother and my home. At eighteen I led men and fought in my first battles. Since then I have served my brother in wars in Scotland and France. I would that I had no need for violence and that my life had been peaceful. It may be yet. I hope that my actions – here this week, today, whatever comes tomorrow – will lead to a kingdom where my son, you – and, yes, this boy King – can grow up in peace – where cousin will never fight against cousin again for power. It may be yet.'

He fell silent, cradling his cup and gazing into the fire again. And I knew it was time for me to leave.

I dropped to my knee in front of him and felt his hand on my shoulder one last time.

'Good night, Matthew. May tomorrow bring you all that you desire. And yes, I will remember to call on you if I am in need. It seems that you do indeed have the makings of a fine chivalrous knight.'

I was used to his gentle mockery, but somehow now, although his tone was light, there was a seriousness about his words. Perhaps that was unsurprising after the events of recent days.

All this raced through my brain as I rode with Master Kendall away from the procession in London, together with my last parting from the King earlier that morning.

Edward had clasped my hand warmly, given a last treat to Murrey, and urged me to visit him when he was lodged at the Tower. There I could marvel at his menagerie of wondrous, exotic animals and his fabulous treasure – when it was returned to him. A momentary darkness had crossed his brow at that reminder of his uncle Sir Edward's actions, before being banished by thoughts of the coming joyous celebrations.

Perhaps I believed that I would one day pay such a call on the King about as much as I believed that Duke Richard would ever summon my aid. As I followed Master

Kendall through the emptying streets on our way to Master Ashley's townhouse, I told myself I had to put that part of my life – my brushes with nobility and royalty – firmly in my past and look only to the future.

5

'A Bag of Snakes'

The familiarity of Master Ashley's house and many of the
people within it were a great help to me over the following
weeks as I adjusted to this second immense change in my
life. My new master greeted me formally that morning,
holding the apprentice papers ready for my signature, but
the friendliness with which he and Master Kendall
conversed reminded me of the strong links between their
households. It gave me hope that I would still be able to
see my friends in the Order.

The two men spoke about the late King – 'He was
a good man, but would have done better to have spent
more time governing than in pleasure' – and of the
dangerous times ahead – 'Master Lewis – remember him?
– he was talking of Westminster and its cliques as a bag of
snakes ready and waiting to be opened – I do not envy the
new Protector his task.' And, of course, being Englishmen,
of the weather.

'It has been so fine these past weeks that the
strawberries are ripening in the more sheltered part of my
garden,' Master Ashley said.

Master Kendall shook his head in disbelief.

'It will be another month at least before the
Duchess will be eating them at home in Middleham.'

At which my new master called at once for his
steward.

Master Lyndsey, whom I remembered well from
my time here in the winter, entered carrying a covered
basket.

'Master Lyndsey has had some gathered to take
back with you. I know how much Duke Richard enjoys
them. And there are peaches for him too.'

'Now you are jesting with me!'

'Brought in from France this morning,' Master Lyndsey assured him.

They would have been nestled in straw in shallow crates for the journey as I now knew, having seen the arrival of golden oranges during the winter, shipped in by Spanish merchants from the far-off groves of Seville.

Being reminded of the exotic sights and sounds and smells of Master Ashley's house and store rooms at last rekindled my interest after the shocks of recent days. After all, many good things could come of my change of situation.

Another presented itself almost at once.

'Before I forget,' said Master Kendall, 'the Duke has requested that you arrange for Matthew to continue with his lessons in singing and his instrument. He will gladly pay for them. He believes the boy has a talent that should be encouraged.'

'I will be pleased to,' said Master Ashley, 'at no cost to His Grace. I have no singer in my household at present. Although it may be some weeks before I can find him a suitable tutor. He will be accompanying my party to Flanders in a few days.'

I was astounded that the Duke should have had time to think of music lessons, although I must confess that I would have preferred to keep up my weapons training. But mention of the journey drove all else from my head.

'To Flanders?' I asked without thought.

Master Ashley glanced at me. His smile suggested not anger at the interruption, but rather amusement at my enthusiasm.

'Aye, lad, to Flanders. I have cloth and printing concerns to attend to in Bruges, and you have much to learn about both. Will that suit?'

The next few days were almost as busy as the previous ones as I settled in to my new household.

I shared a small attic room with only one other boy, which was paradise after the cramped pages' quarters at Middleham. He was a fellow apprentice called Simon, a year or two older than me. At first I feared he was avoiding me, but soon discovered that he assumed I would be too big for my boots, having been in the household of a royal duke. We rubbed along well enough after that. For both of us it was to be our first visit over the sea when later that week we packed our few belongings to prepare for the journey to Bruges.

Before we left, mindful of my promise to the Duke, I wrote to Ed about all that had happened since last I had seen him, especially about my renewed acquaintance with his cousin, the King. I made sure to write much of it using the code we had created, so that it could not be understood if it fell into the hands of our enemies. Or at least those of Hugh or Lionel... I had been careful to bring my copy of the cipher away with me, although I had taken the sad decision to leave behind with Alys the sacred list of the Order's rules. I had scribed them in my best handwriting during those glorious days of our early friendship last summer. I had to force my thoughts away before any pangs of homesickness crept up on me.

Master Ashley told me to place any letters with his own.

'They will be taken with mine to His Grace's house, and from there they can be sent on to your friends in the north. And do not fret, lad. We will be back home again in London in time for the young King's coronation. I hear the date has now been set by his new Royal Council.'

Then we were on our way to Flanders.

Though we stayed there four weeks or more, I have few clear memories of that first visit to the majestic trading city of Bruges. Important events were playing out back in London, though I did not know it at the time, and looking back, they colour the little that I do recollect. But remembrance of the churning stomach of my first rough sea voyage will remain with me all my life, the slapping of the white sails of Master Ashley's ship cracking my tender head as I lay retching in my bunk, the salt taste on my lips as, on calmer waters, I stood on deck watching the thicket of ships' masts and the bustling harbourside slide towards us. The ride through endless, flat, poplar-fringed fields that stretched towards every horizon, until I saw piercing the sky the slender finger of a bell tower, its roots at our destination.

The town walls rearing up, the arched barbican over the open gates, traders, farmers, citizens, their beasts and wagons pouring through on to the cobbled streets, mirror-like canals hemmed in by high brick buildings, their gables crazily stepped up towards the clouds, their foundations deep beneath the heavy wooden barges cruising slowly past.

The guttural voices of local stallholders as they hawked goods in their native Flemish tongue, the softer tones of French merchants in their fine robes striding on their way, the clopping of pack asses and mules laden with bales of cloth or sacks of unknown wares, the screeching swifts and twittering martins as they swooped for insects far above our heads, the clang of a single bell in a church on the corner.

The warmth and sweetness of new baking wafting from windows, the earthy stench of dung from below, the reek of sweat amidst the mingling crowds, the smoky smell of meat roasting on a brazier that made the water spring in my mouth, the fruity burst of my first bite of a lattice pastry offered up by a passing trader in exchange for a small unfamiliar coin.

The greetings of my master in that strange local tongue to old friends and acquaintances from atop his slender grey mare, the laughing, waving responses, the immense carpet of paving as we rode into the expanse of the main square, the fine tall buildings jostling for space around its edges, topped always by that towering town hall belfry we had spied from afar.

Master Ashley of course kept a beautiful townhouse close to this central square, though far enough away from the market bustle to be peaceful in the day as well as night. Its main doors opened straight on to the street, but at the rear its walls plunged into the depths of a canal. The window of the tiny room I shared with Simon gazed unseeing down upon the still, dark waters, and across them, into the fruit-tree-filled walled gardens of houses on the far side.

Our days in the city were full of business, learning the ways of clothmakers and merchants, entering strings of numbers in giant ledgers, jotting notes to our master's customers or suppliers, finding our way, hesitantly at first, around the dense maze of streets and waterways to deliver messages or order goods. Once, even, feeding my intense curiosity, having demonstrated to us the working of a printing machine such as Master Caxton now used to make books in his workshop crouched under the walls of St Paul's churchyard.

Tiny metal letters clutched in hands of iron, smeared with ink by apprentices like us, pressed down on immense sheets of paper or parchment, and lifted to reveal neat lines of words on page after page – again and again and again. So far from the painstaking work of copyists I'd watched in the scriptorium at York Minster – labouring all day with goose quill, knife, ink pot, scraper, to produce a single page or less of handwritten Latin text.

This of all that I encountered on my first trip abroad excited me more than any other. With my brother Fred learning his trade as bookbinder at home in York, perhaps, one day, when I had served my apprenticeship too, we might set up in partnership with this wondrous machine. If ever we could gather the funds to afford one...

Finally our weeks in Bruges came to a close and we prepared to retrace our steps back towards the coast and London.

I had had little leisure to think of what might be happening back in England, with all my tasks during the day and singing and playing for Master Ashley in the evenings. Nor had I received a letter from any of my friends, despite sending at least one myself to each of them with Master Ashley's post. I told myself that it would take a very long time for my letters to arrive in London and then be sent far north to Middleham. But still I was disappointed.

The crossing back over the sea to England was calmer than the outward journey and I passed much of the time on deck, marvelling at the sailors' agility in the rigging and gazing at the English coast as it came ever nearer. The sun had set on another day and lights had bloomed in the gathering dusk before we docked. Our party spent that night in a habourside tavern before starting out at first light on the road to London.

After my weeks in foreign parts, the city seemed very strange when we finally arrived, although little of substance had changed in my absence. The river still flowed in its usual course, the main buildings were no different – although they appeared odd to my eyes, now used to the steep roofs and stepped gables of Flemish towns – and the same stench rose from the streets. But as we rode towards Master Ashley's house, I became aware of a whispering in the streets, knots of people talking on corners, a buzz of expectation.

On our arrival, almost before I had passed Bess to a groom to be unsaddled, fed and watered, a servant thrust a small note into my hand. Recognizing the handwriting, I hurried off to my attic room, there slitting open the folded paper, eager to discover its contents.

To my disappointment the letter contained nothing beyond a single sentence in our code:

'*Wigy ni myy om un Wlimvs Jfuwx um miih um sio wuh – Ufsm.*'

I checked when it had been written – a Monday more than a week before. Then I could translate it using our cipher for that day. Revealed were the words 'Come to see us at Crosby Place as soon as you can – Alys.'

Despite the shortness of her message, seeing Alys's name again, and knowing that she was in London too, drove away my momentary unhappiness. No matter now that she hadn't written before. She had clearly been too busy with preparations for her journey and then settling in to her new lodgings in the city.

It was just supper time and I already knew Master Ashley did not require me to sing that evening. So I resolved to take advantage of the long hours of daylight remaining to visit Alys that day if I could.

The atmosphere at supper was subdued. All the party must have been as tired as I was following our long day's journey, and after more than a month away it was no surprise that our master rose early from the table with his wife, steward and secretary and retired to his private chamber. At that, I also rose, declining Simon's offer of an evening spent playing dice. Soon I was treading the familiar streets towards Duke Richard's townhouse, Murrey sticking close to my heels.

Those streets were busier than I recalled from earlier in the year, but I put that down to the better weather and the lighter evening. It was less easy to explain why the stout iron gates of Crosby Place were barred against me when I arrived, with double the number of men at arms on guard. Given the events of the Duke's journey to London, however, perhaps I should not have been surprised that greater security was required. As I stated my name and business, and showed the guards the Duke's little silver boar badge that I now wore proudly on my doublet at all times, Master Ashley's remark about the 'bag of snakes' at Westminster wormed unprompted into my mind. What had unfolded while I had been away?

I was ushered into the courtyard to wait while a servant went to announce me. Before long Elen, Alys's companion, emerged from a side door. Her dark eyes brightened at the sight of me standing there, Murrey perched neat and upright by my feet, and with a smile she beckoned me forward.

'It's so nice to see you, Matthew,' she said, as she led me through passages and up staircases into the heart of the house that, not long ago, had briefly been my home too. 'We have been stuck so long in London now with so little to do. Your tales of your new life will be a welcome distraction.'

Her words surprised me, not only because it was rare for Elen to speak so openly, but also her complaint about lack of amusements. Surely the capital was full of entertainments for two young girls?

As I murmured something about hoping to be of service, we reached a small door towards the topmost part of the house. Elen opened it, drawing her full skirts aside to let me past, and there, in a small parlour, with her embroidery untouched on her lap, sat Alys.

She rose to greet me, and she at least had not changed. As ever her unruly reddish curls were escaping from her linen cap and, standing with her hands upon her hips, she raised one eyebrow as her sharp green eyes looked me up and down.

'Quite a man about town now, I see,' she said with a curl to her lip.

I had of course swapped the Duke's murrey and blue livery for that of Master Ashley, an altogether more elaborate uniform with a touch of lace at the collar and cuffs. And my boots were of smart black leather, no longer the battered pair of our rides together at Middleham.

Where once perhaps my cheeks would have glowed at her words, now I simply lowered myself on to one knee and pressed my lips to her offered hand.

'But still not fit to woo the lady of my dreams, alas. I must continue to wander the world until I have found my fortune.'

To my relief, she laughed as she pushed me away.

'Fool! But did you not find it in faraway Flanders?'

'Thank you for your letters, Matt,' Elen broke in from where she was now seated on a stool to one side. 'Bruges sounds a beautiful city.'

'It is,' I said, and at her prompting, launched into a description of some of the delights I had met with on my travels. Before long, however, her questions tailed off and my own chatter dwindled away in its turn. Uncertain what to say next, I leaned forward to fondle Murrey's ears.

After some moments of silence, Alys burst out,

'So while we've been kicking our heels here, under siege, you've been out and about enjoying yourself!'

I almost laughed at the drama of her words.

'Under siege? Whatever do you mean?'

Elen's dark hands plucked at her arm, but Alys threw them off.

'Well, it seems like it. We're not allowed to go out unless three or four guards are there to protect us. More than a fortnight we've been here and we've seen almost nothing. With the Queen in sanctuary, there's no court to speak of. And now the coronation's been postponed there are hardly any ladies in the city at all. My first visit to London in six years – it was meant to be glorious. I didn't expect it to be like this!'

What she said stunned me.

'What do you mean, the coronation's been postponed?'

'Don't you know what's happened? Have you heard nothing while you've been away?'

'I – we were so busy. And – and I had no letters.'

It wasn't meant as a rebuke, but her face was suddenly aflame.

'Oh, Matt, I'm so sorry. Everything was in an uproar after we received the Duke's news from Northampton – then we were travelling – then more uproar when we arrived here. Your letters did reach us – but we didn't know when you would be returning...'

Her voice trailed away, before rallying again.

'Not that I should make excuses. Ed managed to write to you.'

'Ed?' I asked, casting my eyes around the chamber. Was my little friend hiding in some dark corner as when I had first met him in his father's library? 'Where is he?'

'He stayed behind at home. The Duchess was worried he might become ill in the heat and smoke of London. At least that's what she told him. Although with everything that's happened to the Duke... He wasn't happy. We kept his letters for you, as we weren't sure where to send them. I suppose he'll have told you himself.'

Elen was on her feet, searching in a small trunk on a side table. Turning back, she passed me four or five folded and sealed papers.

I broke with a snap the wax seal on the uppermost, into which was cut a primitive 'E'. Within was a densely packed page of Ed's childish writing.

'He's written it in code, hasn't he?' said Alys, pale once more, her lips curved in a faint smile.

'Every word.'

'I knew it. He always uses the code now, whenever he can. Even just for the briefest notes. He says, "What would Matt say if I didn't use it?"'

'And tells us how much he misses you,' Elen put in.

And I him. But I didn't say the words. That was a different life. When I had been the friend of a Duke's son.

Folding the letter up again to save for later, when I had my cipher to hand, I dragged my thoughts back to the present.

'But what were you saying about the coronation? And the Queen – she's still in sanctuary? Why?'

'I can't believe you don't know anything. Surely Master Ashley did?'

On several days my new master had been agitated when he received his letters and had taken himself off with his secretary Master Hardyng to his study overlooking the quiet canal. But he had never shared news with us lowly boys.

'Perhaps. But don't forget, I'm just an apprentice now – not party to great events.'

'All of London knows it,' she cried in exasperation. 'Lord Hastings has been executed!'

6

St Paul's Cross

I was too shocked to speak at first.

The old King's closest friend, Lord Chamberlain of England, the huge bear-like man I had seen laughing and riding and drinking with the King and Duke at Christmas? Executed?

'How?' I stammered. Then thought – stupid question. I knew. A sharp axe to the neck, of course. Rather – 'I mean, why?'

'They say he'd been plotting with the Queen and the Marquess of Dorset,' said Alys, her eyes alight, though agitated, at the story she had to tell. 'That they were aiming to seize back power along with the King. That he didn't like Duke Richard being Protector and favouring the Duke of Buckingham when he – Lord Hastings – thought he should be in charge of the Council. The Bishop of Ely too, and the old Chancellor, Rotherham – oh, and Lord Thomas Stanley – they've all been arrested as well.'

'Arrested? But you said executed?'

'Well, Lord Hastings – they say that when he was accused – at a Council meeting in the Tower – they found a hidden weapon on him. Master Kendall says his lordship called for the men at arms to support him, but they overpowered him instead. So he was tried at once and executed almost straight away. Master Kendall thinks the Duke acted on the spur of the moment – decided that removing Lord Hastings would take away the main focus for the plot.'

'And has it?'

'Maybe. A couple of days later the Queen allowed the King's little brother, Richard, to leave sanctuary. He's joined Edward in his apartment in the Tower to prepare for the coronation. Perhaps that means she thinks the game's up.'

Edward's last words to me before his glorious entry into London came back to me – about my visiting the menagerie of exotic beasts near his lodgings at the Tower. How close had the boy King been to the place of execution? Had he heard the commotion or the dread sound as the axe fell?

Alys was watching me, as though awaiting my reaction. As I pondered, her earlier words came back to me.

'But you said the coronation's been postponed.'

'Well, yes. There had been a rumour that it would be before all this happened. I think something else is afoot.'

'Why do you say that?'

'Well, Master Kendall knows something, but he's keeping tight-lipped about it for once. The Duchess looks worried all the time – at least whenever we see her, which isn't often. She and the Duke are staying at Baynard's Castle with his mother as often as here. And anyway, I daren't ask her. When all's said and done, we're just children.'

'So's the King,' I said, 'even younger than us. Do you think he knows what's happening?'

She shrugged.

My mind went back to my talks with Edward on the road to and from Northampton, his confusion and questions about his family, his uncertainty about Duke Richard, his worry about being a good king. I recalled also the Duke kneeling to him, unprotected, on the cobbled yard of the manor house, his kiss of the ring, the oath he had led in York Minster, his words to me about being brought up in violent times. His smile when I had pledged him my loyalty. The flash of his sword when threatened by Lord Grey.

'I'm sure the Duke's doing right by him – by us all. He's an important man. He has to make big decisions, he's always had to. And the old King trusted him to make the right ones or he wouldn't have made him Lord Protector.'

'But it's all so far away from our life at Middleham. And I wonder what will happen next. Sometimes it seems as though everyone is holding their breath, waiting to see. It's all so frustrating. And we have no distractions from it here.'

She bit her lip.

'I suppose that sounds terrible, to complain about being bored when a man has just lost his life. But I truly wish there was more for us to do. It might take our minds off all this. Even if we could just ride more often.'

I was glad to think about something other than the bewildering news.

'Perhaps we could ride out together. I have no duties on Sunday.'

Alys clapped her hands together at my words. Elen's eyes were shining too as she said quietly,

'Are you sure, Matthew – that you wish to give up your holiday?'

I bowed to both of them.

'It will be my pleasure. Duke Richard let me take Bess to Master Ashley's, but I've hardly have a chance to ride her since, except for the journey to the coast. And he gave permission for me to see you if you came to London.'

Alys screwed her mouth into a pout.

'Despite Lord Soulsby?'

The reason for my being sent away from Middleham swam back into my head.

'The Duke said we must give his lordship no cause for complaint. But what suspicions can we attract just riding out in the city – two girls and a boy in full view of the whole populace? Nothing, surely, to upset the marriage plans for his son.'

A shadow seeped into Alys's eyes, like a cloud shielding the sun from view. Aware of my mistake in reminding her of her betrothal, I gabbled on.

'We could see some of the most famous sights hereabouts – the Guildhall, maybe, the great bridge, St Paul's. It really is a most wondrous church – almost as fine as the Minster.'

Elen helped me out in my discomfort. She stood and gave me her hand, saying with her gentle humour,

'That's very kind of you, Matthew, to think of us and our entertainment. And if you're escorting us, perhaps we'll need only three men at arms this time.'

Indeed, when I called again at Crosby Place on Sunday morning, the girls were attended by no more than two of the Duke's soldiers, already astride their horses, halberds hefted in their gauntleted fists. Perhaps, as the city had remained calm in the days since Lord Hastings's death, there was little risk in ladies venturing forth. For me, the shock was still fresh – that this man I had met and who had seemed Duke Richard's ally should have met such a brutal end. And on the Duke's orders.

Like Alys I suspected there must be more to the story. Everywhere in Master Ashley's household and throughout the streets of the city, people appeared to be waiting, watching, whispering in shadows.

Bess's coat had been brushed until it shone and Murrey's royal collar also polished for the occasion. Alys was once more atop her pretty chestnut pony and Elen had borrowed an old palfrey from the household steward. He said that, though large, it was sweet-tempered and would be ideal for carrying a lady safely about the bustling streets. As we set off for St Paul's, we soon appreciated the value of horses not readily disturbed by crowds.

Sunday was of course a holiday for all the citizens of London, whether master, journeyman or apprentice, and the streets were always thronged after morning service. But today, as we approached the great cathedral, it was more difficult than usual to force a path through the seething hordes of people. The soldiers had at first trailed in our wake, chatting and little resembling the bodyguard Alys had lamented. But now they pushed their way to the front. At sight of their dark red and blue livery, the townsfolk melted away to either side.

I thought nothing of it and was just telling Alys and Elen something of the first of Ed's letters that I had painstakingly deciphered, when we rode out on to the square about St Paul's Cross.

This roofed stone pulpit I knew to be a place for meetings and preaching to the populace. So it was scarcely surprising to glimpse a tall man clad in a brown habit standing upon it, the morning sun glinting off the dome of his tonsured head. Around him clustered an enormous crowd, as though half the population of the city had collected there.

What I did not expect was a sizeable gathering of horsemen on the far side of the square, ranged before the soaring walls of the cathedral itself. The swathes of velvets, silks, lace and fur trimmings they displayed, and the rich trappings of their horses, marked those at the front as among the wealthiest men in the land. All lords had been summoned to a special sitting of Parliament due to begin in a few days, but I wondered to see so many here.

Beside me, Alys murmured, 'Look. Duke Richard.'

Running my eyes along their ranks a second time, in their midst I spied my old master's slight form upon Storm. Both man and horse were arrayed in deepest purple cloth. In previous weeks I had become so accustomed to seeing the Duke in his sombre black mourning clothes that I had not observed him before.

'And as ever at his side nowadays, my lord of Buckingham,' Alys went on. 'I wonder what we shall see or hear if we remain?'

The Duke of Buckingham had reined his midnight stallion to a halt a little in front of the other lords. Seeing him, attired in vibrant purple shot through with gold thread, a stranger might have imagined him to be the leading man in the government of the realm. But now the friar at the cross started to speak and what he said soon drove away all thought of Duke Henry.

First of all the man raised his hands as though to silence the crowd. This was a gesture so unnecessary it made me want to laugh. Here as elsewhere, it was as though everyone was holding their breath, waiting. The silence was broken only by the shifting of horses and the faint cry of a child, hushed as soon as it began.

He cleared his throat.

'I take as my text this morning a verse from Solomon, chapter 4 verse 3: Bastard slips shall not take root.'

His voice was strong and distinct and it caught the attention of everyone there.

Following a brief discussion of the meaning of his biblical text, to my surprise he spoke in glowing terms of the old Duke of York, Duke Richard's father, of how he had been a great nobleman of England, heir to the true kings of old, before his betrayal and brutal murder by the usurping Lancastrians. And of all his sons, the friar said, only one, Richard, Duke of Gloucester, had been born in our great realm, in England itself. He was therefore the most truly English, as well as a man of firm moral standing and authority.

I glanced at Alys. What did she make of this?

But like the crowd hemming us in, she was transfixed. Whether she was staring at the friar or at the multitude of lords beyond, I could not tell.

'As for legitimate authority, it seems he alone possesses it,' the man's voice rang out. 'For it has come to the attention of the highest lords of our kingdom that our late King, Edward, the fourth of that name, was intemperate in his ways. Before he married the lady Elizabeth Grey, known as Queen, he had been wed to another, one Eleanor Talbot. And it was while that lady was still living, that he took as his wife also that said Dame Elizabeth Grey who bore him his two sons and numbers of daughters. Therefore in the sight of God and our holy mother church, those children are not fit heirs to the throne of England.'

He paused and the faintest whisper or a sigh ran through the assembled people. Then the friar spoke once more.

'The late Duke of York's second son, Edmund of Rutland, died without issue. His third, George of Clarence, having been attainted for his treason to our late King Edward, his offspring are also unable to inherit. So it comes to the final son, Richard of Gloucester, who alone is fit to rule.'

He continued to speak, praising Duke Richard for his nobility, his honour, his steadfastness to his royal brother, his valour in battle, his love for the church, and again, his father's descent from kings all the way back to the Conqueror.

But I couldn't take it all in.

I turned to Alys in bewilderment.

'Alys, what does it all mean?'

She remained staring straight ahead, her face unreadable, as she said softly,

'It means that Duke Richard will be King.'

I looked across to where the Duke sat unmoving on Storm, but he was too far away for me to make out his expression.

7

To be a King

Over the next few days the full story filtered down even to me, a lowly apprentice.

All London was agog with the news, although many who had been in the city these past weeks had had some inkling of what might happen.

'I knew it, as soon as the coronation was delayed again.' A woman's voice had floated up to our ears as we pushed our way through the crowd out of the square. The friar had finished his speech and the lords had turned their mounts' heads to follow the two Dukes away from the cathedral. 'I knew something was amiss.'

And, 'I had my suspicions after old Hastings lost his head,' said one groom to another as I left Bess to be unsaddled on my return to Master Ashley's. 'They say he'd been keeping secrets for the old King for years. Maybe this was one of them. It was bound to catch up with them in the end.'

News had travelled through the city faster than summer lightning on that day.

I accompanied Alys and Elen straight back to Crosby Place, the soldiers preferring to usher them back to the safety of its walls and barred gates after the friar's pronouncement. Yet the crowd remained calm and drifted away alongside us, barely glancing at us or our escort's livery as we passed wordless through the bustling streets.

Alys's thanks were muted as we parted at the townhouse entryway and, each wrapped in our own thoughts, we did not speak about what had happened or of meeting again. But a day or two later another note in code arrived, again summoning me to her side.

'*Qcas og gccb og dcggwpzs – Ozmg.*'*

73

By then the talk of my master's journeymen and servants was all of my lord Buckingham having spoken to certain collections of lords and great men of the city about Duke Richard's right to the throne. And it was said that on this day the matter would be discussed by a meeting of Lords and Commons in Westminster that would be a Parliament in all but name.

As before, I walked to Crosby Place after supper.

Elen met me in the courtyard, this time with nothing more than a simple greeting, and retired with her sewing to a stool by the hearth after showing me in to the parlour.

Alys was standing staring out of a window, but swung round as we entered.

'Well, is it true?'

I was taken aback by her abruptness.

'Is what true?'

'What they are saying. What everyone apart from us in his own household knows about. That Parliament will ask the Duke to be King.'

I sat down, even though she hadn't invited me to.

'That's what I've heard. Master Lyndsey, my master's steward, he says all this is why Parliament wasn't postponed when the coronation was.' He had been speaking of it to Master Hardyng, the secretary, in the dining hall. Not that I'd been eavesdropping... 'He says the Bishop of Bath and Wells told the Duke and the Council that the old King had been married before he met the Queen. That he had himself performed the ceremony in secret. So when King Edward married the Queen, he was already married – to someone who was still alive.'

'So poor Edward and the others are...'

She couldn't bring herself to say the word, dropping into a chair next to mine with a mixture of emotions chasing across her face. I carried on to save her.

'The King's second marriage was bigamous, so it wasn't legal, yes. So Edward can't become King because he's not the legal heir.'

Silence reigned for some minutes, before Alys spoke again.

'So who was she? His first wife.'

'Lady Eleanor? Master Lyndsey says she was the widow of a Lancastrian knight. Her first husband died some time before King Edward took the throne.'

'A widow? Just like Queen Elizabeth was when she met the King. And her first husband was a Lancastrian too.'

'Was he?' I asked. As usual, the intricacies of the royal family were a mystery to me. 'How odd. According to Master Lyndsey, both ladies were older than the King too – by five or six years.'

Alys's green eyes narrowed in thought.

'And both marriages happened in secret, didn't they? When the King and Queen married, they didn't tell anyone for months. Until the Earl of Warwick said he was arranging a marriage for the King with a foreign princess. Then it all came out. It was quite a scandal. The King should have asked the Lords for permission, of course. And the Earl was especially angry. All his plans went for nothing.'

Another silence. Were we all thinking about how similar the stories were?

Elen said quietly, 'There was a rumour too that the Queen had used sorcery to bewitch the King.'

Alys rounded on her.

'Sorcery – pah! Beautiful women don't need to use sorcery to bewitch men. And everyone says the Queen was very beautiful when she was younger.'

She still is. The words teetered on my lips, as my memories of Christmas surfaced in my mind, but they didn't spill out. Instead, smiling at Elen, who had shrunk back at the sharp words, I said,

'Master Lyndsey says there were lots of rumours about the King. That he promised to marry several beautiful ladies before the Queen, but he didn't honour his promises.'

Alys nodded, as ever taking no more notice of Elen.

'I heard that when he married the Queen, it was because he wanted to show that he could make his own decisions – that he didn't need the Earl to do it for him.'

'And meanwhile poor Lady Eleanor was in a convent.'

'Why do you think she never said anything?'

I shrugged.

'Who knows? Though they say she died not long after. But I wonder whether the Queen knew.'

'Well, it might explain a lot if she did.' Alys sat back again in her chair, her long pale fingers playing absently with a red-gold curl that hung down loose from her linen cap. 'Why the Woodvilles wanted to keep the Duke away from London. Why the Queen went into sanctuary so quickly. Perhaps they feared it would all come out once the old King was dead.'

'And maybe that's why they were so keen to get Edward crowned as quickly as possible,' I added, thinking back to those days before we reached London.

Then I remembered with a start what else had been spoken of at Northampton. Should I mention it? Perhaps not.

But Alys's sharp eyes had somehow caught my thought, even as I bit it back, and she stared at me now, expectant.

'And what?'

'And – well, the Duke of Buckingham said then that there was a rumour the King had been poisoned.'

'Poisoned?'

'I know he'd blame the Queen's family for anything,' I hurried on, 'but he said it wasn't a coincidence that the Marquess had just taken charge of the Tower and treasury.'

'Really?' Alys didn't appear shocked by the notion. Her calm face recalled that of Duke Richard as he had listened to my lord of Buckingham bluster on. She

76

said thoughtfully, 'Well, whether or not he was poisoned, perhaps they believed that everything was in place for a smooth, fast takeover if they hurried Prince Edward on to London. That he was young enough to be controlled while they hung on to power. No one would have dared to question his right to the throne once he'd been crowned.'

'But surely they must have known Duke Richard wouldn't be happy about it all – particularly if he was to be in charge as Protector. And isn't it well known that he doesn't like the Woodvilles? I remember Roger mentioning it – something to do with the death of another brother.'

'The Duke of Clarence?'

'I think that was it.'

'He rebelled with Warwick against King Edward, but it was only years later that he was executed for treason. Some people think the Queen persuaded King Edward not to pardon him, because he'd spoken up against their marriage – and that was when the marriage was believed to be legal. And they also say that Duke Richard stayed so much in the north later to avoid her.'

'Did she and her family hope he'd stay in Middleham out of the way?'

'I suppose it's possible. Maybe they didn't know he'd be named Protector and would have to come down to London.'

I cast my thoughts back to the days after news of the King's death had reached us.

'Didn't the Duchess say the Queen would have expected to be regent? When we heard her and the Duke speaking about it. They sounded surprised at the Duke becoming Protector instead.'

'I do remember Master Kendall saying after we arrived in London that the King changed his will just before he died. Perhaps that was when he appointed the Duke as Protector.'

'So it might have come as a surprise to the Queen and her family as well, if they thought she'd be ruling the country through her son,' I said. 'But – but, really, do you think it's possible? That anyone would kill a King? Especially his own wife.'

It was Alys's turn to shrug.

'I don't know, Matt. But they do say power and wealth do strange things to people.'

'I don't suppose I'll ever find that out,' I tried to joke. Our talk had become serious – treasonous even, with mention of killing a king.

But Alys didn't laugh.

'The Queen's family had all their power and rich appointments direct from the King too. Perhaps they feared losing them.'

'Would Lord Hastings have been worried about that too? I heard someone say that maybe he knew about the first marriage, that he'd helped keep it secret. Did he think that if Duke Richard discovered he knew all about Lady Eleanor...'

'That the Duke might not want him on the Royal Council?' Again Alys read the notion that was only just half-forming in my mind. 'That's possible. He'd never been the Queen's friend, but maybe that pushed him to plot with her and her family – the fear that they'd all lose everything because of the Duke.'

We sat in silence once again, but from a tightening of her lips and the fingers twining in the lock of hair it was obvious something more was gnawing at Alys. It wasn't long before she spoke up.

'And then there's my lord Buckingham. Master Kendall says he's been acting like another Kingmaker this past week or two – pushing the Duke to take the crown if it's offered to him.' A shadow passed across her face, like a stray cloud veiling the moon. 'But I can tell you – each time I've seen the Duke since we've been here, he's looked very unhappy. Not as though he's in any hurry to get any more power. Money, now – Master Kendall says he could certainly do with more of that.'

'Why? Surely the Duke is not short of it.'

'It's because the royal treasure has disappeared. Duke Richard's been paying for everything out of his own purse – and that includes arranging the coronation – until it was postponed of course... Though they'll be arranging another one soon, if all they say is true.'

In the quiet that followed, Murrey, curled up as normal on my feet, whimpered as she twitched in her sleep. Was she chasing rabbits in her dream, or being chased herself?

Nudging her with my toe to rouse her, it occurred to me that something was missing.

'Where's Shadow? I haven't seen her.'

'Have you only just noticed?' Alys replied with some scorn. 'She's back home in Middleham. The Duchess said she wasn't a suitable dog for a lady at court. I don't see why. But at least she's company for Ed. He's desperate for a hound of his own, especially since you left with Murrey.'

'The Duke said he probably wouldn't come for the coronation.'

'He wasn't pleased. I heard him shouting at his mother when she told him, then sobbing. But she promised she and the Duke would be back before summer's end.' She hesitated. 'Though that may not be likely now.'

Yet more of Duke Henry's words at Northampton came back to me.

'Perhaps they thought he'd be safer at home. My lord Buckingham hinted...'

'Yes?'

'Well, he hinted that not only Duke Richard, but Ed and the Duchess might be at risk from the Woodvilles' plotting.'

'Then it's just as well that the Duke and other lords in the Council and Parliament have taken charge and removed them from power. I hear that Lord Rivers and Lord Grey are to be tried for treason. If they're found guilty, they'll be executed like Lord Hastings.'

The Earl's handsome, courteous face forced its way before my mind's eye, and Lord Grey's, contorted by hatred as he tried to strike Duke Richard. As I rose to take my leave, aware from the creeping twilight that the evening was growing late, my thoughts were in turmoil. How complicated were the lives of great men and women – and how dangerous could be the roads that they chose.

*

The next day Master Ashley did not appear at dinner, having left the house during the morning formally dressed in scarlet robes. When he returned to supper, it was to a house abuzz with talk and rumour of events that day in Westminster.

We apprentices were waiting in line to wash our hands before entering the dining hall when Mistress Ashley bustled out to greet her husband.

'So, is it done?' she asked without ceremony, as a servant helped him off with his mantle.

His face grave, he nodded.

'Aye, wife, it is. And done well. His Grace is no longer Protector, but King.'

And after he sluiced the city dust from his face and hands in the bowl held up for him, he spoke to all of us now thronging about him, apprentices, journeymen and servants.

'This morning Parliament called on His Grace the Duke of Gloucester to ascend the throne. In front of a large gathering of lords and citizens, he agreed and at once was hailed as King Richard the Third.'

A murmur arose from the assembled household and Simon, standing next to me, whispered something in my ear. But I had attention for no one but my new master as he continued his tale.

'Then His Grace, followed by all the nobles and men there present, rode to Westminster Hall, to the King's Bench, to take the royal oath. He was a sight to behold –

seated in that great marble chair surrounded by all the justices and great men of the kingdom, with the cheers of all of us gathered there ringing in the very rafters. He spoke those words so solemnly, and called for all persons, rich or poor, lord or commoner, to be treated equally in the law. Then he summoned Sir John Fogge, the Queen's cousin, from sanctuary and clasped him by the hand, swearing to be his friend.'

Master Ashley paused, running his eyes around all the eager, listening faces, then nodded as though answering a silent, but important question.

'To me, wife, boys, that is the mark of the man who is now to be our king. And let us hope that Queen Elizabeth hears and herself comes out of sanctuary before long.'

With that, he strode into the dining hall. In a few moments we were all seated at the tables, our heads bowed as grace was said, followed by a prayer for this special day. Though my mind still raked over the confusing events of recent weeks, my voice joined with fervour in the call for our Lord to protect our new sovereign.

8

Men from the North

Over the following days the tension in the city relaxed. Even the arrival of troops from the north was met with good humour rather than the Londoners' usual suspicion.

Master Lyndsey had overheard Master Ashley speaking with friends who had witnessed their reception. And as ever I overheard Master Lyndsey discussing it with Master Hardyng the secretary as I laboured over a tally of numbers in a ledger.

'The talk among the city folk was all of hordes of northerners being on their way,' said the secretary. 'Three or four thousand, they reckoned. And of what it meant. What the King might intend by summoning them.'

'And afraid that London's rights and freedoms might be threatened, I'll be bound,' scoffed Master Lyndsey. He was a man from the Midlands, who had travelled much with Master Ashley before settling down in the capital as his steward. 'That's always the way in this city. Ever worrying about its own affairs, never those of the kingdom at large, let alone the person of the King.'

'Well, the people have a right to be concerned, here as anywhere else.' Master Hardyng of course was a Londoner. 'These have been difficult times – not knowing from one day to the next what will happen. Who will be in charge.'

'Aye, perhaps. But Duke Richard knew who he could trust when things were uncertain. No doubt that's why he summoned men from the north when he was protector. When he didn't know what the Woodvilles meant to do, or how much support they would have.'

'But now things are settled. Parliament has made him King. Why are they here?'

'They're still camped outside the city walls at the moment. Nothing to worry about. And Master Ashley's guests say they'll be dismissed back home once they've patrolled the streets during the coronation. You know how ruffians and vagabonds delight in thieving amongst crowds of people. But they also said how much the local people laughed and mocked at them.'

'Why so?'

'Because of their ancient gear. Tatty and worn, apparently. They said these northern troops weren't fit to clean the boots of their own city guard.'

What Master Kendall had once told me about Londoners' sense of their own superiority sprang into my mind and I was thankful that my brother Fred was not among the troops this time.

A day or two later I was running an errand for Master Ashley when the sound of many men and horses tramping resounded through the streets. People from all around hurried to discover what was afoot.

I followed, pushing my way to the front of the growing crowd lining Thames Street.

Trumpets blared, and on all sides cheers rose and kerchiefs were waved.

Behind the lines of scarlet-clad trumpeters, and at the head of marching columns of soldiers and horsemen, rode two men. One was a nobleman I did not know, atop a bay charger, a blue lion rearing on the yellow shield slung at his saddle. Beside him rode Duke Richard – or rather, King Richard. The sunshine glinted off the gold thread of the royal standard fluttering above.

Storm bore him on towards where I stood hemmed in by the cheering crowds. The stallion's hooves stepped high across the cobbles, the crest of his neck curving proudly beneath his murrey and blue trappings.

My old master raised his hand in response to the acclamation, and smiled up at a baby held out at an upper-storey window, waving its pudgy little arms at him. But his eyes were shadowed with tiredness, dark lines etched beneath them as on the day he'd learnt of his brother's death.

What he had said of the burdens of kingship flashed across my mind, and with it also the haunted face of his nephew Edward when he had spoken about becoming king so soon.

Before I gave thought to my action, I stepped forward and called, 'Your Grace!'

One of his companions spurred his horse towards me, no doubt concerned at any threat such a sudden movement might pose. But somehow my cry reached the King's ears above the tumult, and he recognized me despite my new livery.

'Matthew?'

He reined Storm back and the whole column of troops behind came to a halt.

'Hold your hand, Richard. It is Master Wansford, my late page.'

It was Master Ratcliffe who had driven his mount forward, and who now swung away to face the still cheering crowd.

Beyond him rank upon rank of soldiers stood to attention, alert to all around them. From their liveries and banners of yellow and blue, alongside men in the Yorkist colours of murrey and blue, I took the other nobleman to be the Earl of Northumberland who had led the troops down from the north. He was, I knew, little liked in my home city. He watched in curiosity as the King leaned towards me, resting his forearm on Storm's crest, and spoke again.

'Well, Matt, are you proud of your northern countrymen? They rallied promptly to my call in case aid was needed in these past weeks' upheavals. You know of the great changes that have occurred? Though I hear Master Ashley has been in Flanders.'

'Aye, Your Grace. We returned some days ago. I was with Alys and heard the friar's sermon at the Cross.'

He gazed down at me, the expression on his face difficult to read.

'Great changes, indeed,' he repeated. 'But Alys – she is still the late Queen's ward, though she will remain part of the royal household until Elizabeth should decide to leave sanctuary. Then – then Elizabeth can do with her as she wishes. But in the meantime... I see you still wear my badge.'

I seized the fabric of my doublet where the silver boar was pinned and thrust it towards him as though in proof.

He nodded.

'You may use it to enter the Abbey for the coronation – if your new master allows a holiday. It may be that you will see Alys there.'

'Thank you, Your Grace.'

Behind him, the Earl edged his mount forward as though in impatience.

'Sire?'

As the King straightened up at his voice, the face of the boy king Edward swam before my eyes again.

Perhaps fearing to lose this one chance, I blurted out, without thinking,

'And Edward, Your Grace? He who was to be —'

I stopped, knowing I was impertinent.

King Richard's expression didn't change.

'You mean my brother's son? He and his brother lodge still at the royal apartments in the Tower. They will be safe there until their mother comes to her senses and can take them again into her charge. I doubt he will be at the coronation. His change of circumstances will be hard enough for him to bear. Too often children must deal with the consequences of their parents' mistakes. But he is young and will adapt.'

Master Ratcliffe turned his horse back towards us.

'Your Grace. We are expected at Baynard's Castle. The lady Cecily...'

'You are right, Richard. We must not keep my mother waiting, though I am now King.' His familiar wry smile. 'God speed you on your life's path, Matt. Offer prayers if you will for your new King and his Queen.'

'I – I will, my lord,' I stammered.

I stood back as he urged Storm into motion once again. With a barked word from their commander, the whole body of troops streamed after him, their vibrant banners whipping into life above the tide of leather and steel.

As Master Ratcliffe passed, he leant down and slipped something into my hand. Murmuring the words 'From the King's bounty', he then kicked his horse on to follow the retreating backs of the King, the Earl and their companions.

I opened my hand.

A bright coin lay on my palm, crisp and new, a head with a crown adorning one side, a tiny boar stamped nearby.

It could have been the head of any king, such was the crudeness of the features. But the name 'Edward' was scribed around the edge.

I shoved the coin into the pouch at my belt. Then, though I should not have delayed my errand further, I watched the rest of the procession as it passed.

Among the hundreds of men marching beneath banners of Gloucester, Northumberland and York, I recognized here and there neighbours from my home town. I drew a grin or a nod if they spotted me.

One face, however, I did not expect.

In the last cohort of riders, resplendent in the murrey and blue of the King's livery, I glimpsed my old adversary.

Hugh Soulsby.

I had not seen him since I had left Middleham. Since his revenge had led to my dismissal.

His eyes were fixed resolutely ahead as he was carried forward by the dark brown colt I remembered from the castle, his harness gleaming in the spring sunshine.

At first he did not see me. But then something – what was it? – made him glance to the side. And his eyes caught mine.

A moment, a hesitation.

Then he recognized me. His eyes narrowed. And his lips parted, mouthing words I could not hear above the tramp, tramp, tramp of the marching feet and clattering hooves.

But I guessed his meaning, as those lips curved into a smirk. Triumphant in his victory over me.

As always.

And then his hand stole towards the pommel of his knife.

Emotion rushed within me. Not hatred, perhaps, but raw resentment. That he, rather than I, should be serving the new King as his loyal supporter.

I pushed through the crowds to get away. Surprise showed on the faces of people around me. That surge in my chest must be reflected in a vicious twist to my features.

I hurried on, eager to leave those ugly thoughts behind me.

*

The day of the coronation was duly declared a holiday by Master Ashley, but though I hastened to the great Abbey at Westminster as soon as breakfast was over, I was too late to gain entry. Guards stood with their halberds crossed to keep back the crowds and only laughed at my attempt to pass on to the expanse of crimson carpet leading from Westminster Hall to the huge door of the Abbey's west front.

'I wish I had a groat for every one of those I've seen today,' grumbled one as I showed my boar badge and tried to explain. 'I'd be the richest man in London.'

'The church is full to overflowing,' said another. 'Only nobles or churchmen allowed through now. Take your place out here with the other little people.'

I bristled at his last words, but I could do no more. So I stayed where I was, hoping no one taller would push in front. But when the proceedings began not long after, I had as good a view as anyone not within the buildings themselves.

First to emerge from the Hall, to the blast of trumpets and cries of heralds, was a procession of churchmen, clothed in the finest regalia. A tremendous gilt and jewelled crucifix the size of a man was carried aloft before them.

Next came a line of noblemen, sumptuously dressed, each bearing a symbol of kingship – swords, a mace, a sceptre, the golden crown itself. Among them were the Earl of Northumberland and, striding just behind, the King's great friend, Lord Lovell, his features solemn.

A further fanfare burst forth.

And from the shadows of the tall doorway, flanked by several bishops and clad in purple velvet trimmed with ermine, stepped King Richard himself.

The crowds around me shouted and applauded and hurrahed as one.

But I found I had not the voice to join in. Now, only now, at last, I grasped the full truth of what had happened. The Duke – my Duke – had become King of all England and would today be confirmed such.

He walked forward beneath a richly embroidered canopy held high above his head on golden poles. His slow pace allowed all those present the time to behold him. Thunderous cheers crashed against the towering buildings, echoing about the square.

A few steps behind, bearing the hem of the train that cascaded from the King's shoulders, paced the Duke of Buckingham, almost outshining his sovereign in a gown of blue stitched with gold cartwheels. Beyond him flowed a stream of other lords, the last carrying another gem-studded crown.

The Duchess came next. More than two months since I had bid farewell to her at Middleham, her face above her silver gown was no less pale than it had been then. Her train of cloth of gold was held by an older lady with pinched cheeks and eyes shrewd as a weasel.

And then, in the cluster of ladies following, I espied Alys, her reddish curls for once demurely caught up in a netted cap of silver thread dotted with seed pearls. She spotted me and the serious look upon her face fell away. But her joyous wave was shushed away by the more mature ladies around her. In moments she was swept on past me and into the Abbey's cavernous depths.

Though I was not within the great church itself, the torrents of music and song that washed forth and what Master Ashley had told us of the ceremony meant all unfolded before my mind's eye. The swelling song of the choir as the King and Queen entered St Edward's shrine to take their seats of estate. The Latin service intoned before their approach to the high altar. Their anointing with the holy oil. The Mass celebrated in front of the enormous sword of state. The solemn oath sworn by all the nobles. The King kneeling as the Archbishop held the crown above his head...

I waited with the restless crowd on the cobbles of the Abbey precinct. Then a fanfare of trumpets blared, a deafening cheer went up within, the bells in the tower pealed, birds, startled from their perches on the roofs and stone sills of the ancient building, flew up into the glowing blue of the sky, and Duke Richard I knew now was King.

9

Rebellion

'Well, boy, you've settled in here with your new master and no mistake.'

My father's hand was heavy on my back as we strolled together around the garden of Master Ashley's townhouse, aflame now with early autumn colour. Pride radiated from him and from his voice like warmth from the October sun.

'The mayor asked after you when he heard I would be visiting. It's been the talk of the council chamber, your having fallen on your feet again. First with the Duke – though I suppose I should say King – and now here. I trust you know how fortunate you have been.'

'Yes, father.'

Did I sound convinced?

'It's not every boy who could be disgraced at the Minster one minute, and the next be apprenticed to one of the richest merchants in London.'

'No, father.'

The memory of that disgrace – the choir master's black eye and his anger at the riot I had caused – surfaced in my mind for the first time in many months, but I thrust it away. That was a different life, I was a different boy.

My father was on only his second ever trip to London in the course of his own merchant business. This was mostly in woollen and other cloths, but he also branched out into various luxuries, such as the books that Master Ashley had recently begun to print in the capital. The two men had met for the first time this morning and my father had been greeted as a welcome guest before they conducted a little business. I had waited outside my master's study door, wondering if I had been forgotten, despite my father's insistence in his letters that he was eager to see me in my new life.

The weight of his hand lifted from my shoulder as he paused to admire a cluster of blushing grapes hanging from a vine that clung to the sunniest wall of the garden. He plucked one of the smallest and popped it into his mouth, chewing once or twice before speaking again.

'And of course we all had a glimpse of your old master last month. It's been many years since York was honoured by a visit from a king, let alone one so newly crowned. I'm sure ours is the most loyal city on his progress around the kingdom.'

As I was constantly being reminded by town criers and household gossip and letters from Alys, only weeks after their coronation King Richard and his wife had set off on a regal tour around England. They had wended their way up to my home city by way of Oxford, Gloucester, Worcester, Warwick and other like towns, meeting the most important men of the kingdom and showing themselves to their people.

'He cannot have been entertained half so royally anywhere else,' continued my father. 'And his entry was a far grander sight than any I've clapped eyes on – ten times the spectacle we laid on for him last spring when he was still Duke. No doubt that's why he chose to make his son Prince of Wales in the Minster.'

His hand, holding another grape, stopped halfway to his lips as he gazed down at me, his eyes quizzical.

'How strange to think that the little lad was once your friend, Matt.'

Not 'once', I wanted to say as his hand carried on its way and the grape burst between his teeth in a shower of juice. Ed was still my friend, though he was so far distant. He had told me all about his special day at York in a letter I had received only a week or two before, decorated as always with his tiny drawings. He had not given up on our friendship, even if my father had, for all that he was now a prince.

'It was certainly a sight to behold, his investiture,' said my father, walking on again between trees laden with fruit and leaves of brilliant red and gold. 'More splendid than the coronation itself, some say. And the gifts that were given to the King and Queen – dishes piled high with gold – and the feast afterwards at the Archbishop's palace! Hundreds were seated there that night!'

Ed – too excited by the events to translate everything into our code – had written of his new gown of cloth of gold sent specially from London, and of the golden wreath with which he had been crowned by the Archbishop, and of walking back along the aisle of the Minster at the side of his mother and father, also wearing their crowns. And of the cheers and shouts of the gathered crowds as they showed their love and affection for their new King and Queen and their small prince.

Alys's most recent letter, nestled in my pouch alongside Ed's, had also likened the day to that of the coronation, but said that these celebrations had been more joyous. In York the King and Queen acted as though they were among friends, she wrote, not touched by the intrigues and gossip and rivalries of the court at Westminster. As the royal party had travelled further north from the capital, though he was always busy with work and petitions the King had at last relaxed. He had even laughed when councils of towns he visited tried to give him presents of money to help with his expenses. Alys said he always refused them, declaring he would rather have his people's hearts than their money.

These letters from Alys and Ed, a few from Elen – none at all from Roger, of course, just odd lines scribbled at the end of others' messages – were the most precious things in my life now, together with Murrey – my only remaining links with that part of my life that had gone and now, looking back, seemed so brief. I kept them safe always, hidden in my bundle in my attic room or, the most recent, tucked in my pouch with other of my treasures, to be read and reread in any moments of leisure. My fingers itched to retrieve them now as my father spoke more of my old master and his family.

'It's said the King plans a great council to rule in the north – to show that he will not neglect us now he must live here in the capital. His sister's son, the Earl of Lincoln, will be a great man thereabouts in his place, no doubt to keep my lord of Northumberland in check. And little Prince Edward will stay on in northern parts and learn to govern alongside him.'

Ed's howl of disappointment on being told this news tore through my head as though I had been there with him. His last letter to me had been full of the dread of being left behind when his beloved mother and father made their way back to London, as had happened in the spring. Now his fears were shown to be well founded. He would see it as a further cruelty, although my father obviously approved.

Our conversation turned then to our family matters – the coming marriage of my eldest brother, John, how my baby sister was growing, that my new mother was praying for a baby of her own – and soon it was time for my father to say his farewells. Once he had embraced me, Mistress Ashley arrived in a rustle of silk skirts to relay her husband's apologies at having been called away on business. She pressed into my father's grateful hands a basket of grapes and violet plums from the beautiful gardens, and then he was gone.

All that was left was his familiar smell of lanolin, leather and ink lingering in the air, the warm memory of his pride in me and loyalty to our King – and his usual reassurance that York would ever be my home if I should need it.

My mood was mixed as I returned to my work in the printing house – happiness at my father's praise, longing to see the rest of my family again, sadness at not witnessing the festivities in York with my friends, sorrow for Ed. But I had little time to rake through such thoughts as there came a hollering and a hammering at the main door – loud enough to reach us above the clacking and groaning of the printing press at work.

Master de Vries, the new print master lately arrived from Flanders together with the mint-new printing press, told Simon and me to keep working as he hurried off to investigate. But of course, intrigued, we followed him out and through the connecting passageways, to find in the entrance hall half the household staff clustered, chattering like an excited flock of starlings.

In their midst was Master Lyndsey, clapping his hands and raising his voice, calling for calm. Beside him Mistress Ashley was speaking in an undertone with a stranger clad in dusty leather armour, who clutched a sealed letter in one hand.

As Simon and I lurked in a doorway watching, Mistress Ashley led the man away towards her husband's study. The hubbub quietened and at last Master Lyndsey's words could be heard above the uproar.

'Our master has already been called away to the city council, so no doubt we shall soon know more. But this messenger says the call has gone out for men to rally to the city's defence. The militia will be gathering at the usual muster points. All men of fighting age are free to attend.'

With that he followed his mistress and the soldier into the study and the crowd splintered off in all directions.

Master de Vries caught sight of us hovering in the background and flapped his hands at us.

'Away you go, boys,' he said in his heavily accented English. 'Work is over for the day. But you must keep to the house. It may not be safe on the streets.'

'But what has happened, Master?' Simon asked, as the print master took us each by the elbow and steered us back towards his workshop.

'Nothing is quite clear yet, boys, but they say that there have been rumblings of discontent in some areas since the summer. Since King Richard stood against the old King's family and then became King himself. Now rebels have declared themselves and are marching on London.'

'On London!'

Simon was a local boy and terror was splashed across his face.

'Aye, lad. But fear not – it will take several days for them to march in from their lairs in Kent.'

'Kent? But that isn't so very far,' I protested, remembering the country I had ridden through with Master Ashley's party on the way to the port on the coast.

'They will be trying to gather supporters on their way – that will take time, if they manage it at all.'

Fear was still in Simon's eyes, despite Master de Vries's calming words.

'But what will happen when they get here? My family —'

He fell silent as the print master raised his hands.

'Master Lyndsey says the Duke of Norfolk has been making preparations for some time. He has already called up his men to take the field against any rebels. And once London's own defenders are gathered, there will be nothing to fear. Master Hardyng tells me that Londoners are most valiant in their city's defence.'

'But why? Who are they – the rebels?' I asked.

'The word is that they are Lancastrians – and supporters of the old Queen's family.'

'The Woodvilles?' said Simon. 'Why?'

'They'll no doubt be men who fear they may lose their jobs and preferments under King Richard,' Master de Vries replied, searing scorn in his voice. 'And maybe they would if they carry on their corrupt lives and don't adjust to the new King's ways. It is said they plan to place the old Queen's son, young Edward, on the throne, despite the boy's bastardy.'

My thoughts snapped back to the events of early summer. And to the old Queen, Elizabeth Woodville, who was still living in sanctuary after more than five months.

'But how would they do that? And would Parliament allow it?'

Master de Vries's face was grim.

'They've timed it well, I'll allow them that. With the King away in the north of the country, with few men about him, and most of the great lords out of London... If the rebels are able to capture the city and the Tower, and prevent the King from returning... If they can raise enough men to face him...'

He shook his head, then shrugged.

'But I am sure the city will stand firm against them. And my lord of Norfolk has rallied many men to him already, with more to come. It seems there were warning signs... I doubt the old Queen and her family will win out and get the chance to put their case to Parliament – whatever case they believe they have.'

By now we had cleared away our work tools and with the dark bulk of the printing press brooding still and silent as at the end of a normal day, Master de Vries dismissed us. His last words were a reminder not to leave the house.

But of course I could not heed him, not today, not with rebellion brewing against my old master.

Saying nothing to Simon, or any of the household, I slipped out of a back door and into the bustle of the city, uncertain at first where to direct my feet. But it wasn't long before I was aware of small groups of men, in twos and threes, some clutching bundles, hurrying away from the river. I guessed they were on their way to join the defence.

With Murrey sticking close, I chose two men to follow, winding my way behind them through the crowds of people thronging the streets – peaceful still, carrying on with their usual business. Had they, perhaps, not heard of the threat on its way?

Unlike Simon I had no worry for my own family. My father had said he would be leaving London the next day to return to York, and if Master de Vries was right, it would be some time before the city would be facing any real danger.

The two men I was trailing had the appearance of young craft journeymen, around the age of my elder brother, perhaps leatherworkers or cobblers from their clothes and the calluses on their hands. They joked and laughed together as they jostled their way through the townsfolk, heading always north through the maze of alleys and courtyards in this part of the city. They seemed not to observe they had two shadows on their heels – one human and one hound. All around us other men, most older, a few younger, some grim-faced, more of them lighter-hearted like my guides, strode purposefully in the same direction. Soon we all merged with a stream of men flowing along a wider street, lined by a mixture of fine merchants' houses and craft workshops. Far ahead of us loomed one of the massive gates through the city wall.

In all my months' apprenticeship and, before that, my time in London during the winter, I had never ventured into this area. But as the stone gatehouse rose above us and I passed with the others through its dark archway out into sunlight-flooded open fields, I guessed where we were. This must be Moorfields, the marshy land where the men of York had camped before the coronation and before their triumphal entry to the city behind the King and Earl of Northumberland. Where Master Lyndsey had said Londoners had turned out to mock them and their ancient gear. Now Londoners themselves were collecting together here to repel a real threat.

Hundreds were there already as I trudged out on to the tussocky ground. Within moments I had lost my two guides amidst the hustle and bustle, as busy as a summer fair back in York. My eyes were drawn this way and that by men shouting to each other, greeting friends and clapping them across the back, leading horses, mules, asses, pushing and shoving every which way to find a path through the gathering. Two or three times I had to skip smartly out of the way before a boot or a hoof stomped down on my foot. Murrey's sharp barked warnings reached my ears above the clamour as her warm flank pressed comfortingly against my leg.

After a while a pattern emerged in the chaos. Here and there huddles formed around soldiers clad in leather armour like the messenger at Master Ashley's. These officers clasped wood-bound wax tablets such as I had used in lessons at the Minster school and were busy jotting on them as they spoke to the men clustering about them.

Attaching myself to the nearest knot of men, I hovered on the fringes, straining to hear what was being said over the racket all around. I stood there only a minute or two before the officer spotted me and beckoned. The men to either side pressed back to let me pass.

My steps forward were slow, despite my earlier eagerness to join the city's defenders, aware as I was of all those eyes upon me. The officer waved me to him once more.

'Hurry up, boy.'

His eyes narrowed, his stylus poised above his writing tablet.

'Have you brought me a message from your master? Will he or his journeymen be joining us later? Just give me his name and I will write it down.'

I swallowed, my face warm under his stare.

'No, sir, not my master, but me. I've come to offer my service.'

My voice sounded high and hesitant to my ears, a boy's voice only still, and all about me laughter flared. I wished then that I had not come. But I was heartened both by Murrey's growl and that the officer himself did not laugh.

Instead he squinted at me again, looking me up and down.

'Nay, lad, you're rather small to join the muster. The city's not so desperate yet. Nor likely to be, from what I've heard of these paltry rebels.'

The laughter changed to cheers and the officer allowed himself a smile.

'So, be off with you. Or your master will be missing you. Next?'

I stood my ground, stopping those around me from stepping up.

'But, sir, is there no way I can be of use? I want to serve my King. Look!'

Remembering my boar badge – for all it had been no help at the coronation – I pointed to where it was still fastened to my doublet.

His face altered. Was it suspicion or –?

His next words confirmed it.

'So you wear the King's badge? Who did you steal that from, hey?'

I was shocked at the idea.

'No one!' My fierce response prompted another rumble from Murrey as I protested, 'He gave it to me with his own hands. When he was still Duke. I was his page.'

'Any thief could say that.'

'You can ask my new master. He'll vouch for me.'

To my surprise, the officer roared with laughter.

'Don't fret, lad. It's just my little joke. You're not the only one here today who wants to serve the King – nor who has a badge to show. Though,' he leaned in close, peering at my chest, 'not all perhaps such a pretty one. Most I've seen have been hessian ones, given to all and sundry at the coronation. Maybe we can find you a job after all. Have you keen sight?'

'Aye, sir,' I said, drawing a breath in relief.

'Perhaps the watch will have a use for you. If your new master can spare you.'

He laid a heavy stress on the word 'new' as though he hadn't believed my earlier words. But I didn't care.

And that was how I came to be atop the great wall of London at midnight.

10

The Watch

It was a fine clear night, the faintest nip of early frost in the air as I paced along the walkway on the top of the city wall.

Above me, a dusting of stars, no moon; behind me, any lanterns still burning in the city blotted out by the ancient fortress known as the Tower.

People said a castle had stood here since the Conquest, guarding the crossing of the river. That it had never fallen, even during the cousins' war more than three centuries ago, when Queen Mathilda and King Stephen had fought each other for the crown. I prayed tonight that its venerable stones would prove invincible once again if the rebels should attack.

The elegant square building called the White Tower dominated the castle complex, overshadowing every other structure in the several acres enclosed on three sides by the deep moat, on the fourth by the river. This night few lights shone through its arrow slits. Its defenders were not on high alert.

Master de Vries had been right. More than seven nights now I had paced for hours along the wall top, before handing over the watch to my replacement and tracing my way back through the pitch-dark streets to throw myself, bone-weary, on my narrow attic bed. And still there was no sign of the Kentish rebels.

This morning, on an errand for Master Ashley, I had watched as a hundred horsemen or more and several companies of footsoldiers had filed through the city streets, despatched across the river to seek the rebels. At their head, beneath a banner of a silver lion rampant, rode the Duke of Norfolk, newly honoured with that title by King Richard before his coronation. Watchful eyes in a face lined by many summers scanned the cheering crowds even as he raised his mailed hand to salute them. I had seen him once or twice before on visits to the watch or city guard, speaking to officers and men as if he were one of them. They touched their caps or doffed their helmets, but soon they were joking with him with no mind to his noble status.

A shiver ambushed me as I gazed across the country beyond the wall. A keen breeze carried with it the scent of burnt stubble from the autumn fields, mingled with the salt smell of the tide as it raced up the river towards the bridge. Not a glimmer of light in that direction, save one on the mast of a merchant ship I had marked before sundown, tethered downstream of the city, no doubt awaiting the ebbing of the tide. No movement or sound either. Nothing that could herald the approach of the rebels.

The darkness and silence were split by a shattering, drawn-out roar, answered at once by Murrey, starting up, snarling in her turn.

I grabbed at her collar before she flung herself off the wall to find the source of the challenge. I knew it well enough now, though my little hound still could not understand. For there within the Tower precinct was the famous royal menagerie of exotic beasts.

I had never seen them, but my fellow watchmen had told me of the graceful long-necked creatures which reached far above a man's head, colossal grey thick-skinned animals with snakes for noses, sandy-coloured horses with splayed feet and hills upon their backs, ferocious giant cats with shaggy manes upon their heads and roaring voices that split the night. Lions. The noble beasts of kings and emperors.

How I longed to see them! And had thought several times to take myself to the great gateway into the Tower and ask to be admitted.

I recalled how young Edward – then King – had invited me to visit him there and view his wondrous exhibit. But also to mind came the reception of my boar badge by the officer at Moorfields – how it was a two-a-penny thing, perhaps no more to be considered a key to the Tower than it was a key to the good graces of the militia.

I fingered it now as I relaxed my grip on Murrey, her snarl having subsided to a grumble deep within her throat. I knew it was not a tuppenny-ha'penny thing, not really. Forged of choice silver, not cut from drab cloth, and handed to me alone by a royal duke, soon to be King. But by that token, not to be employed for tawdry purposes, such as fulfilment of a base desire to spy on strange, savage beasts.

For just that reason I had refrained from attempting entry to the Tower to find Edward himself – lodged there still as far as I knew, with his brother Richard, in the luxurious royal apartments of the Garden Tower. Its dark bulk, close to the menagerie, was visible from my vantage point, its wide windows facing the river black squares now, only one or two still outlined with flickering firelight.

I had thought often of Edward these past nights, as I had during the summer. Of what he did, how he spent his time – and how he bore the thought that he was now never to be king. Perhaps he had been relieved. His words to me on our long rides together had suggested as much. Yet what was in his mind now, if he knew of the rebellion in his name? Did he hope that the Kentish rebels, and those also recently reported south of the city in Surrey, would prevail, seize him from his lodgings, defeat his uncle Richard, and put him back upon the throne? Did he even still believe that was his place after the revelations about his parents' marriage – or lack of it – and his declared illegitimacy?

I bent down and stroked Murrey's tufted head, my touch rewarded by her raising her eyes to mine. Reflected in their velvet depths, stars glowed like the dying embers of a fire.

'Matt!'

The voice hailing me was Simon's.

He had caught me leaving Master Ashley's on the evening of my first watch and had insisted on coming with me so he also could serve King Richard. The officer in charge had shrugged and told him to relieve me for the second watch of the night.

The stretch of wall that we patrolled was only short – maybe half the length of that guarded by adults of the watch. Perhaps the officer was merely humouring us young boys in our zeal to be of use. But I was glad even just to do this. And, having found among our master's many books a volume on the basics of swordplay, Simon and I had pledged that once this danger was past, we would join together in training. We had already lodged an order for two hardened chestnut swords with a local woodturner.

'Is all quiet?' he asked now.

'All quiet,' I agreed. 'Save the lions.'

He flashed a smile, just perceptible in the darkness.

'Maybe they're hoping to greet the rebels with a warm welcome.'

'I could do with one of those. It's a chilly night.'

'The brazier's still lit in the guard house. Captain says there will be spiced ale if you don't dawdle.'

We clasped hands and, whistling to Murrey, I picked my way down the nearest flight of narrow steps clinging to the inside of the wall. A little way along, snug against the ancient stonework, crouched a small building. A warm, wavering orange glow spilled from its open doorway, illuminating to one side two seated men, casting dice and talking quietly. At my approach, one rose, while the other reached for an axe lying upon the ground next to him.

I stood still and cleared my throat.

'Matthew Wansford of the watch, sir.'

The standing man nodded, his face hidden in the gloom.

'Aye, lad, I knew from that shadow by your side. Rest easy, Dan.' He waved his hand to his companion, who replaced the axe upon the cobbles. ''Tis only the lad who takes the first watch and his little hound. There's nothing to worry about – you'll have time aplenty to win back your pennies from me.' Then again to me, 'All's quiet, lad? Neither hide nor hair of the traitors?'

'Nothing, sir.'

'Long may that continue. Take yourself off to your bed, lad. Or if you prefer, warm yourself at the fire and sup what mulled ale the guard have left.'

My nostrils twitched at the enticing scent of clove and cinnamon wafting in the night air and, with a bow to the captain and his friend, I stepped into the outer chamber of the guard house.

A scatter of stools, a small table or two, an earthenware cauldron suspended above the iron latticework of the brazier in the middle of the room, crammed with glowing coals, tiny flames licking at their edges. Snores penetrated the stout door from the inner chamber, where the company of guards rested while awaiting any alarm.

I ladled out some steaming ale and took myself off to a stool against the far wall. Murrey settled herself at my feet as I took a first sip. The liquid scalded my tongue, leaving behind grittiness from the spices.

Setting the cup upon a table to cool, I fished in my pouch, drawing out the small leather-bound volume of 'The Death of Arthur' given to me by the Duchess – now Queen, I corrected myself. Safe within it were folded the most recent letters from my friends, so far away. I opened the book now, and with it the letters. I couldn't read them in the poor light thrown by the brazier, but I didn't need to. As my fingertips brushed the smooth papers and the faint spider-scrawls of ink, I recalled them almost word for word, I had read them so often.

My glimpse of the Duke of Norfolk in the morning brought to mind Alys's lively tales from the court, and how his wife had been slighted on the day of the coronation. Though a great friend, she had been robbed of the chance to hold the new Queen's train for the ceremony by Lady Stanley, wife of a Royal Council member, who claimed seniority. Alys had been scathing in her letter:

She claims her first husband was an Earl, but even a newly made Duchess is senior to a Countess – in everything, except perhaps age. The Queen and Duchess laughed about it later, but Lady Tyrell – who has quite befriended me since I've been here – said the Duke of Norfolk had words with Lord Stanley about it.

And indeed this morning my lord of Norfolk had appeared the sort of steadfast gentleman who would display such loyalty to both his wife and his King.

Voices broke through my musing, above even the cacophony of snoring from the sleeping guards. Outside, the captain was speaking, not quietly to his friend as before, but challenging a newcomer.

The new voice stirred something deep inside me, unnerving me before I could even distinguish any words, although the captain's tones had become friendlier. Murrey uncurled her lithe body and pushed her head up against my hand. I felt rather than heard the rumble in her throat, then the fur bristled on her head. Was she sensing my strange disquiet, or had the voice itself provoked her?

Among the snores, now, snatches of the conversation became audible – single words, odd phrases. 'Rebels – West Country – His Grace – royal seal – Grantham – Duke of Buckingham – foul traitor – ready to take up arms – Tudor – the south coast – string 'em up.' As I struggled to make out what was afoot, the familiarity of the second voice grew, until at the captain's final words, 'at the fire', it at last struck me with the force of a blow who stood outside, reporting.

I sprang to my feet, my hand flying unbidden to the knife at my belt as a broad shadow cut across the doorway. It stepped forward, the firelight grasping at its face, and my fear was confirmed.

It was Hugh Soulsby.

His eyes met mine, but for a second he didn't recognize me. Then his features twisted, and the brazier's flickering flames and their pitch-black shadows transformed him into all the red-painted demons from hell I'd ever seen daubed on church walls.

The moment passed. Moving to one side, he revealed the captain's companion, Dan, following in his wake.

Hugh dropped the helmet he was carrying on to a nearby table and shrugged his thick travelling cloak from his shoulders. Beneath was the iron-studded leather armour now worn by so many men around the city.

Dan scooped out a cup of spiced ale and handed it to him, turning back to the cauldron to fill another. Seeing me there, he gestured with the ladle as though offering to replenish mine, but I shook my head in silence.

'Sit you down, lad,' he said to Hugh as he poured ale for himself. Then to me, 'And you, lad, if you want to hear this squire's report. He's brought word of the rebels. It seems the treachery is spreading.'

Inside, a part of me was screaming at me to leave, to get far away from this boy who had been such an evil influence on my life. But he and Dan stood between me and the doorway. And, for all my loathing of Hugh, I dearly wanted news of the rebellion.

Hugh didn't glance at me again as he drew up a stool close to the brazier. He seated himself and rubbed his hands, stretching them towards the fireglow, before picking up his cup again, rolling it in his hands to warm them some more. Dan also sat and I lowered myself back on to my stool, tucking my book and letters away in my pouch. Murrey rested her head upon my knee, letting out a faint whine as I caressed her silky ears.

'Come, lad,' Dan was saying, 'you were in full flow to the captain when I came back from relieving myself. Can you start your report again, briefer this time, if it suits you?'

'Aye, sir.'

Hugh took a taste of his ale and his shadowed eyes peered at me a moment above the rim of his cup. As he lowered it again, a hint of his usual smirk fleeted across his face, before he turned again to his questioner.

'As I told your captain, sir, I've been sent by order of the Royal Council to report to all the guards along this stretch of the defences. Your company is the last. The Council reports that the rebellion is swelling. There has been word from the King that rebels are marching also in Wales and the west country. His Grace has ordered the Great Seal to be sent to him at Grantham.'

The little I knew of how the kingdom was governed told me that mention of this royal seal was important, but what Hugh said next drove all thought of it from my head.

'And he has proclaimed the Duke of Buckingham a traitor.'

'Buckingham? A traitor?' Dan's amazement was no greater than my own.

'Aye, sir. It seems he is leading the rebels in the west, marching out from his stronghold at Brecon. The rebels in Kent and Surrey have already declared him their leader.'

'Is it possible?' Dan's question echoed that careering round my own head. 'Can he be so rash? I heard the King had granted him all the lands and titles he coveted. What can he seek to gain?' His shook his head in disbelief. 'They say few men have rallied to the rebels so far. And with the King mustering a great army in the midlands, the north steadfast in its support – and London holding firm for him – what hope can my lord of Buckingham have of taking the city and putting the boy Edward back on the throne?'

'They say that is not his aim.'

'Not his aim?' Dan spluttered. 'Not the aim of these Woodville lackeys who dare to take up arms against their rightful King? What then can be Buckingham's plan? And why has he thrown in his lot with them?'

Hugh gulped again at his drink, lengthening the expectant moment as though to increase its drama.

'They say, sir, that he has taken the cause of Henry Tudor.'

Dan was shocked into silence. His mouth hung open, a dark void in the firelit oval of his face.

A coal fell with a clatter within the brazier, breaking the stillness, before I dared to speak.

'Henry Tudor? Who is he?'

Hugh shot me a glance, but said nothing.

Dan shook himself and closed his mouth, before opening it again to spit out the words,

'A traitor from the line of Lancaster. He calls himself the Earl of Richmond, but that title was taken away from his family for their treachery. He claims he has more right to the crown than any Yorkist – and he fled to exile in Brittany years ago rather than bow down to King Edward. And Buckingham's family were of course Lancastrians in the past.'

Hugh's face showed no expression as Dan turned to him again.

'And is there news of Tudor's movements in all this?'

Hugh shrugged.

'None that I have heard. Though there have been rumours that the Duke of Brittany has been equipping ships and soldiers for him.'

Dan spat into the brazier. It sizzled and flared.

'Pah! Rumours. There are always rumours. And Brittany, France – always keen to stir up trouble for us. Old King Edward should have dealt properly with them years ago. But, no – he preferred their gifts and promises of friendship and weasel words.'

'But we have had peace with them.'

'Peace? At what cost? Their constant manoeuvrings, helping our enemies behind our backs, harbouring them as they plot against us, allowing pirates to plunder our ships and disrupt our trade – maybe encouraging them. That's not a peace worth the name. And now this. Lady Stanley should have been told to deal with her son long ago.'

The familiar name prompted me to ask, 'Lady Stanley, sir?'

'She's wife now to Lord Thomas Stanley, who is close advisor to the King and Council. But she is mother to this Tudor by her first husband. And they say she has some influence.' Dan was thoughtful for a moment. 'Though it must be said, Lord Stanley and his family's loyalty to King Richard and King Edward has been questionable at best.'

'Sir!' Hugh protested. 'My uncle, Lord Soulsby, is Lord Thomas's man. Who questions his loyalty questions the honour of my family too.'

At this, the man stood quickly and bowed to him.

'Then I beg pardon, lad. I repeat only what I have heard. Take no offence, I pray you. We are all here united in our loyalty to the King.'

'Indeed, sir, we are.'

Hugh buried his face in his cup once more and I could not read his expression.

'Yet still I cannot understand why Buckingham would throw in his lot with this pretender,' continued Dan. 'If anything, he himself has as good a claim to the throne as Tudor does. Better, even. And word was that the rebellion sought only to restore old King Edward's son to the crown.'

Hugh placed his cup back upon the table and raised his hands again towards the brazier, as though still cold. He looked at neither me nor Dan as he said,

'Perhaps other news can explain it, sir. My uncle tells me that word has come from France that King Edward's sons are...' he paused, '... are dead.'

The word plunged like a stone into the room.

Dan's mouth fell open again.

'Dead?' I choked the word out.

Hugh stabbed me with a look.

'Aye. Dead.'

'How so?'

'Murdered.'

I could not speak again. It was as though hands were upon my throat, squeezing it, stopping my words, my breath.

Dan picked up where I left off.

'It cannot be. They are safe within the Tower.'

'And who has charge of the Tower?'

'King Richard, of course. And the Constable.'

'The Constable. Aye. Since the summer, the Duke of Buckingham. And the Deputy Constable, Brackenbury. Both loyal to the King. Yet now... As you say – and my uncle too – what cause should my lord of Buckingham have to turn rebel against the King?'

Thought after thought could be seen chasing across Dan's face, mirroring the turmoil in my own mind. What was Hugh suggesting?

'You cannot be serious, boy. That our King... that King Richard...'

'Why not?'

'But King Richard...'

'God's teeth, sir! He has already taken their crown. Placed himself on the throne in their stead. My uncle says this would be the next sensible step. He says he would do it himself if he were in the King's place.'

'What next step?'

'To rid himself of the boys. Once and for all.'

His eyes wide, Dan looked about him and back through the dark entranceway, as though afraid of who might be watching or listening in the shadows. Hugh took another mouthful of his ale.

'Have a care, lad. What you are saying is treason. And for what reason would King Richard commit such a crime? Parliament set the boys aside. King Richard is the rightful King. There's no need for – for murder.'

'Maybe so. But it's the talk of Brittany, they say.'

'Who says?' I found my voice again. Hugh glanced my way.

'My uncle. He has contacts. People who hear things. Who know things.'

'More rumours, you mean?' I remembered what King Richard had said to the Duke of Buckingham of rumours – when he was himself still Duke, all those months ago in Northampton. 'They're dangerous things. You should not believe them lightly. And these people who've said this. They don't know him. And they're miles away. How could they know anything?'

'Word gets around.'

'Or it's sent around,' Dan put in. 'Brittany, you said? Maybe by Tudor, then. He wants to be King himself, if the rebels defeat King Richard and are spurred on by this. And the boys would stand in his way too.'

'But they're not in King Richard's way,' I insisted. 'Their father's bigamy ensured that.'

'Aye,' said Dan. ''Tis true. Though what he was thinking of... But he was ever reckless, they say, old King Edward – especially when it came to women...'

I turned to Hugh.

'And how could you repeat such evil about him. You know him.'

Hugh glared at me.

'Know who?'

'King Richard, of course. You know what he's like.'

'Aye, I do.'

'Then you know he could never do such a thing.'

Hugh's face betrayed no emotion. But he raised one eyebrow.

'Do I?'

My hands curled into fists as I leapt to my feet.

Murrey, dislodged, sprang up too, her lips drawn back in a snarl, baring her white dagger-like teeth.

I grasped hold of her collar before she lunged towards Hugh.

Restraining her gave me time to think – about what, on impulse, I had been about to do. About the mistake it would have been. And what my then master had said when I had resorted to violence against Hugh once before.

With King Richard's words circling in my brain, I brought my breathing back under control, though my heart still thumped against my ribs, the torrents of blood rushing in my ears.

I drew myself up to what height I possessed.

'I'll listen to no more of this... of this treasonous talk,' I said with all the dignity I could muster. And, dragging a wriggling Murrey along with me, I stalked out of the chamber.

Behind me, Hugh's laughter pealed out, pursuing me as I headed off into the night. And as I strode across the cobbled yard towards the street, his shout assaulted my ears:

'What are you so upset about? By the devil, I've heard the boys are both brats – just like their good-for-nothing milksop cousin.'

11

Return of the King

I slept little for the rest of that night and showed up to work on the morrow bleary-eyed and yawning.

Simon, whose watch ended long after mine, wondered at my shortness of temper as we laboured together over the printing press, helping Master de Vries sort the tiny letters in their cases, positioning the vast sheets of paper, raising and lowering the weighty platen. When we ceased work for dinner, he took me aside before we entered the dining hall.

'What ails you today? You're as irritable as Murrey when she snapped at that wasp in the summer.'

Poor Murrey had had a terrible time after the wasp had stung inside her mouth. She had pawed and pawed at her swollen cheek until it bled, and I had been forced to bind all four of her feet in cloth to stop her clawing her face to ribbons. I wished now that I could scratch in the same way the sore, raw spot left by Hugh's words.

I told Simon as briefly as I could what had passed the night before. He too was horrified and dismissed the rumours as lies and slanders that should never see the light of day. But I overheard him later telling the journeyman printer as we returned to work – and I regretted mentioning it to him at all.

But, as Hugh had said, word got around – even without my help. By the time of Alys's next letter, the rumours had reached even Middleham, where she and Roger had remained with Ed and the Queen when King Richard had ridden south at the first stirrings of the revolt. Her horror at them and scorn for those who could spread such lies dripped like caustic lime from her words as she told of how the rebellion was viewed from far away in the north.

The Londoners are no fools. They clearly don't believe the King could be so wicked if they have rallied to his defence as you say. And the same in all other parts of the kingdom. Very few people seem to be supporting the Duke of Buckingham, or this Tudor. But now I understand a conversation I overheard weeks ago between the Duchess of Norfolk and Lady Tyrell.

She had switched to our code, as she always did when writing about gossip or anything that might be confidential.

Qb eia ijwcb epmbpmz bpm jwga apwctl jm uwdml nzwu bpm Bwemz· Q bpwcopb qb eia bw abwx bpmu jmqvo i nwkca nwz zmjmttqwv, tqsm bpmg pidm jmmv – jcb uigjm qb eia ijwcb bpmqz ainmbg· lvl eqbp bpm Lcsm wn Jcksqvopiu ia Kwvabijtm wn bpm Bwemz...*

She had broken off, as though she could not bear to think any more on the subject, and had turned to telling of how the Queen was sick with worry and had had to be stopped from following the King.

Master Fleete said King Richard had enough to worry about without her safety too. Best for her to remain in Middleham, in the midst of their most loyal subjects. Although Master Fleete himself immediately took horse with other men from the castle and rode to join the army.

Real news of the course of the uprising was hard to come by over the following days. But in time came the word that we had all been waiting for.

Master Ashley had been summoned again to attend the city council, and I was on an errand for Master de Vries to collect supplies from a shop in St Paul's churchyard, when a gathering crowd attracted my attention. I joined its very fringes, clutching to me the various bundles and packages to keep them safe from cutpurses.

A crier had mounted the steps of St Paul's Cross and was holding aloft a proclamation. Damp stains were spreading on the pale paper in the heavy drizzle. The crisp golden days of early autumn had descended into a dreary, wet November.

'God be praised,' the crier bellowed, as the whispering and mutterings of the crowd died away. 'Let us offer thanks to the Virgin for our deliverance. For the rebellion is over.'

Cheers rose into the air as though pigeons taking flight, but many of the people hushed their neighbours, eager to hear more without hindrance. The crier obliged as the uproar settled back into expectant silence.

'By the Grace of God and with the aid of his loyal subjects, our lord King Richard has defeated the rebels. No battle was needed. On the approach of the King and his army, men fled in terror before his righteous cause, deserting the great rebel and traitor the Duke of Buckingham and his allies in malice. The said Duke, like a base coward, in turn fled in disguise, but was captured and taken to Salisbury to be tried for treason. On Sunday last he was beheaded in the market square as a condemned traitor.'

A shiver rippled through the crowd at these words, like a chill breeze lifting fallen leaves on a winter's day. The crier waited for a moment before speaking again.

'His Grace the King declares that no yeoman or commoner who took arms with the said rebels shall suffer his wrath. But all are urged to deliver up to his commissioners those well-born rebels and traitors still at large. By name these are: the bishops of Ely and

Salisbury,' a gasp rose from the gathering, 'the Marquess of Dorset,' knowing nods were exchanged between two men in front of me, 'Sir John Fogge,' the man embraced by the King on the day of his oath-taking, 'Sir John Cheney, Sir William Stonor, Sir George Brown, Sir Giles Dawbeney...'

The list continued – names unknown to me – of knights who had taken up arms against their King in Wales and the west country, and in counties south of the Thames. There a last stand had been made at Bodiam Castle in Kent – taken finally by the Duke of Norfolk. Along with the names were the sums of money to be paid as rewards for their capture – a thousand marks for the Marquess and bishops, five hundred for each knight.

As I listened I wondered that such men could break their oath of loyalty to their King, that churchmen could involve themselves in such affairs (though I later learnt that one bishop was himself a Woodville, the other a close friend of Lady Stanley) – and how the Marquess had escaped from sanctuary at Westminster, where his mother, the old Queen, was still holed up. I marvelled less now at her decision to remain there.

On finishing his litany, the crier rolled up the proclamation and stepped down from the cross. The crowd were left to chatter among themselves and potter away to their business.

Over the days to come, more word arrived of events in the west country as the King travelled through Dorset and Devon to restore order there and reward men who had remained loyal. More executions were reported, but fewer by far than the names read out by the crier. Later I heard that some men had fled with the Marquess to Brittany, but still others had been pardoned – and often even allowed to keep their lands and wealth. Later still, even the Marquess himself was offered a pardon – but I get ahead of myself...

Among other familiar names mentioned was that of Lady Stanley – and of her son, Henry Tudor. For once a rumour had had some truth in it. Around the time of Duke Henry's execution, Tudor was sighted along the Dorset coast, then off Plymouth, in command of two ships crewed by men in the pay of the Duke of Brittany. On receiving the news of King Richard's victory, he had turned tail and was presumed to have slunk back to his foreign lair.

Alys's next letter wrote of the disappointment of his mother, Lady Stanley, and how she had been at the heart of the rebellion – the centre of a web of intrigue between Buckingham, the bishops, Tudor and others of her Lancastrian family exiled on the continent.

Nyrk r nzkty!* She showed her true colours during the coronation. Yet the King has chosen to be merciful to her. Her lands are to be confiscated – but just given to her husband, who stayed loyal despite her plotting. So it's not much of a punishment. But as the Queen says, the King needs to keep such men as Lord Stanley happy – though she didn't look too happy about it herself.

Mind you, Lord Stanley and his brother William were not always loyal to King Edward, though they were later forgiven. Did you know? How difficult it must be to be King, when everyone is after power and wealth. Why can't they all just live in peace and enjoy the quiet life and prosperity it brings?

Hugh's words about his uncle being Lord Stanley's man nudged into my mind as I read the letter – and the story Roger had told me all those months ago in Middleham, about the execution of Hugh's father for treason. And I too wondered at this endless desire for power – at any cost.

Two or three weeks later, just at the start of Advent, news tore through the city that the King was to return from his progress back through the southern counties.

Crowds flocked to see him as he was led into the city across the great bridge by an escort of mayor, aldermen and chief citizens, my new master among them. All clothed in rich robes of crimson and violet, they offered a splash of colour on this drear day. Above, against the pale blue winter sky, fluttered the royal standard and the familiar banner of white boar upon its field of murrey and blue. The silver lion of the Duke of Norfolk shone alongside. Behind the high-stepping horses of the standard bearers rode the King, astride Storm as usual, and the older Duke, with Lord Lovell and Master Ratcliffe heading the host of gentlemen bringing up the rear.

I had stolen away from my duties to snatch a glimpse of my old master, back in his capital city after an absence of more than four months. Unable to push my way through the throng, I had only a distant view. But even from so many yards away, the change since I had last seen him was unmistakable. He and the Duke laughed with one another, raised their hats to the cheers of the people, touched their breastplates over their hearts, bowed and waved to those who called to them from the overhanging house-fronts, and reached into their own purses to scatter coins to those at the front who begged for alms. Lord Lovell and their other gentlemen, though, were watchful, eyes scanning the crowd as though they feared there might still be trouble, even here in this loyal city.

As I straggled behind the procession of soldiers who marched in their wake, the mayor reached the steps of St Magnus's church and stood with his fellow councilmen awaiting their honoured guests. The King strode up to him, the Duke a step or two behind. They accepted bows, gifts and a speech of welcome, then embraced the mayor and several of his companions. Turning, the King spoke some words himself to the gathered multitude.

Though too far away to catch his speech, my head soon rang with the roars of the people, rolling back to me in waves, until everywhere around me was awash with noise. As I thrust my hands to my ears to deaden the sound, King Richard threw up his arm in salute, and then was gone, swallowed up in the church by the following flow of purple and red of the principal men of London. Master Ashley told us later of the service of thanksgiving and immense feast laid on by the council to celebrate the King's triumphal return.

It was the start of a joyous run-up to the Christmas season, though, for me, one very different to that of the previous year, when I had been guest at the court of the old King. All the solemnities of religious services were interlaced with the customary feasting and gifts, but the highlight for me was the practice of 'topsy-turvy' on Twelfth Night.

I had heard tell of it at the York Minster song school, but, living always at home and not as a boarder at the school, I had never been a part of it, or seen the Dean serve the choristers and canons at table, or any other of the customs involved. So to witness Master Ashley don rough clothes and place an apprentice cap upon his head, and Mistress Ashley tie a housewife's apron about her oldest gown, and both carry trays of meat and drink to tables, and bow to us boys and journeymen as they served us and poured our ale – and even sing for us during the meal, poke the huge Yule log in the hearth and clear away the empty dishes – it was all remarkable to me. It was a tradition in such households across the city and beyond – although it never reached as far as my father's house in York's Stonegate.

Ed enjoyed a memorable Christmas-tide too, though upset that his mother had travelled to London to join his father without him. In his many welcome letters, he also sorrowed over the loss of Alys who had headed south with the Queen, but he revelled in riding out each day with Roger and the other pages, despite the snow and warnings about his health. Once again, little snow fell in London – though in Middleham Ed said there were icicles as long as his arm hanging from the stable roof in celebration of Jesus' birth.

But one letter in particular almost bubbled over with his delight.

But my big news – can you believe it? – I have a hound puppy of my very own! Roger says my father feels guilty that he was not with me at Christmas – again – so he decided I should have one. I don't care what the reason is. Sir James Tyrell, the new master of the pages and squires, surprised me with her on Twelfth Night. It almost made up for my mother and father not being here.

She's beautiful, Matt – pure white like Florette and Shadow. I've called her 'Belle', because that means 'beautiful' in French. When we went out, I had to carry her in my doublet just like you did with Murrey, otherwise I would have lost her in all the snow! These past few days she's snuggled up with me since I've been unwell – it's nothing much, just a chill caught on one of our rides. (Fqq'v vgnn Oqvjgt!*)

I'm sure I'll be better soon and perhaps in the spring I'll be able to travel to London – I can't wait for Belle to meet Murrey. Or maybe you can come with my mother and father when they return here after Parliament is finished in the spring? Oh, why are you not still part of their household?

But, despite Ed's lament, I was no longer part of his family's close circle, and must accept it, cheerfully if I could, no matter how much I missed the company of all my friends.

Time passed. All was quiet in the realm. And so, 1483 – the tumultuous year of the three kings and the great rebellion – turned to 1484.

12

The Visitor

'Master Wansford, you are wanted in our master's study.'

One of the household servants stood before me in the print house.

I paused, the roller in my hand slick with ink, poised to run it across the frame full of type. Simon glanced at me, his eyebrows raised.

'Me? Are you sure?'

Bemused at the summons, I handed the roller to Simon and removed my heavy apron, folding it and placing it carefully on a nearby table.

Master Ashley I knew to be away from London on business in East Anglia. Mistress Ashley, though kindly to all the apprentices, had little to do with us unless we were ill or otherwise out of sorts. Master Lyndsey? I searched my memory for any reason he could wish to see me and I could discover none. While perhaps not the perfect apprentice, I had committed no misdemeanours of late that would prompt the mistress to charge the steward to punish me.

With Murrey as ever at my heels, I made my way through the entrance hall to the narrow door tucked away towards the rear. I knocked once, and the door was opened straight away by Mistress Ashley herself. One hand clutched a spray of spring flowers – sky-blue forget-me-knots, pink gillyflowers – and a small pair of iron shears, as though she had been interrupted in gathering her usual posies from her garden.

An oddly familiar expression shadowed her eyes for an instant and her free hand stretched out to squeeze my shoulder.

'Matthew, lad, come in, come in. Here is a friend come to see you.'

She drew me into the room, where the fresh sunlight slanted in through diamond-paned windows overlooking the garden. As I passed her, she patted my back again.

'I shall leave you alone to talk.'

And she glided out, pulling the door to behind her.

To my astonishment, there before me – strangely small against the magnificent carved stone fireplace of my master's private chamber – was –

'Roger!'

I had not met him for more than a year – in person or in letters. Though I wrote to him often enough, it was seldom any response came my way. As he had insisted on our first encounter, he was made for dancing and sport, not classroom learning – or, so it seemed, letter-writing. I had resigned myself to that long ago, though the loss of our fellowship and his unfailing cheerfulness had left a gaping void in my life.

As I stepped forward to greet him, I thought at first that he had not changed at all. Except perhaps he had gained a few more inches on me. But was there something else too? For a moment, I struggled to pinpoint it. But, when I shook his hand before heartily embracing him, it dawned on me. The usual laughing light had vanished from his eyes.

He drew away from my hug at once and shifted from one foot to another, his fingers fiddling with the strap of his pouch, before he leaned down to stroke Murrey.

Puzzled that he would not meet my eyes – what had I done wrong? – I forced myself to break our silence.

'I did not think to see you here in London, Roger. How are you? And your family?' His father's estate was not far from London, I knew, and that he had a townhouse in the city. 'There is no trouble at home, I hope?'

'No, not at all, though I am on my way to see them.'

'I thought you were to stay in the north and help Ed rule this new council of his.'

Roger's gaze slid sideways towards me and, as he straightened up, his mouth twisted as though in unhappiness.

'Do not joke, Matt. It is hardly a time for jests.'

His words and uneasiness worried me not a little.

'It's no joke, Roger. I would not dare. I leave that sort of thing to you. Yet today... Why so serious? Why are you here? Is Alys well? Elen?'

'The Queen has sent me to visit my parents. She thought it might make me feel better. But she said perhaps I should see you on the way.'

'Why? Have you been ill? Ed has not told me of it in his letters. Nor Alys. Though maybe she had not reached Middleham before you left. Although you said the Queen... Alys was travelling with her and the King...'

Roger stared at me.

'What? Haven't you heard?'

'Heard what?'

'But I wrote you a letter. At least, I thought I did.'

I laughed, a hollow, strained sound to my ears.

What hadn't I heard?

'You? A letter? I've received only one from you since I left Middleham. And that was just four lines asking what I knew about the rebellion. But perhaps there were others and they've all gone astray? Though Ed's and Alys's always arrive.'

I was gabbling, I realized, wondering at his seriousness, my alarm growing. My final words emerged in a stutter.

'This letter, what – what was it about?'

'About – it was about Ed.'

'Ed? What about him?'

There had been rumours. There were always rumours. About this or that. Master Ashley said they were sent around to confuse people, demoralize them, stir them up against the King, as in the late rebellion, or against this noble or that alderman, to thwart his ambition, or –

But this – about Ed – this –

123

'Matt,' Roger swallowed, forced himself to go on. 'Ed – Ed's dead.'

It was as though my heart, my very core, had been torn from my chest.

'Dead? But... but he can't be. I had a letter from him, only last —'

When was it? Last week? Last month?

This spring had been so busy. A trip to Friesland early in the year, the return delayed by storms in the channel, the need to catch up on work. The letter had been waiting for me on our return. Before I heard tell of any rumour...

In it he had written of... of longing to see his father and mother when they rode north again in the spring... of training his new pup with Roger, and... of having caught a chill, when out riding.

But it was nothing, he'd said. And he'd begged me not to tell his mother – as he always did if he'd done something amiss. As if I would now have the chance! She was worried about his health, he said, had given instructions that he was not to ride in the wintry weather.

And yet he had. Behind his tutor's back. And delighted in it. In cantering through the snowy water meadows, up on to the moor, overlooking the patchwork of strip fields in the valley, edged with drifts of snow and dark stone walls and the skeletons of thorn trees.

'He had been ill,' Roger said, his voice cracking. 'Not so serious. A chill. But it lingered.'

Yes, I knew.

'But then he would go riding again. Too soon. Although Doctor Frees had told him he shouldn't. And his mother in her letters. Though we all told him...'

Yes, yes, of course. That was Ed. Impatient to be well, to do what everyone else did.

'It was a cold day. And when we were on the moor, he... We didn't know what to do... Perhaps if you had been there...'

Haltingly, Roger told me all that had happened. And as he told it, I could see, hear, feel, as though I had been there.

A cold, sharp spring day. The knifing of the breeze in the nostrils. Plumes of breath rising from boys, ponies, grooms as they hurried about making all ready.

The clang of shod hooves on cobbles, the dull thud across the water meadows. The musty smell of last year's heather brushed by horses' legs up on the moor tops.

Black points of mud. Leaden sky above.

Boys laughing gaily, the snorting of their mounts, the sounds carrying across the still moor.

Then a gasp. And another.

Ed's breath rasping in his throat.

Boys clustering in concern. Leaden grey of his skin, bluish lips, eyes wide.

The rising scent of panic in the chill air.

A page remounts, dashes for the castle, the physician. A cloak, another, bundling Ed. Somehow, somehow, get him back to safety.

The thunder of hooves across the water meadows, up on to the moor. Adults' cries.

Master Fleete passing the small bundle, racked with coughs, struggling breaths, up to Master Gygges. Gentle hands, holding, supporting, before him on his mount.

The straggle of pages watching, the riders picking their way down and across the final fields. Following more slowly, dread weighing heavy inside them.

Back within the cold stone walls. Gloom cast by drawn curtains, paling only in the smokiness of lighted tallow.

Hushed, whispering.

Waiting on the steps, outside Ed's tower room.

The tang of herbs burning, warding off bad humours.

Nurse bustling, in, out, fetching, carrying. Bowls of steaming liquid, trays of this and that.

Master physician... closing the door behind him. Head shaking, eyes moist.

Small white pup whimpering, scratching at the wood.

Tap, tap, tap.

Then – silence.

Darkness.

Candles quenched.

The pungent fumes of incense, drifting.

Muttered words in Latin. The wails of women.

Men with trails of tears upon their cheeks.

The sad tolling of a single bell at the parish church.

Wetness upon my cheeks too. I buried my face in Murrey's fur. Her warm tongue licked the hand that clutched her.

'It was so quick.'

Roger's voice seeped into my sorrow.

'Too quick to summon the King and Queen. They were far away, still journeying north. Nothing could be done. It was days before they came. Alys was distraught. And Belle...'

The shivering white pup. Curled up against the cold, grey, still little boy.

Gently lifted away, crying to go back. Whimpering, scratching at the door.

'We nearly lost Belle too. She didn't want to leave him, wouldn't eat for days. Shadow had to care for her, almost like a mother. But she kept going back to Ed's chamber, trying to get in.'

Tap, tap, tap.

Roger's words faltered to a halt. He had no more to say.

His face glum, he stared out of the window as I wiped away my tears with my cuff.

Silence.

Save for the birds trilling their lilting spring songs among the fruit trees beyond the splintered glass.

A soft knock.

Mistress Ashley's lace-framed face peered around the door.

Roger started. He swung back to me, his eyes not meeting mine.

'I must go. My mother...'

I nodded, unable to trust my own voice.

'I will write,' he said. 'I promise. When I – when I go back. I'm to join the household at Sheriff Hutton, with the Earl of Lincoln. Now Ed – now there will be no household at Middleham.'

And he was gone. No farewell, not a backward glance.

Mistress Ashley guided me to a chair, sat me down, patted my shoulder again.

'Stay as long as you wish. I have told Master de Vries. If you need anything, just send the servant for me.'

Her tone was pitying. As she left the room, her last words to herself reached me.

'Poor little lad. And the Queen's only child...'

And I recollected that she herself had no children of her own, despite long years of prayers to the Virgin and St Anne.

I heard no more from Roger – I did not expect to, in truth, though all year I had hoped – but in a day or two a letter arrived from Alys. In it she told of the moment when the King and Queen had received the news of their son.

I've never seen such grief before. The Queen was overcome. The King could do nothing to comfort her, though they clung to one another as though they would never let go.

The royal party had journeyed sadly up to Middleham instead of the joyous spring progress it was to have been. A quiet funeral for Ed, then it was back to business for the King. For word had reached him that Henry Tudor had not given up his ambition, despite his flight after the failed revolt. In a ceremony in Brittany on Christmas day he had sworn an oath to marry Princess Elizabeth – old King Edward's eldest daughter.

He says it is to unite the houses of York and Lancaster, to stop the rivalry once and for all – though most Lancastrian supporters gave that up long ago, under King Edward. But it's said that the French King is helping him plan for an invasion of England, to challenge King Richard for the throne. I don't think he'd dare to land here in the north – no one would give him their support, their loyalty to the King and Queen is too strong. But there is talk of the King travelling round the north country to check the defences anyway. I think perhaps he doesn't want to go far from Ed too soon – or at least the place where he now lies.

I'm not sure whether the Queen will return to Westminster as planned – maybe she won't want to be apart from the King. She has been so distracted with grief. After the funeral, she walked for hours alone on the moor – she wouldn't let any ladies join her. The King was so worried when he heard – he had been in important meetings all day. And when she returned her gown was all torn and muddy, and she had lost her favourite jewel – do you remember, the beautiful necklace the King gave her after you returned from Christmas in London? The servants searched everywhere, but the Queen couldn't recall where she'd wandered and they never found it.

I did remember it – the vivid blue stone clasped in gold that I'd seen about the Queen's neck in happier days, when she was still Duchess. And when I had still been servant to her and her husband – and friend to their only son.

13

Paths Cross

Spring turned into summer, and summer passed slowly.

My grief remained raw, and now I had only one regular correspondent whose letters lit up the ordinary days of my apprenticeship. And even that source of enjoyment appeared under threat following a long-awaited event.

After almost a year, the old Queen – now to be called Dame Grey after her first, legitimate husband – had finally emerged from sanctuary, together with her daughters. And on her return to Westminster from the north, Alys was warned that her fate might soon be decided.

She tried to look on the bright side in her letters, despite her lingering sadness at Edward's death. As she told me straight away, this change didn't mean she was to marry Ralph Soulsby just yet. Nor was she to be made to join the household of Dame Grey, who had taken up residence in the countryside. Instead she was to attend her guardian's daughter, the lady Elizabeth, who had remained at court.

Elizabeth has been very friendly to me since she came out of sanctuary. She's only a few years older than me, but she says she remembers well when my mother was lady-in-waiting to her mother. She's even said I may keep Shadow with me now I've brought her back from Middleham. She loves hunting and hounds too – she used to hunt with her father as often as she was allowed. I'm sure I'll be very happy with her.

And who knows where I might end up? Lady Tyrell says the King must surely find Elizabeth a husband soon – if only to ruin Henry Tudor's plan to marry her himself. But the Queen pointed out that the King promised good husbands for Elizabeth and each of her sisters before their mother agreed to leave sanctuary, and he says there's no hurry. He wants to find the right match for her – a royal husband, if he can, though she is no longer seen as a true daughter of a King of England – and Tudor's threats don't worry him. So maybe I will get to travel abroad as you have!

Yet, for all Alys's cheerfulness and hope for the future, her regret at leaving the Queen and King after so many years was clear. And especially only months after their loss of Ed.

'They send their respects to you,' she wrote, 'and their thanks for your prayers when Ed died. They're still grieving, despite the show they must put on for courtiers and diplomats. I see the sadness in their faces at quiet moments.'

Although the King had said Alys could continue to write to me, as Dame Elizabeth had not forbidden it, perhaps the pleasures of a young princess's household distracted her, as her letters became less frequent. Then, as my second summer in the city drew to a close, they ceased altogether.

I continued to write – how could I not? Alys, and Elen who had accompanied her to Elizabeth's new house, were my last link to the chapter of my life that meant so much to me, the last link in a chain that was falling to pieces. Yet our lives had drifted so far apart now that I did not wonder at the change. I was after all only a merchant's son, and now a lowly apprentice. Our paths had brushed against one another for a brief time, like the closing of a butterfly's wings as it alights on a beautiful flower, then fluttered apart, perhaps to touch again no more. I dutifully wrote of the humdrum events of my existence, of the bright interlude of our late-summer visit to Bruges. But though I had on my return enclosed a kerchief of web-like lace as a gift for each of them from my travels, I no longer expected any reply.

Yet reply, of a sort, I did receive, unlooked-for though it was.

Autumn was gathering pace, and the early evening mists were rolling off the river into the embrace of the smoke rising from the city's coal fires, when one evening I was returning through the dusk from an errand. I was almost safe back at my master's house, when rounding a corner out of an alley, I all but bumped into a couple strolling together, as it seemed, along the street outside his gates.

The lady uttered a cry. The gentleman took a step backwards with a curse, lifting up the lantern he carried.

I bowed my apology swiftly. As I straightened up, a familiar voice spoke my name.

'Matthew? Is it you?' A gentle laugh. 'I see it is, for here also is Murrey. I hope she has not forgotten me.'

The lady was in fact a girl. It was Elen.

The light cast by the lantern slanted through the strands of mist on to her dark cheek as she leant to pet my hound. Beyond her, a mounted groom led two horses, one the palfrey I remembered from Crosby Place, the other a dark brown colt, tricked out in the murrey and blue of the royal household.

Her companion laughed too.

'Ah! So it is. Well, perhaps it is not unexpected. One must be ready to meet the rat if one ventures near its lair.'

The words were spoken lightly, but with a mocking undertone. For Elen's companion was also known to me. Hugh Soulsby.

My delight at Elen's appearance after so long was matched by my distaste at seeing him. I returned his slight bow of greeting, hooking a finger through Murrey's collar in case I needed to restrain her.

'So, Master Wansford, this is where you've been hiding from us all this time.' He threw a glance about him, holding his lantern aloft though the darkness was not yet pressing in upon us. 'I can understand why Mistress Elen has not ventured here herself before today.'

Elen stared at him, her lips parting, then closing as though she was uncertain what to say. But I brushed his words aside, not even looking at him. Master Ashley's townhouse was one of many fine merchants' residences hereabouts, for all they were hedged around by workaday artisans' dwellings and shops.

'I'm very pleased to see you, Elen. Do you wish to come and meet my master? I'm sure he will welcome you warmly.'

'No doubt,' said Hugh, before Elen could utter a word. 'I'm sure he'd welcome anything that brings him closer to a royal household.'

I could not ignore that – not after his many insinuations against myself in the past.

I turned to face him.

'Why do you say that, Master Soulsby? Do you not know my master has long been a friend of the King?' For Master Lyndsey often spoke of their lengthy friendship, as well as of the many deals they had conducted together.

Had Hugh grown even taller since our last meeting? He stared at me as though scrutinizing an insect on the ground before him.

'Of the King, indeed? Oh, of course, the *King*. From when he was just a *Duke*, I suppose. His royal brother's *dog* of all *works*.'

My skin crawled at these words and the stress he laid upon them, and Elen plucked at her skirts as though in discomfort. Murrey's ears pricked up and her snout lifted, alive to the rising emotions. My hand tightened on her collar.

Hugh carried on regardless, his all-too-familiar sneer now unfurling across his handsome face.

'And these jumped-up merchants – of course, they'll do *anything*, with *anyone* – so long as they gain a *profit* by it.'

That was more than I could bear. Not only a slur on the King and Master Ashley, but also on my father.

But as I let go of Murrey's collar and thrust myself at Hugh with my fists upraised, Elen threw herself between us, both hands flung up to grasp mine.

'No, Matt, no!' she gasped out, clutching at my balled fists.

Behind her, the lantern light flared on Hugh's face. A spasm clenched his jaws together, before they relaxed in a smirk and he tossed back his head with a bellow of laughter.

'Ha! And you – a jumped-up merchant's son yourself – having to be defended by a girl!'

Her sudden release and the sudden movements and the sudden noise were too much now for Murrey. She wriggled free from between Elen's skirts and my legs and exploded in a fury of barking and snarling and snapping.

His guffaw cut short, Hugh backed away abruptly, swinging the lantern down like a scythe in front of his legs to ward her off, while he groped for his knife. Murrey in turn shied away, but then lunged forward again, still barking ferociously at him as he tried to draw the dagger. As I made a grab for her collar, and missed, Hugh swiped at her again with the heavy iron lantern, this time catching her a glancing blow on the shoulder that sent her tumbling over across the cobbles, yelping. But she twisted back up and leapt forward once more, throwing herself back towards him, while I flung myself at her and Elen snatched at the flailing lantern, shouting at Hugh to stop.

In all the commotion I hardly noticed the click and creak of the opening gate, before a voice thundered above the tumult,

'What is all this? Why this uproar?'

At last I managed to catch Murrey by the scruff of her neck and drag her away, but not before Hugh, unable to use his other weapons, lashed out with his boot, clouting her in the ribs as she wriggled helpless in my grasp. Murrey squealed, then squirmed around and snarled as I hauled her with me towards the courtyard wall. A moment later, realizing she was in my grip, she calmed down and stood quivering while I ran my hands over her back and side, checking for any wounds. Though she winced and grumbled in her throat, I was soon satisfied she was no more than bruised.

Stroking her still-bristling head, I looked back to see Hugh resheathing his knife and lowering his lantern, while Elen smoothed down her skirts and tucked away the wisps of hair that had been dislodged from her cap.

Before them stood Master Ashley and a companion, a tall man clad in a travelling cloak and hood, both their backs towards me.

Hugh bowed with something of his usual swagger, though his face was pale at the shock of the attack. His mouth opened, but before he could speak, my master cut in.

'No, say nothing more. I heard what you said about the King. Have you no respect?'

'But, sir —'

'Don't try to explain. Be off with you, boy!'

Hugh was now easily a finger or two taller than Master Ashley and far broader, and he stood his ground a moment, staring at him, his chest still heaving beneath his royal livery. His lips moved as though he would speak again. But my master's companion took a step towards him and Hugh thought better of it, proffered the slightest of bows and turned to Elen. His voice was icily polite as he said,

'My lady, it has been a pleasure. We must ride out together again another time. Pray remember me to your esteemed friend, Lady Alys.'

And, seizing her hand before she could snatch it away, he pressed it to his lips. Then he strode to the brown colt, whisked its rein from the groom's hands, passed him the lantern, mounted and, spurring the horse's sides, was gone.

Elen wiped the back of one hand on the other, a deep red tingeing her cheek, just visible in the twilight.

Master Ashley took her hand and, patting it once, drew it courteously through his arm.

'My dear, you are trembling. You must come in and my wife shall give you a restorative. Matthew – follow us.'

Murmuring a word to his companion, he led Elen through the gates into the courtyard. The other gentleman walked at her other side as though supporting her, and the groom, now dismounted, led the palfrey and his own horse towards the stables.

I trailed behind my master, still clinging on to Murrey's collar so she stuck close to my side, and wondering for the first time why Elen was here at all – and why Hugh had been with her.

A servant had hurried ahead and Mistress Ashley met us at the top of the main entrance steps, her concerned face lit up by torches newly flaring to either side. Master Ashley relinquished Elen's arm to her as she said,

'Come in, come in, my dear. What has happened?'

The mistress urged Elen into the dining hall, waving away her quiet protest that all was well, and I was left in the entrance hallway with my master and his companion, uncertain what to do next. They gazed after the ladies through the still-open door, then spoke together in an undertone. Their speech was not clear to me as I lingered near the main door, but its rhythms betrayed that it was not English.

His hood now thrown back, in the glimmer of candles ranged in sconces around the hallway the other man was revealed to be not only tall and lean, but also the possessor of skin and hair as dark as Elen's, perhaps darker even. He was attired beneath his fur-trimmed cloak in outlandish robes of vivid silks, and, with black eyes that glinted like the eyes of a hawk, he had the air of one used to being obeyed. It was no wonder that Hugh had had second thoughts about confronting my master when he stood beside such a man.

He took his leave a moment later, and I watched with my master as he strode to the stables. There another man in similar robes held the bridle of a dapple grey stallion with a proud, curving neck, alongside his own, similarly noble horse. A groom helped the gentleman to mount and soon the gates clanged behind the two strangers as they rode away.

Master Ashley placed his hand on my shoulder, driving out of my mind all thoughts of who they might be.

'Shall we see how your young friend is? She is Lady Alys Langdown's companion unless I am mistaken.'

Given the closeness between his household and that of the King, I was unsurprised that he knew of Elen. I was perhaps more surprised at his next words, and the mild manner in which they were spoken.

'And the squire? Is he perhaps Lord Soulsby's nephew, Master Hugh?'

'Aye, sir, he is.' Though I did my best, my voice was not so calm.

'I heard that you two had a disagreement while you were at Middleham. I see that it has not been forgotten. You would do well perhaps to avoid him while in London if you can. His family were ever ones to bear a grudge.'

This also was no surprise to me, and no doubt excellent advice – if I could avoid all accidental meetings too.

I followed him into the dining hall. Within, Mistress was fussing over Elen, now resting upon a bench, sipping deep-red wine from a crystal goblet.

'Ah, husband, let Matthew come in. Elen here says she was on her way to visit him when this unpleasantness occurred. She has quite recovered herself now.'

With smiles and reassurances, Mistress Ashley retreated with her husband and I was left alone with Elen.

A single candle on the nearby table cast a corona of light around her.

'Are you well now, Elen?' I asked.

'Yes, I thank you, Matthew,' she replied, her colour rising again. 'It was nothing, indeed. Just Hugh...'

A pause, before she continued.

'I did not wish him to accompany me. He was outside Lady Elizabeth's stables as I left, chatting with the stable lads. When he saw me, he offered to ride with me. He said the way might not be safe.'

'Although you had your groom?'

'He was just being polite.'

Another pause.

To distract her from her discomfort, I pulled up a small stool for myself and then changed the subject. I had no wish to speak more of Master Soulsby.

'And how is Alys?'

'She is well, thank you.' Elen brightened at the words. 'She is the reason for my visit. Though she did not want me to come.'

'Not?'

My disappointment must have been obvious to her, for she went on hurriedly,

'Only because she would rather have come herself. Or have written.'

'But she has not?'

The weeks without letters had bothered me more than I had known, for all that I had justified them to myself. The words cut as they came out, and Elen's eyes flinched as at a wound.

'She would have written if she could. Believe me, Matthew. It is not her intent to neglect you. She is as frustrated as you can be, but she would not let me write to you in her stead.'

I regretted my words now. My tone softened.

'Why? What has happened?'

'She was thrown from her pony.'

'What? But you said she was well.'

'Don't worry – she is not badly hurt. But the bones in her wrist were broken and so she cannot write. Her arm is all swathed in bandages. She says it does not pain her greatly, but it may be some weeks still before it is strong enough to hold a quill.'

'I hope she may recover more quickly than that. But she was thrown, you say. Yet she's such a good rider, and knows her pony so well.'

Elen smiled her quiet smile.

'Yes, Matthew, we all know she's a fine rider. But – and she would tell me off for saying this – she was riding recklessly. She had just heard she was not to travel to Gipping, and she was annoyed. I believe she took it out on her poor pony and spurred him more than he was used to. He jibbed and threw her.'

'Gipping?' I racked my memory for a trace of the name.

'To visit Lady Tyrell. It is her husband's estate in Suffolk. Alys has not seen Lady Tyrell since she left the Queen's household and they had become such friends at court. Sir James Tyrell is now master of the King's henchmen. I'm sure Roger will have told you. He is his master now, and of all the pages.'

I shook my head. Despite his promise, Roger had written hardly a letter to me since his return to the north.

'I don't often hear from Roger. And I have not seen him since the spring. Since he brought me news of...' I swallowed, pushing away the memory. 'Since he came to visit his parents.'

Elen bowed her head and reached a hand down to stroke Murrey's ears, but the tear growing on her long black lashes sparkled in the candlelight like a star on the darkest night. She blinked once or twice and after a moment, lifted her head again. Her emotion left no trace upon her face as she continued her tale.

'Lady Elizabeth was to visit Lady Tyrell with her mother, Dame Grey. Naturally Alys was to join them. But Dame Grey sent word at the last moment that Elizabeth was not to go with her.' She glanced about her, as though the shadows in the dining hall teemed with listeners, then went on. 'The older ladies in the household say it's because there is a rumour that a Portuguese Duke wishes to marry Lady Elizabeth. They say he has sent an ambassador to London just to see her.'

I remembered Alys's letter about the King's marriage plans for his brother's daughter – and her words about perhaps travelling abroad with Elizabeth herself.

'Is the rumour true?'

'I don't know,' Elen replied. 'There are always rumours swirling about at court – about this and that. Always gossip and intrigues, lords and ladies plotting and vying against one another for royal favour and attention. Alys says it's one of the reasons why the King and Queen stayed away from court so much when old King Edward was alive. They do all they can to prevent it now, but Lady Tyrell said it's impossible to go against centuries of tradition.'

'Then maybe there is nothing in it, just talk among idle folk.'

How would I feel if it were true? If Princess Elizabeth were to marry and take Alys with her to Portugal or any such foreign land – and perhaps Elen too? And with Roger so far away in Sheriff Hutton. And Ed... Even after more than a year I had not made such good friends in London, for all that Simon and I worked together, trained together, lived and laughed together. Yet, I should not grudge Alys her chance to travel and see exotic lands if it should come. But how would it affect her future marriage too?

Perhaps Elen read some of my thoughts scribed on my face, despite the dimness of the light cast by the single candle in its silver holder.

'It may not happen. We must wait to see how the King's diplomacy fares. Yet I for one hope Lady Elizabeth marries this Duke, or someone similar, soon.'

'Why do you say that?'

'Because other rumours say that the King offered her hand in marriage to Henry Tudor, in hope that in return he would come back to England, pledge his allegiance and give up his claim to the throne.'

'What? King Richard?'

Elen nodded.

'Do not look so shocked. They say King Edward, her father, did the same when the French prince ended his betrothal to her – though he was no more successful than King Richard has been so far. If the rumour is true.'

'But Tudor is an enemy. Why would they do that?'

Elen's lips twitched, though whether in a smile or a grimace I could not tell.

'Because there are many ways of turning an enemy into a friend, Matthew. To offer them a young lady – and the land and wealth and titles that come with her – is one of them. Perhaps the best one if you are a king.'

In the silence that followed my mind flitted to another such case. Almost without thought I asked,

'Is that why Alys was promised in marriage to Ralph Soulsby?'

Elen stiffened as though offended by the question, but maybe it was pain rather. Her dark eyes glistened like molten glass in the candle's gleam.

'In a way, perhaps. Though Lord Soulsby has long been an ally, not an enemy, of the King, and King Edward before him, for all that his brother was a traitor.' She hesitated. 'Yet perhaps that is another reason to hope Lady Elizabeth will marry someone other than Henry Tudor. Alys might go to Portugal or another royal household with her, if the Soulsbys would give up their claim to her. We can but hope it will happen.'

Even though it would take her far from me too...

'And,' added Elen, casting a glance about her again with a small conspiratorial smile, 'for Lady Elizabeth's sake. She told Alys she would refuse to marry Tudor if she could. Not only has she never met him, but she says she knows his mother, Lady Stanley, too well to want her for a mother-in-law.'

I joined her in her smile, Alys's words about that lady's actions at the coronation and after coming unbidden to my memory. Yet still the effect of such a change for myself pricked at my mind.

'If it should happen, I wonder whether we can remain friends. Portugal is so very far away.'

Indeed I had only a vague idea of where it was. I had not often encountered its merchants in London – never in York – although I knew them to be dark of skin like those of the Spanish kingdoms – and to be courageous seafarers who had for generations traded with distant lands.

Elen's eyelashes fluttered down again, hiding her eyes from my sight, as she said, her voice a little husky,

'I'm sure we can. Whatever distance should separate us all. And we do not know what will happen yet.'

Silence reigned. The candle guttered, throwing flickering shadows across the walls and making the fantastic beasts leap and gambol on my master's fine silk tapestries.

Then Elen stood, her abrupt movement dislodging Murrey, who had been lying asleep across her small booted feet.

'I must go, before it grows too late.'

'I'm sure my master will send a serving man with you to guard you.'

'There is no need. My groom —'

'Was no defence against Hugh.'

She waited while I called a household servant to send in search of the mistress. As he scurried away, she laid a hand upon my arm.

'Thank you, Matthew. It has been good to see you after all this time. I – I know Alys has missed your company, and she – we both welcome your letters, and all your news. Your life is so much more interesting than our own.'

Her words surprised me. For me the life of a simple apprentice could never match that lived by fine ladies and gentlemen at court.

'But,' she went on, 'Alys says it would be safer to use the code more often now. She says we can never know what spies there may be in Elizabeth's household – or at court. I think she is being perhaps a little dramatic. But all these rumours and intrigues have to start somewhere.'

Master Lyndsey the steward himself came to escort Elen to the stables. There her palfrey and groom stood waiting, along with one of Master Ashley's own stable lads, hefting a halberd in case there should be cutpurses or footpads lying in wait on the journey back to Westminster. Affixed to the groom's saddle was a covered basket, no doubt a gift of fruit and autumn blooms picked from the garden for Lady Elizabeth's household.

Once mounted, Elen leaned down to offer me her gloved hand. As I pressed my lips to it in farewell, she said softly,

'Stay in touch, Matthew. And be sure to tell us of your mother's happy event when it comes. I so long to hear news of your new baby brother or sister.'

I watched her ride away into the darkness flanked by both grooms, until the twinkling of their lanterns turned a distant corner and could be seen no more. And as I retraced my steps to the light and warmth of my master's house, I marvelled for the first time at all she had said. In the many months I had known Elen, she had not uttered half so much before. Yet in all that evening, only once, perhaps twice, had she spoken of herself.

Elen's prospects, her future, were at least as uncertain as those of Alys, or the Lady Elizabeth, yet her thoughts and words were only for them. What were her own dreams and desires?

But then she, like myself, was but a small person, entangled in the lives and affairs of those greater than ourselves. We had little say or sway over events, or even, sometimes, choice in the paths that we had to follow.

14

The Light Fades

Another autumn. Another Advent. Another Christmas-time.

Another chill, grey London winter.

Alys was as good as her word – or as Elen's, at least. Once the physician pronounced her wrist healed, she took up her quill again and penned more of her usual lively letters – even if they were shorter and not so frequent as they had once been. Perhaps her duties were more onerous now she was a young lady at court, or perhaps it was the tedium of always writing in code. But, still, they were full of the colour and finery of the royal festivities of which she and Elizabeth were a part.

And her words about the King and Queen heartened me, filling me with the good cheer suitable to the Christmas season – although amongst her happy news was the faintest of shadows on the horizon.

During Christmas they have looked happier than I had seen them for months, at least since that terrible time in the spring. The Queen and Elizabeth and all the ladies have been wearing the most sumptuous gowns of cream and gold, while the gentlemen have dressed mostly in blues and greys. But on Twelfth Night – what a spectacle! We were all clad in red or gold, like flames in the great fireplaces of the palace. The Queen had made a gift to Elizabeth of a gown exactly like her own, and the King had presented them both with the most beautiful jewels. He then led both of them out to dance while everyone cheered and clapped.

We learned later that earlier in the day the King had been brought reports that Henry Tudor is again planning an invasion in the summer. Lady Tyrell told us that the King was pleased, saying he wished to deal with that problem once and for all.

I do hope you have enjoyed Christmas too. Did Master Ashley and his family wait on you apprentices topsy-turvy fashion like last year? I meant to suggest that to the King and Queen this Christmas season. I hope your new baby brother is still well. The Queen laughed with delight when I told her your father had named him Richard in thanks for all that the King has done for you. She said that on her next trip to York, she will visit your mother to thank her, though that will not be before springtime at the earliest. Do you think that will be time enough for your mother to prepare?!

In friendship,
Alys

And so 1484 had turned into 1485.

Then, with no warning, came shattering news, as heartbreaking in its way as the news of Ed's death almost a year before.

A glorious morning in early spring. I was at work with Simon and Master Ashley in the counting house. A huge leather-bound ledger lay upon the table before me and I was busy tallying up the figures neatly written in long columns on the open page. But gradually the numbers grew dim and the sunlight streaming into the room faded.

A quizzical look touched Master Ashley's face and he went to open the door.

Cries of alarm filtered in from the distant streets. But my master, glancing upwards, only laughed.

'Come, boys,' he said, beckoning to us.

Bemused, I laid down my quill and, with Simon, followed him out of the doorway.

As we walked down the narrow alley, no clouds darkened the ribbon of sky above us, and few enough floated in the expanse that opened up when we emerged on to the tiny riverside wharf. But all colour was bleeding from the heavens, the world around us turning grey as though night were falling.

On all sides wharvesmen were muttering prayers, dropping to their knees, crossing themselves. Out on the water boats drifted with the current as sailors and steersmen likewise abandoned their tasks.

But Master Ashley remained standing, pointing towards the far bank.

'There, boys, look at that. Do you see?'

A single ray of sunlight glinted off the blue stone of the ring on his index finger, but I looked beyond it, past the tower of Southwark Priory across the river, darkest black now against the grey sky. And I saw.

It was as though the sun were a lantern partly shuttered, its light now coming only from a thin crescent like a fiery new moon, its horns pointing earthwards. A dark, dense disc blotted out its radiance, moving slowly, oh so slowly, across it. Then my eyes hurt and I had to look away.

'Mother of God!' Simon's voice, beside me, was muffled.

'Do not be afraid,' said Master Ashley. 'It has been foretold by learned men and is not a portent of evil things. It is just the dance of the spheres in the heavens, as the ancients explained. The moon travels across the sun and hides his light from our sight. Soon she will move on and day will return.'

And so it did. But not before long minutes had passed, as that dark shadow crawled further across the failing orb, and dread had gripped my heart also.

In the eerie twilight, the birds ceased their song, but the men's quiet pleas to God and the Virgin Mary murmured on, vying with the slap of water against the wharf timbers. On the river, lamps were raised on masts, casting strange glimmers across the black oily waters. And from far to the west, a vast distance behind us, a single bell tolled. Its sad note crept through the darkness, giving a rhythm to the mumbled prayers, as slowly, so slowly, the light seeped back into the world.

Only later did we discover why the great bell of Westminster Abbey had rung. Master Ashley, it seemed, had been wrong about the bad omen. As the light of the sun had drained away, so too had the light of the King's life. Queen Anne was dead.

A letter arrived from Alys a few days later. It could hardly contain her sadness. Sorrow flowed from every word she wrote.

She told of her visit to the Queen the day before her death, of how that lady lay pale and thin and exhausted after her long struggle with illness, her hand cold to the touch beneath the furs and rich coverlets of her sickbed. Of how her voice rose scarce above a whisper as she told Alys to be good and obedient and to live her life well. As she joined her in a simple prayer and then bid her farewell.

I recognized the stain of tears on the letter and could barely hold back my own, though it had been long since last I had seen Her Grace.

Murrey pressed her wet nose against the hand that held the letter and whined, her brown eyes wide gazing up at me. I caressed her head, but read on. She leaned her flank against my leg as though to warm it. As so often she was a much-needed comfort.

What makes it even sadder – if that's possible – is that one of Elizabeth's ladies says the Queen may have been with child. That may have made things worse, or even have been why she was ill. If that were true, and not just another rumour, it might explain the King and Queen's happiness at Christmas-tide, especially after losing poor Ed. But if it were that that led to Her Grace's death...

I asked Elizabeth if she was not afraid of what might happen in her own marriage when it came. She just laughed and said her mother and grandmothers had had lots of babies, without

problems, and it's well known that that is what's
important for girls. I think she can't wait to marry –
though no plans have been spoken of recently – not
since the Queen became ill...

As I read the final expressions of friendship in Alys's letter, my thoughts were only of her words about the Queen, and then the Lady Elizabeth. Was Alys afraid for herself? She had never struck me as someone who thought that having lots of babies was important for girls. But perhaps the knowledge that she herself was destined to marry Ralph Soulsby – and presumably bear his children – was becoming all too real.

A week later, I slipped away from my duties in the city to stand with my cap in my hand and head bowed as Her Grace, the late Queen, was carried in her richly carved oak coffin the short distance from the Palace to Westminster Abbey. Many in the dense crowd around me, both men and women, wept openly, mourning this beloved daughter of the Kingmaker, as the great bell of the Abbey tolled for her final journey.

I learnt afterwards that, in keeping with age-old tradition, her husband was not seen to attend the solemn requiem Mass or witness her body being lowered into her grave near the high altar as the choir sang the Te Deum. But I recalled our evenings together in the private chamber of the castle at Middleham, the lady's careful training of a boy to sing her husband's favourite songs, a toast with a silver cup before a hunt, the kiss of a hand, a man staring into a fire as he thought of his family far away, his grief on the day he learned of his brother's death, the swinging of a small son into the air in the joy of a return. And my heart ached for the loneliness of a king.

15

'Still the Chivalrous Knight'

I stood waiting at the panelled oak doors. My heart thumped fast inside my chest and below it bubbled up an unsettling sensation like a pit of serpents coiling and uncoiling within me.

I had not thought ever to stand here again, and now that I did... would my nervousness overmaster me?

The guards to either side, resplendent in their murrey and blue livery, were motionless, but their eyes watched my every movement. I had already straightened my doublet, dragged my hand through my unruly hair, ordered Murrey to sit close against my boot. Now, as a murmur of voices trickled from beyond the doors, I forced myself to study the beautiful grain of the wood, casting my thoughts back over why I was here, in hopes that it would steady me.

The message had arrived a few days before. At first I had not known what to do. Surely I could not be so bold as to do what it asked? Then, my mind at last made up, I had come as soon as I could, before my fears got the better of me. For what it would be worth. I had little expectation of success.

As I waited, my restless fingers brushed the corner of the letter folded up in my pouch.

Dear Matthew
Forgive me for writing, but I know that Alys won't –
her pride won't let her. She thinks because she is
now a lady of wealth and position, she must suffer in
silence. But I don't see why she should – not while
there is still one person left who might help her.

We've tried everyone else, all her friends at
court or elsewhere, but they all say the same thing –

that her marriage has been arranged and she must go through with it.

But I remember you saying that the King – when he was still the Duke – and his brother King Edward before him, after you saved little Edward on the boar hunt – they said that if they could ever help you, you need only ask. Alys was with you on that day in the snowstorm. If you can get to see King Richard, surely he'll not refuse your request?

Dame Grey always said Alys should marry once she turns fifteen, but Lady Elizabeth persuaded her mother to wait until after the summer. She wants Alys to attend her as long as possible, perhaps until her own wedding – though we still don't know when that will be. But now we hear Lord Soulsby is becoming impatient.

They say the King is planning to leave Westminster for Windsor and then the north in the middle of this month, so there isn't much time.

Please, Matthew, try to see the King and do what you can. Alys will ever thank you.

Your good friend,
Elen

So, begging from Master de Vries an early end to my day's work, I had ridden on Bess out towards Westminster, and made my way from the streets into the royal stables. Once there, enough stable boys and household servants recognized me – or, if the truth is told, Murrey and her dancing – for me soon to be ushered into the chamber of the King's secretary.

Master Kendall had welcomed me with a smile, almost soothing my worries at my impudence, and he agreed to take my boar badge to the King on my behalf. But it was a full hour or more after he left, when the hollow deep in my stomach was roiling again, that a servant had finally come to guide me through the maze of passageways to these doors.

At last one of them opened, and the servant waved me through.

'Master Matthew Wansford, Your Grace,' he announced, before bowing and backing out of the room, leaving me standing there alone. On the hard stone floor of the private chamber of the King of England.

The room had changed little from the late winter's day more than two years ago when I had been ushered into it before. As then, a fire was even blazing in the cavernous fireplace, this May-time being unseasonably cold. All that was missing was the colourful swarm of noble lords and ladies – and, to my relief, the many cages and their imprisoned songbirds. The only sounds as I straightened up from my deepest bow were the hiss of the flaming logs and a voice I did not know, fussing.

'If Your Grace would please be still, just a little longer, I can perhaps finish this evening, and then I need bother you no more.'

In one of the wide bays of the chamber were two figures, flooded by the late afternoon sun streaming in through the windows.

Closest to me was the man who had spoken. His back towards me, he was standing at an easel, dabbing with a fine-tipped brush at a painting upon it.

Forgetting my fears for a moment, I stepped forward to gain a better view. It was plainly intended as a portrait of King Richard, but in truth it was very different to the man seated in a carved and gilded chair beyond.

There was an unnatural stillness to the painted, unfurrowed brow and the distant, haunted gaze of the blue eyes below it. A gem-encrusted chain was draped across shoulders arrayed in a sumptuous embroidered gown of crimson and gold. In the one suggestion of movement, the long thin fingers of one hand played with a unadorned ring on the third finger of the other.

But the man who sat deep within the window recess was clad all in unornamented black. And far from unlined, his face was pale and drawn, dark shadows beneath his eyes, his lips pinched. In looks he had aged more than just the year or two that had passed since my last glimpse of him – from afar on his triumphant return after the rebellion.

Yet, as I recalled the events of those brief years, particularly the sorrows of recent months, it was a marvel to me that he – king of all this great land – should catch sight of me and smile in recognition of a mere page. He beckoned to me, and a light and life shone in his eyes that were not captured on the canvas.

'Matthew. It has been a long time since last we saw you. Come forward.'

My insides lurched again, but I did his bidding, kneeling before him and kissing the great jewelled ring on his hand, as I had seen him do to his nephew Edward – as seemed so very long ago. His hand rested an instant on the top of my head before the painter tutted.

'Your Grace, please. How am I to capture your likeness if you will keep moving?'

'Will you wait awhile, lad?' the King murmured, and I withdrew a little to one side. Finding a footstool nearby, I sat with Murrey curling round my ankles, grateful to watch the scene and allow my nerves time to settle.

Also in the room, at the end distant from the artist's tableau, several gentlemen were talking in hushed tones, gathered about a table upon which was strewn a mess of papers. Master Kendall winked at me and Lord Lovell nodded in recognition, but the unknown faces of the others expressed surprise, as though unused to seeing a boy such as me in the King's private chamber. But they continued their discussion, one from time to time carrying a document to the King to sign. He would take each paper and read it through, before flourishing the quill handed to him, perhaps turning to comment or ask a question. In between times his black-shod foot tapped as though in impatience, or he twisted his red-stoned signet ring as I had seen many times before.

A frown like gathering thunderclouds grew on the painter's face and he moistened his lips with his tongue as though about to speak again. Perhaps King Richard also noticed, for, before a word was uttered, he sprang to his feet and clapped his hands.

'Enough! No more today,' he cried. 'We shall finish another time – if more time is really needed.'

'But, Your Grace,' the man protested.

'No more, I say. Get out, get out!' And the King flapped his hands towards him as if he were actually going to shoo him out of the room.

Flustered, the painter collected his things together and bowed his way from the chamber. Soon only the easel, the painting upon it and the faint echo of his retreating footsteps remained.

Lord Lovell laughed.

'Dickon, you terrify that man. You have done it so often now. If you are not careful, he will depict you as a tyrant.'

'Me? It is he who is the tyrant. With his "Pray be still, Your Grace," "Just one more sitting, Your Grace," "Perhaps another hour in the morning when the light will be better, Your Grace." How many hours does it take to paint one man's face? Does he not understand I have work to do in the mornings?'

'And in the afternoons and evenings, Your Grace,' said Master Kendall, advancing with another document for the King's signature.

Sighing, the King took up his quill again.

'Yes, indeed, John. But let this be the last today. There may be other more pressing matters needing my attention.'

As he bent his head to read the paper, his glance flicked towards me, and curving his lips was that half-smile I well remembered. Heat rose in my face and my stomach churned again at the thought of why I was here – in contrast with the important royal business he had no doubt been conducting.

Within a few minutes all the gentlemen filed from the chamber. I stood out of respect. Lord Lovell inclined his head once more as he passed and Master Kendall patted me on the shoulder, murmuring words of encouragement. Then the King and I were alone.

Going to the table, he poured ruby-red wine into two long-stemmed glasses. He handed one to me and took the other over to the easel. His expression was unreadable as he inspected the painting. Then he glanced across to me, where I stood waiting for him to speak.

'Well, Matthew. It has indeed been a long time. It seems that you have grown.'

I bowed low. 'But not so very much, Your Grace. No more than you might expect.'

King Richard laughed that short laugh of his.

'No, perhaps not. But you are yet young, and have time ahead of you. Does Master Ashley feed you well?'

'Aye, Your Grace – meat or fish every day, save on fast days. He is a good master – I thank you for that.'

'You are most welcome.'

He eyed me a moment, then, stepping back towards the crackling fire, waved me to a seat. It was an ornate, high-backed, cushioned chair this time, not a footstool, and he settled himself into its twin across the hearth. In one hand he cradled his wine-glass and, now, in the other was my silver boar badge. His fingers turned it over and over, his eyes following the lights it caught and scattered from the flames.

My training as a page had taught me that I must not speak before he did. Yet several minutes passed in silence. Perhaps unwisely, I took refuge in swallows of the rich, smooth wine, seeking to quell the nerves rising again within me. I had drained almost half the glass before the King spoke.

'They told me you wished to see me, but couldn't tell me why.'

'That's because I didn't – I – couldn't tell them.'

'Couldn't?' Looking up, he raised one eyebrow. 'Why? Is it a matter of honour again? About a lady?'

My memory was sharp of that morning at Middleham more than two years before – the day of my beating. When I had told him of my letter to Alys, but refused to say how it had fallen into Hugh's hands – that he had snatched it from Elen. Did the King remember that too? Had he ever known who the 'lady' had been?

'In a way, yes, Your Grace.'

'You have not changed your tune then? Still the chivalrous knight?'

That stung a little. But he could not know of all the hours I had trained since leaving his service, mostly alone, learning to wield my chestnut sword. And I knew it was not meant unkindly.

I bowed my head.

'It's about Alys, Your Grace.'

'Alys Langdown? Then you are still friends?'

'Aye... At least, I think so. I haven't seen her for almost two years. Since your coronation. And then only from a distance.'

The King sat back a little in his chair.

'Ah, that was a day to remember. And yet... it was a difficult time, that summer —' He frowned, then his eyes cleared, snapping back to me. 'But what is this about Alys? She is well, is she not? I understand she attends my niece.'

'Yes, Your Grace. I believe she is well. It's just that she...'

'Yes?'

'She is to be married. This summer. To Ralph Soulsby.' I hesitated. The King continued to watch me.

'And?'

'She doesn't wish it, my lord.'

'Why not?'

'Because... because she has not chosen her husband herself.'

'That is usual for a young lady of noble birth.'

'But she doesn't even know him. Not really. She's met him only once – years ago.' I searched my memory for Alys's tale about Ralph long ago at Middleham. 'She was just a little girl, no more than eight or nine, and he was spiteful to her. She says he had just been made squire when he came across her reading in the Duchess's garden. He took away her books and threw them down the well because he said girls should not be taught to read and write.'

'That was a long time ago, Matt. People can change – they often do.'

'But if he was a bully then... Your Grace, please can you stop this marriage?'

King Richard was quiet for a moment, as though considering. But then –

'I'm afraid I cannot. Alys is a ward of Dame Grey herself, not the crown. Alys's mother was one of her ladies. When... when Elizabeth was Queen, she arranged the marriage to secure the loyalty of Ralph's family for the King, my brother. She has not chosen to break the betrothal since.'

'But now you are King, Your Grace. Surely you could step in and prevent it?'

'But, Matthew, as King I also need the loyalty of the Soulsbys and their allies. That has not changed. Nor, to my knowledge, has Elizabeth's mind on the matter. And you may not have cause to worry – love can grow after marriage, even when that is arranged. I saw it with my parents.'

His gaze drifted towards the fire's glow as he took a sip from his wine-glass.

I knew I should leave it there, that I shouldn't argue with a king – no matter how much familiarity he had allowed, both this evening and in times past. But for Alys's sake – and maybe the wine I'd drunk was half to blame – I carried on, not thinking at first what I was saying.

'But, Your Grace, you married for love, didn't you?'

His glance swung back to me, and I realized what I had done – barely more than a month after he had buried his beloved wife.

But in his face was no anger at my words, if that was what I feared. Far worse was the deep sorrow inscribed there, in the shadow darkening his eyes and the twisting of his mouth.

It was a moment before he mastered his emotion and said in a soft voice,

'So I did, Matt, so I did. But a king must look on these matters differently – as I have learnt. Marriages are not just about two people. They're about families, dynasties, countries even.' He swallowed another mouthful of wine, before placing the glass on a small table at his elbow. 'My brother also married for love – twice. And see the outcome of that.'

He chose a sweetmeat from a dish on the table and leaned down to entice Murrey away from my feet. As always when food was offered, she deserted me to go and beg for the tidbit. The firelight glinted in the King's eyes as the hound danced her pirouette for him.

'It may be that you and Alys can remain friends after her marriage.'

'I don't think that will be possible, my lord. I cannot think Lord Soulsby would allow it. He objected to my letters before.'

My words, the tone – their impudence struck me to shame, but it was too late to bite them back. Yet the King remained calm, as Murrey sat to attention, awaiting another treat.

'I was sorry to send you away, Matt. But I could not jeopardize Lord Soulsby's loyalty to my brother. His family had turned traitor before and Edward had worked hard to win them back to his cause. It is difficult always to keep noble men happy, as I have found too. Had it been up to me, I would have laughed off Hugh's tale-telling and kept you with us.' He coaxed Murrey to dance again, slipping her another morsel and smoothing the dark red tufts of her fur. 'My wife especially was sad to see you leave.'

'She was very kind to me. From my first days at the castle.'

Silence enshrouded us.

The King's hand rested still on Murrey's poll, his own head bowed.

Was he caught up in memories, as was I? Of that first time I had seen the Queen – Duchess as she was then – step down from her carriage to the cheers of the household. When she spoke to me that evening of all my troubles and asked me to sing. Her tears as she listened to the French lovers' lament.

Perhaps, again, I should not have spoken. Perhaps my shame and regret goaded me, making me think I could make amend. Once more the words spilled out before I could check them.

'Her Grace told me then – the first time I saw her – that if she were to die, she wished that you would marry again.'

Another silence.

Then he said softly, 'All those weeks of her illness, we did not speak of it – I – I could not speak of it.'

'She said – she said, it was so that you might be happy again, and because she hoped Ed would have a brother or sister.'

He raised his head and the pain in his eyes was raw. And as he spoke again it was as though I, a boy only, were not there.

'My wife dearly wanted more children. But after Ed was born, the physicians counselled her against it – warned us it might kill her. And then, when Ed died —'

He broke off. Reaching for his wine-glass, he sat back again and took another gulp. Twisting the glass about in his hands, he watched the swirl of the crimson liquid for a moment or two.

'My advisors also urge me to marry again, that I must have an heir. But – it is too soon, much too soon. And not, of course, my niece. That poisonous rumour...'

I knew, of course, what he meant.

It had been all round London, not long after Queen Anne's death. The whisper that the King planned to marry his brother's daughter, Elizabeth – to gain an heir, to appease the Woodvilles – to thwart Henry Tudor's plans. So far had the rumour spread – it even reached the ears of my family in faraway York – that the King had been forced to deny it publicly in front of the mayor and citizens of London.

Alys had been most indignant, both for the King and for Elizabeth. She abandoned the code and her handwriting became spiky and ragged, the quill point almost tearing through the paper at her angry underlinings.

How ridiculous it is! She's his underline(niece), and he's so much underline(older) than her, and she's... well, if her brother could not be king, what advantage could King Richard gain from marrying underline(her)? Why do people not underline(think) before they repeat these things?

Elizabeth is mortified. She says that she has grown to underline(like) her uncle, now that she knows him better, but she could never underline(love) him like underline(that)! She'd much rather marry 'her' Duke Manuel. He's nearly the same age as her, and her friend Lady Brampton has told her so much about the beauties of Portugal. She so longs to marry. She can't understand why it's taking underline(so) long to arrange...

Watching King Richard now, perhaps that delay was no mystery. He had been quick to dismiss his gentlemen, as though he had no heart to continue his business. A tiredness hung about him, a heaviness, that brought to mind the tail-end of our Christmas-time at his brother's court.

And also into my mind nudged the image of my own father in the weeks after my mother's death – when he was not seen at his workplace for days on end. It had been as though he could not bear to think that his own life would go on as normal. Only a visit from his great friend the mayor persuaded him that he must pick himself up and carry on – otherwise his business would fail and his children starve. And then, later, came the gentle smiles and soft words of the nursemaid who became my new mother.

Again, unbidden – except perhaps by the wine – I spoke up.

'My father married again. Some months after my mother died. For weeks, though, I think he wished he could join her. But now he is very happy. And I have another brother.'

This time, perhaps, I did not need to worry that I had spoken out of turn. A faint smile played around the King's lips – hard to discern in the fading daylight and the flickering fireglow, but it was there.

He raised his wine-glass as though to toast me.

'All my advisors say the same, Matt – all have a similar story to tell me. Yours, at least, I know to be true. And I thank you for it.'

Placing the glass down again... was that a sigh as he did?

'Were my life to end tomorrow – yes, sometimes I wish I could join my wife and son. But life goes on... Your father is a fortunate man. To have found happiness twice in his life. And to have such a son as you.'

I thanked the saints for the failing light. Colour was rising in my cheeks and a boy of my age was too old to be seen blushing like a child.

The King perhaps didn't notice.

'Well, I shall make a bargain with you. I shall consider your advice on remarriage if – ' I waited for what I should have to do – 'if you continue to wear my badge loyally and come to me again when I am in need.'

'But, Your Grace...'

Now I was confused, as his hand stretched out towards me, the silver boar on the palm gleaming in the firelight. The words of our last conversation at Northampton, when he had first handed it to me, tumbled through my brain.

'Your Grace, it was I who came to you with my request.'

His half-smile became a half-laugh.

'Aye, so it was. And yet it seems to have been you who has helped me. At my present time of need. So I shall make an addition to our bargain. I will ask Dame Grey to reconsider Alys's marriage. I can promise nothing, mind – legally I have no right to ask, so do not raise your hopes or hers too high. Do we have a deal?'

'Of course, Your Grace. Thank you.'

I took the badge and pinned it to my doublet in its usual place, over my heart. I sensed his eyes following the practised movement.

'You still wear it proudly, I see.'

'Aye, sir, and always shall. And... and loyalty will always bind me.'

Those words of his motto had not crossed my lips in two long years since riding with... with another King on the road to St Albans – Edward, the boy King as was... When he had passed me the fragment of parchment with this King's signature on it. That scrap remained in my bundle with other treasures I had collected, safe alongside all the letters from my friends in the Order, Ed's drawings, the book his mother had given me and the shiny coin Master Ratcliffe had handed me at our last brief meeting.

King Richard thrust out his hand, but to my surprise, not for me to kiss his great ring of state, rather to shake my own.

'I thank you for that, Matt. Loyalty freely given is beyond any price. I have not forgotten that you were ever a true friend to my son.'

'And he – and you – were ever friends to me.'

Then all my sadness from the past year welled up in me.

I bowed low to hide the tears that were shining in my eyes, and, as the King bid me farewell, I backed out of the room, still bowing, as I had seen the servant do earlier. Minutes later, as I passed through the towering gatehouse of the palace, it struck me that, for the first time ever, I had not sung for my lord, the King. Would I ever have another chance?

That night I begged a rushlight from Master Lyndsey and sat up late composing, for once, a letter to Elen. It saddened me that I could not write with better news, but I hoped that such a promise from the King would be welcome. But I received no reply. Only some time later did I learn that the Lady Elizabeth and her household had already travelled north to join Ed's cousins, the young earls of Warwick and Lincoln, at Sheriff Hutton.

Alys's letters also ceased. Did she no longer want to write to me as I had failed in my task? Or had she been warned off because of her coming marriage?

The lack of letters from Roger – also of course at Sheriff Hutton – was nothing strange. Perhaps the Order was truly at an end, despite our solemn oaths, and I would have to seek for new friends in my future life. But I resolved that I would ever be true to my own pledges.

And so spring turned towards summer.

16

Dangerous Days

The month of May drew on and the King left the capital as Elen had written, wending his way north to his castle at Nottingham, crouched on its crag at the very centre of his kingdom. There he seemed to be waiting.

For rumours were being blown about London like the blossom of fruit trees in my master's garden, scattered by every early summer squall. Henry Tudor would invade. Henry Tudor was on his way. Henry Tudor would land in the south, the east, the west. Never the north, of course. Troops were gathering at all compass points, ready to march to the defence of the King and his kingdom wherever they were needed.

One letter I did receive that summer was from my brother Fred, telling me that he was joining a company of archers. His words brimmed with his excitement.

We are to be ready at half a day's notice, with all our gear to hand, to march wheresoever needed to serve the King.

Our father speaks with pride of his grandfather, who told his tales of the great battle at Agincourt, where he fought with the fifth King Henry. He says, if Tudor lands in England, I too will be fighting the French, as it is only they who support him in his claim to the English throne. Or perhaps King Richard will take the fight to France. Then I will travel to foreign lands like you and our great-grandsire.

My brother, an archer fighting for the King.

Hugh Soulsby – last seen wearing the King's livery.

Troops of soldiers in the colours of great lords daily marching through the London streets.

Enormous cannons, barrels of gunpowder, piles of armour and weapons, hauled on wagons from the Tower out towards the city gates, or shipped on barges across the river.

Everyone was ready to fight for our good King Richard.

Except me – an apprentice only, fingers stained with ink, not calloused by the bowstring, neither donning armour nor gathering equipment ready to rally to the royal banner. And yet I wore his badge. How could I serve my two masters loyally?

I redoubled my efforts with my wooden sword, ashamed though I was that it was all I had, that and Master Ashley's book on swordplay. Simon, whose ardour for weapons training had cooled after the great rebellion, now joined me when he could, fired by my tales of glorious battles and hard-won victories, half-remembered from my time with Master Fleete.

We hid away from the other apprentices, in whatever secluded corner of our master's garden we could find. There, for the first time, I bested another boy with my sword. But I had learned much from Ed too, and helped Simon to his feet, returning his chestnut weapon and praising him on his first attempts.

My footwork was already better than before, after almost two years of lone study, and Simon and I trained hard in our free hours, together exploring how we might improve. During the working day, I also took on more of the strenuous jobs, lifting, carrying, bales, barrels, the heavy bolts of cloth, the weighty platen of the printing press. I could feel myself growing fitter, stronger, as the summer wore on.

Then in the middle days of August came the news for which all appeared to have been waiting.

Henry Tudor had landed – in Wales. Almost as far away from the capital as he could.

With so much distance to cross between there and the centre of government – and with King Richard awaiting him already in the middle of the country – his must be an impossible task. As the King summoned to his side men from every part of his kingdom, east, west, south and north, surely the might of his army would prove too much for Tudor to challenge.

And yet, and yet... rumours again swirled about the streets of London, whisperings that all might not be well, that not all the lords would rally to the King's cause.

'They say some have not forgotten their Lancastrian allegiances,' Master Lyndsey told Master de Vries one morning as Simon and I laboured over the press, printing pages for a small religious book destined to be sold in country fairs. Though great matters were afoot, life and work continued as normal.

'What, despite the King's efforts to unify the country, and those of his brother before him?'

Master de Vries still did not understand English politics despite almost two years in London.

'No, indeed,' snorted the steward. 'Or perhaps that is just an excuse. Perhaps King Richard simply has not done enough for them personally.'

'Do you think that is so?'

'Well, he doesn't always hand out plum jobs and lands and costly gifts to buy men's loyalty as was done before. Nor does he uphold their claims against the common folk just because they are wealthy landowners. For him, justice is justice, no matter whether you are rich or poor.'

'And so he is resented by them?' Master de Vries shook his head in sadness. 'That in these days it should come to that!'

'Such men want to cling to the old ways,' said Master Lyndsey, taking up a close-printed page to check while he spoke. 'They complain that it is no longer enough to be of the right family, to have been born to power and wealth – they can no longer expect to keep them always. Nor to rule in courts of law as was their habit.'

'But the ordinary folk. They must be contented with this new order of things?'

Master Lyndsey laughed.

'There's little I know about such folk beyond the city walls. Perhaps it means little to them what King Richard does for their sakes – even making his laws in English so they can understand. But the merchants and artisans of London, now – they are well pleased with King Richard. His laws protect them and their trade – in England and abroad. To be sure, Matthew,' he turned to me, as I snatched a break from the heavy work to listen in, 'your father in York must feel the same? Merchants are merchants, wherever they may be.'

Indeed my father did – that I could confirm. In his letters he told of how his business was thriving, and how the new Council of the North was governing well, allowing the towns to prosper under the peace with the Scots. And he proclaimed, like Fred before him, that the free men of York and its surroundings would answer the King's summons at a moment's notice.

And yet the rumours continued to swirl. Ordinary men might be ready and willing to fight and die for their King, but perhaps not all the powerful nobles who commanded them.

Before another day passed, my mind was made up. I might be a boy only, just an apprentice, no knight or seasoned warrior, but I would travel to my King's side, to serve him in whatever way I could.

But first I had to gain my other master's permission.

I found him alone in his office after breakfast.

'Go to Nottingham, Master Wansford? You?'

Master Ashley's eyes narrowed as though I had asked him something he did not quite understand.

'Aye, master. To aid King Richard in his fight against Henry Tudor.'

'But, Matthew, the King will have an army of trained soldiers.'

'I have been training, sir, ever since I entered your service.'

'I know, lad, and you have done well to. But such troops train together under experienced captains. They know their commanders and how to obey in the heat of battle.'

My fear had been that Master Ashley would view my efforts as mere play, but he had not simply laughed at me. I was heartened by that, and resolved not to be put off.

'But, sir, men say that not all those commanders will prove loyal to His Grace. The Welsh chieftains have not yet moved to challenge Tudor on his march. They say perhaps even Lord Stanley —' I hesitated, remembering what the King himself had said about rumours – and this rumour was about one of his closest advisors – 'they say even Lord Stanley may play him false. Perhaps I can't make much of a difference, but he may need all the men he can gather.'

'That may be. These are dangerous days, Master Wansford, dangerous days.'

'Then let me go, sir, I beg you. I swear I will return once the King is victorious.'

A few seconds of silence. Master Ashley pursed his lips while he considered. Then,

'Very well, Matthew. You may attend the King. It may be that you will somehow be of service. But you must promise to keep yourself out of harm's way as much as you are able. You may take a note from me to Master Kendall. He will know how best you can serve His Grace – and you must follow any instructions he gives you to the letter.'

I stammered my thanks, not thinking too much on his words and only grateful for his leave to travel. In a few minutes he had, with his own hand, written a short message, imprinting the wax seal with his signet. He gave it to me, along with a handful of coins.

'Go to the armourer on Cheapside and buy yourself jack and sallet for your protection. Ask our cooks for provisions for the journey. And take the pony you brought with you from the north. I understand the King is mustering his army at the town of Leicester. Set off today and you may be able to ride there with men at arms from our city.'

He watched as I placed the money and note in my pouch, then added, his face sombre,

'Fare thee well on your journey and in your service, Matthew. And mind you obey Master Kendall in all he says.'

I swept off my cap and bowed, then hurried up to my attic room to collect some things for the journey. I was sorry not to speak to Simon before I left, but knew I should hasten on my way, and somehow felt this journey was one I must take alone. But I spared some moments to write a few lines of explanation to Alys at Sheriff Hutton where I assumed her to be.

It was only as I wrote the final words of code that the seriousness of what I was undertaking truly came home to me.

If I should not return, think kindly of me. I will have remained true to the Order's oath of loyalty and to the King.

> *Qtdfqyd gnsix rj!**
> *Your friend always,*
> *Matthew Wansford*

Before my thoughts could dwell further on the dangers I might face, I sealed up my note and dropped it with Master Ashley's letters before making my way down to the kitchens. Half an hour later, I was astride Bess, riding to the heart of the working quarter of the city, a bag of food in my saddle bag, faithful Murrey at my heel.

17

The Camp

London had been busy in its preparations for war. As I waited impatiently at the armourers while men for the levies were kitted out before me. As some strapped on their padded jacks, tried sturdy sallets on for size on recently shorn heads, hefted new-made weapons. As their friends and colleagues, veterans of other battles, jeered and catcalled, arrayed already in their own gear, worn, but buffed and burnished for this coming campaign.

As I followed the long column of troops out under the dark stone arch of Newgate, their baggage wagons rumbling across the cobbles behind. As the gathered crowds, faces darkened with anger, cheered or shouted encouragement.

'Long live King Richard!'

'Death to the traitor!'

'Tear those French dogs to shreds!'

'A York!'

Yet it was all as nothing to the bustle and tumult as I rode Bess into the town of Leicester. The company of soldiers I had journeyed with halted in fields outside, awaiting further orders, but I pushed on, past outlying houses, towards the squat gateway through the town walls.

All around us streamed men in leather armour and bold liveries, hollering to soldiers coming out of the town and bumping against us.

'Out of the way, boy!'

'Move that scrawny animal off the road!'

Nervous, Bess shifted beneath me as we passed beneath the iron teeth of the portcullis. Once out of the darkness of the archway, I slipped down from her back and led her into the empty courtyard of a nearby church, its grey spire rising tall into the cloudless blue sky. With one hand stroking her velvet nose to calm her, I surveyed the scene before us.

The main street leading into the heart of the town was lined with shops, but today their store-fronts were battened up out of the way of a seething crush of men and beasts. It was amazing that any were managing to move at all, so pressed were they within that narrow lane. But as I watched some made minute headway in one or other direction.

Everywhere pennants fluttered aloft alongside the sharp steel of pikes, harness jingled, men shouted and laughed, oxen lowed as they towed creaking carts. Women and children leaned out of overhanging windows, their mouths agape at the sights. Some waved kerchiefs and hallooed like the crowds in London. Other faces were clouded with worry or fear. Over everything lay the reek of sweat mingled with the choking dust kicked up by all those feet and hooves and wheels on this warm August afternoon.

How would I find my way to Master Kendall through this strange and busy place?

As I hesitated, a more enticing scent wafted into my nostrils.

A girl about my own age was walking towards me, a tray loaded with rich brown pastries suspended by thick cords from her neck. The air above them shimmered. They must have come straight from the oven.

'Mutton pasty, master?' she asked. 'Only a penny each.'

My mouth watered. I still had bread and cheese in my pack from Master Ashley's kitchen, but it was a long time since I had tasted hot foot.

As I reached in my pouch for the coin, she wrapped a pastry in a clean cloth. I took it and thanked her. And here was a chance to discover what I needed to know.

'The King?' she replied, as I sank my teeth into the juicy pie. Warm gravy trickled from the corner of my mouth. 'I watched him ride out over Bow Bridge with his army this morning. A very beautiful sight it was – with crowds cheering and the sun shining on his golden crown and all the knights' armour.'

I wiped my chin with the cloth.

'He's already left? Then who are all these men?'

'Oh, they're just the stragglers, I suppose. I heard his lordship of Northumberland arrived only late yesterday, and some men from the south today.'

'The army must be very large.'

'Many thousands strong, I think. The King should easily beat the traitor. They say most of Tudor's men are in the pay of the French King or else are Welsh rebels.'

She spat on the dusty ground.

Heartened, I asked another question that had often been in my mind during my long ride north.

'Have the men of York joined the King already? They would wear livery bearing the white rose and sound like me when they spoke.' I now knew from long experience that my accent still marked me, and the northern speech of Fred and his fellows might be even more obvious.

She was quiet for a moment, as though counting back through all the soldiers she had come across over the past few days.

'I don't remember any such. But perhaps they were camped in the fields outside town. My father told me not to venture beyond the walls to sell my pasties.'

I thanked her again. After asking for directions, I finished the last crumbs of the tasty pie and moved off to find the road the King had taken hours before. Leading Bess and with Murrey sticking close, I pushed once more into the stream of men and animals that flowed through the streets of this small town.

As we skirted the high wall of a priory, its bells tolled the hour of vespers. I would have to hurry if I wished to find the King before darkness fell. Minutes later I was astride Bess once again, the west gate of Leicester receding behind us as we clattered up and over a hump-backed stone bridge spanning a rushing river.

Soon, as the narrow streets opened up into wide fields, the bustle lessened, but always there were soldiers to all sides. Men in the livery of the Earl of Northumberland were still breaking their camp and loading equipment on wagons and horses, and at my questions they waved me on in the way they would soon be going. I urged Bess into a trot as we passed into the rolling, thinly wooded countryside.

The red orb of the sun was resting on the horizon ahead when I finally came upon the royal army. Two guards wielding pikes blocked my path, but stood aside at the sight of my silver boar.

As I rode on, to either side the golden evening light lapped row after row of tents spreading across fields as far as I could see. It gleamed on the steel points of stacks of pikes and spears planted on the ground between them, and sparked on the helmets of men hurrying every which way, their calls ringing through the growing dusk. As the sun started its descent below the distant hills, camp fires flared all around and wood smoke was sharp in my nostrils.

Bess tossed her head in alarm as a strident clanging rang out to one side. A burly man was hammering at a dented breastplate, which caught and reflected beams of light from the sinking sun.

I swung down from the saddle and placed my hand on Murrey's head. Her fur bristled against my palm. As the clamour ceased, her low growl crept up to my ears. So, also, to those of the armourer.

Turning, he ran his eyes down me, then up again to my face, before saying,

'And whose company are you in, sir?'

Was that a hint of scorn in his voice? Yet, in the dying light his face appeared friendly enough.

'No man's company yet,' I said. 'But I seek Master John Kendall, the King's secretary.'

Again I tapped the badge pinned to my doublet.

He peered at it, then pointed to a ridge some distance away. Atop its crest stood a tent larger than the rest. Its sides glowed in vibrant reds and blues, and the last rays of sunlight touched to flame the sunburst and rose stitched on the banners flying from its crown. Upon one standard I spied also the proud, pure white boar of my old master, before a breath of wind folded it out of sight. Then the sun set and the camp was in darkness.

I touched my cap to the man in thanks and wound my way through the endless tents, fires, carts, piles of weapons and harness, groups of men and horses, keeping my eye always on the outline of the royal tent, black now against the deepening blue of the evening sky.

As I drew nearer, monstrous shadows loomed between lines of horses and into my nose, mixed with the mouth-watering aroma of soldiers' stews, wafted a peculiar acrid smell. Then the flicker of a cooking fire lit up a gaping bronze mouth and slanting barrel, and I knew these were the King's precious cannon, drawn all the way from the Tower of London. The evil stink hanging in the air was the stench of gunpowder.

More guards sprang up at my approach and this time two seized my arms. Their leader took my badge from me as I tried to explain. He frowned as he listened, the deep incised lines of the boar thrown into relief by the blazing brand in his hand.

'Seeking Master Kendall, and in the King's service? Are you a spy, boy?'

'No, sir,' I protested, but did not struggle. I had dropped Bess's rein, but kept hold of Murrey's collar, hearing the rumbling in her throat again. The men, though their grasp on me was tight, stood clear of her. 'I have a message from my master in London and seek only to serve His Grace.'

The man laughed.

'Be not so afraid, boy. One can be a spy and still serve His Grace. Several have come these past days with news of the traitor and his movements. Give me your message, then. We shall see it gets to Master Kendall.'

He held out his hand, but I shook my head.

'Sir, it is for Master Kendall alone. My master said I must hand it to him myself.'

The man raised an eyebrow in surprise, though his surprise could not be as great as my own as these words that spilled out unplanned. Yet he did not argue. He simply nodded and, turning, strode off up the ridge, his fellows marching me along behind him. Bess remained with the other guards, but Murrey trotted along beside me, my fingers still hooked through her collar. The firelight glinted in her eyes as her muzzle swept from side to side, as though questing for a scent.

Within yards of the royal tent crouched one far smaller, its sloping sides glimmering pale in the glow of nearby fires. We halted before it as the chief guard cleared his throat and called, 'Master Secretary?'

The tent flap was thrust aside and a familiar figure emerged, at first dark against the flickering light within. But then the guards' torches lit up the astonishment on Master Kendall's face.

'Matthew! For the love of God, what are you doing here? You should be safe back home in London.'

'You know this boy, sir? He says he has a message.'

'Yes, yes. I know him. You may leave him with me.'

He eyed me curiously as the guards released their grip and saluted him before marching back the way we had come. As their footsteps died away, he lifted the tent flap as though to usher me through.

I stood my ground.

'If you have a message for me, come in, Matthew – I will need light to read it by.'

But still I did not move. What prompted me, I don't know, but I heard myself say,

'Master, my message is for the King.'

174

'The King?'

'Aye, master. For him alone.'

He studied me a moment and I was thankful the nearest camp fires lay behind me – for I was blushing at this second lie. With my face in shadow, this tell-tale sign did not give me away, as he asked,

'Is it from Master Ashley?'

I nodded without speaking, fearing a tremor in my voice would reveal my untruth.

'Come, then.'

Amazed that my little subterfuge had again worked, I followed him the few paces up to the larger tent. Its now-unseen banners slapped against their poles far above. The canvas flaps were tied back, but a pale curtain was drawn across the entrance to keep out the night air. A warm glow and murmurs of voices and laughter seeped around its edges and the guards to either side snapped to attention as we approached.

'His Grace is within?' asked Master Kendall and, without waiting for an answer, he pulled aside the curtain and led the way inside.

Having seen the royal tent only from a distance before darkness had fallen, I was taken aback now at its size.

More than a man's height above my head, its canopied ceiling was supported by a complex skeleton of poles, and the space beneath almost equalled the great hall in Master Ashley's grand townhouse. In a far corner was an elaborate campbed swathed in luxurious red fabric, beside it a waist-high wooden chest on which stood a tall crucifix, several books and a variety of silver plate. To every side the canvas walls were hung with exquisitely embroidered tapestries, the vivid reds, golds, blues, greens shimmering in the gleam of the many torches lodged in iron brackets all around.

In the centre of it all, a stout oak table laden with platters, bowls, goblets and myriad papers was surrounded by standing men, the faces of several of whom I recognized as they turned towards us, Lord Lovell, Sir Richard Ratcliffe, the Earl of Northumberland among them. King Richard himself was seated in an intricately carved chair behind it.

He rose to his feet as Master Kendall and I bowed.

'Master Wansford, Your Grace. He brings you a message.'

The King strode round the table to stand in front of us before we even straightened up.

'Matthew?' His eyes were wide with surprise as I raised my head. 'Master Ashley has sent you to me?'

'Aye, Your Grace.'

I prayed that my rising colour wouldn't betray me now that my goal was so close. But even my small successes so far didn't prepare me for what happened next.

The King swung round to his gentlemen.

'Go about your business, sirs. Allow me some minutes with this boy.'

'But Richard —' protested Lord Lovell, but the King clapped him on the shoulder.

'Leave us, Francis. All may become clear in time. But now he and I must be alone.'

Lord Lovell nodded, some kind of understanding dawning on his face. He and the other gentlemen bowed low and withdrew, the entrance curtain falling gently into place behind them. Only Master Kendall remained.

The King turned to him.

'You too, John.' Master Kendall opened his mouth as if to object, but the King raised a hand to silence him. 'Though I would trust you with my life, John, that is not the issue here as you well know. And I have no more need of my secretary this night. Leave us.'

Master Kendall made again as though to speak, then, perhaps thinking better of it, bowed in his turn and followed the other gentlemen from the tent.

And I was alone with King Richard.

18

The Eve of Battle

He stood before me, his hand out-thrust.

I fumbled in my pouch for Master Ashley's letter. As I drew it out, a sudden pang of guilt griped at me. How dare I, a mere apprentice, lie and cheat my way into the presence of my King?

I dropped to my knees, passing the small square of parchment to him with my head lowered.

He murmured his thanks and moved away to the table. The tiny crack of the wax seal breaking reached my ears, then the crackle of unfolding parchment.

A short silence. Then,

'But this is to Master Kendall. Why are you wasting my time, boy?'

His voice was sharp.

I hung my head still, waiting for his rebuke. Why had I been so stupid?

But then came his familiar bark of a laugh.

'And just asking that you be found a job here.' Relief washed through me at his change of tone. 'Away from any danger, of course.'

My cheeks burned again and my fists curled into balls. Despite my earlier self-reproach, I leapt to my feet, ready to protest.

The King was leaning back against the table, watching me levelly, a half-smile on his lips.

'Nay, boy, do not be so quick to anger. Your master asks John to find you a job wherever you may be useful to me – as you are so keen to serve and so full of youthful foolishness. But, for himself, Master Ashley asks that you be kept from harm as he has many uses for you.'

I was not so used to his gentle mocking ways as I had once been and I jibbed at the words.

'Do not heed him, Your Grace. I want to serve you in the battle – I know it is coming.'

'Yes, it's coming. Tomorrow – did you know that?'

'Tomorrow?'

I swallowed, but found my throat dry. I had seen the camp, the soldiers, the weapons, but had no idea the battle would be so soon.

The King, however, appeared untroubled.

'Aye. Tudor and his forces are just a few miles from here, at Merevale my scouts tell me. Tomorrow we shall meet face to face with our armies at our backs.'

'Your Grace, I – I wish also to fight at your side.'

'I thank you for your brave loyalty, Matt, but you cannot fight. You have no armour.'

'I have my sallet and my jack, like many of your men. Master Ashley gave me money for them – he must have meant for me to wear them in the fight.'

'Or perhaps to protect you from the jibes and buffets of the older men. They may not take seriously your attempt to join them.'

I had no reply to that after my reception at Leicester. But the King considered me a moment, and his tone softened as he said,

'Yet, Master Wansford, you seem to have grown since last I saw you, though that was so short a time ago. Or is it just your sallet that makes you appear taller?'

I still wore my helmet, though in the presence of the King. Hastily I slipped it from my head and, to cover my embarrassment, said,

'My mother used to say that spring and summer are the time for growing, my lord. And I have been training hard to serve you.'

'Training?'

'Yes, my lord, as best I can. When Master Ashley can spare me from my duties.'

'That is commendable, Matthew. Every man should be prepared for war in case the call should come.' I smiled inside at his use of the word 'man', but then he added, 'Yet I have army enough, as you see. Brackenbury came with his London troops, and the Earl of Northumberland at last with his men from the north. Even Master Kendall will strap on armour tomorrow, though he is a man of words, not of the sword. How could one boy...?'

The rumours that had been circling in London sprang into my mind.

'But they say, Your Grace, that some great lords may not rally to your banner.'

'Is that what you have heard? And you feel that you can make up for the failures of such men?'

'They say the Welsh chieftains are marching with Henry Tudor. Even perhaps Lord Stanley...'

A shadow flitted across the King's face, then was gone.

'Lord Stanley? Aye, his family have betrayed my family before. In the past they have waited to see which way the wind will blow. But this time he will stand firm. He and his brother William... They will see that my army numbers several thousand more than Tudor's rabble of French mercenaries. They will see that the wind blows for the rightful King of England, not that half-Welsh traitor, no matter that he has the ear and money of the King of France. They will stand firm.'

'Yet Lady Stanley, Your Grace – is she not Tudor's mother? Did she not plot against you before?'

'Aye, lad, she did. But I spared her then and let her lands remain in her family. Her husband now speaks for her loyalty. And his son who is in my camp speaks for his.'

'My lord?'

'His son, Lord Strange, Tudor's stepbrother, is here at my pleasure. He is my guest,' a wry smile, 'or my hostage if you prefer. My brother Edward and I – we have forgiven the Stanleys often in the past. Now it does no harm to have a little insurance for their honour. He can remind his father and his uncle who has been the source of their prosperity, and who will reward them richly in the future. Sadly it seems that is the language such men understand.'

He pushed himself up from the table's edge and went to sit again in the great chair.

'But, Matthew, it is your fate we must attend to now. I have thought of the way you can best serve me. Are you ready to do my bidding?'

'Of course, Your Grace.'

'You shall help me by returning to London with an important message to your master.'

'But, my lord —' I protested.

'Matthew, I would not have you fight tomorrow, for all your training and your keenness and your leather armour. You are only a boy —' he raised his hand to stall my further objections, 'and I may have other uses for you once we have won our victory here. You have proved yourself valuable in my service before, and as King, I think perhaps I can make further use of you – if Master Ashley agrees to release you. I imagine Lord Soulsby will have forgotten your youthful misdemeanours by now, and surely can have no reason against my employing you again.'

What did his last words mean?

'Does Alys not have to marry Ralph now?'

'Dame Grey agreed to consider the matter. I have not yet had word of how it shall turn out. But Ralph and his father ride with Sir William Stanley. If all goes well tomorrow, they may look to be rewarded with more lands and wealth than even Alys Langdown can bring to them – and as King perhaps I can find another, greater heiress to satisfy them.'

Was he serious? His expression made me uncertain. And did Alys herself – far away as I believed in Sheriff Hutton – know anything of the matter? Yet I was sad for that other, unknown heiress – if she existed.

Whatever the case, though, I had to take the King at his word.

'Thank you, Your Grace. I will be for ever in your debt.'

'It is the privilege of a king to be able to reward all his followers, whether big or small, and one that I enjoy. But in the meantime, you can serve me best by delivering my message.'

This time I didn't protest. I would do my duty as my sovereign saw fit to order. Even if it were just a ploy to keep me safe from the fighting...

King Richard selected a quill and parchment from among the mess of writing equipment on the table and set to work writing with his own hand. This was a thing unseen by me before, as it had been with Master Ashley in London. At normal times both my masters relied on their secretaries. He took his time, consulting a book that lay among the papers, and it was several minutes before he folded the small sheet and dripped molten wax upon it to seal it. Then he walked around the desk and handed the note to me, together with a small leather purse.

'There, Matthew, my message, with expenses for your journey.' The purse clinked as my fingers closed around it. 'You must deliver the message into Master Ashley's own hands. Into no one else's. Do not use it to find your way into the presence of the Archbishop of Canterbury – or of the Emperor or the Pope in Rome. No more deceptions please.'

I laughed and stowed the parchment square and purse in my pouch.

'No, Your Grace. I'm sorry.'

'Do not worry. It was but a small deception – and I'm grateful that it brought me such a messenger as you. You may perhaps travel more easily than one of my men, should tomorrow —'

He broke off, and perched once more on the edge of the table, fiddling with his signet ring.

''Do you still sing, Matthew?'

'Aye, my lord. Though —' Heat rushed to my face again. Once or twice in recent weeks my voice had faltered at the higher notes.

'Though you find that you are growing up? It comes to us all in time.'

'I can sing as well at the moment – I think. Would you like me to tonight?'

'Why not? For old time's sake. It may be the last time before...'

He swung away and poured deep red wine from a flagon into a pair of engraved silver goblets on the table. Handing one to me, he sat again in the oaken chair and raised his goblet.

'To old times. And old friends.'

We both drank. As the warmth of the wine coursed down my throat, I remembered other toasts he had made – at the boar hunt, the night before we had left Middleham, that evening in St Albans. Old times, indeed, and friends who were no longer with us.

I took another sip, then returned the goblet to the table.

'What would you have me sing, Your Grace? I have no lute with me.'

'You are still learning it?' I nodded. 'Master Ashley as ever keeps his promises. Something perhaps in English, Matt – our own fair tongue. And nothing sad on this eve, in case my soldiers shall think me melancholy.'

As he settled more comfortably in the chair, I reflected that such a song would be suitable for such a man – a King who was the first to write his laws in English, not in French, so ordinary people could understand them. And some in his kingdom found fault with that?

The first song I chose, in praise of our Holy Father, I had learnt at the Minster, one of very few the choir master had taught us that were not in Latin. But the second Master Petyt, the dancing master at Middleham, had himself composed, in memory, he had said, of his own youth spent touring from one castle to another, teaching lords' children to dance. The jauntiness of the melody set the King's foot tapping, and to my relief my voice soared to its heights without failing.

As the last notes died away, a rustling arose behind me.

Murrey, stretched out at my feet throughout, shot up and sprang towards the sound, snarling, her sharp white teeth bared, her lithe red body aquiver. The King also rose, a hand on his sword hilt, and I swung round to face whoever, whatever, had made the noise.

It was Lord Lovell, frozen halfway through the entrance, the pale curtain raised in one hand. Amazement was sketched across his face as he eyed the hound, standing bristling in his path.

Before I could call Murrey back and scold her for her ill manners, the King laughed.

'Let that be a warning to you, Francis. How should she know you are not a spy of Tudor's come to murder me?'

'If I were, Richard, would I come through the front door?'

'Then perhaps you must station guards all around my tent tonight. Or should my safety be left to one small hound alone? A brave little thing, is she not? And to think she was one of Florette's "runts".'

Lord Lovell edged forward, letting the curtain fall behind him, all the while keeping a wary eye on Murrey.

I whistled to her and she padded back to me. The whites of her eyes no longer showed and the fur on her back was smooth once again, the faintest rumble only in her throat. The King threw her a morsel of something from a platter on the table and she caught it and devoured it hungrily.

'Runt she may be,' said his lordship, 'but perhaps she should lie across your threshold tonight. You could do worse. Your young squire has asked to be allowed to join his uncle.'

'Young Hugh?' asked King Richard. I started at the name. 'And have you given him leave?'

'I thought it unwise to. After all, if Lord Stanley...'

His mouth clammed shut as his gaze slid towards me.

'We have one guest already, Francis,' the King replied, unperturbed. 'We will have no need of more. Let him go – if he can find his way to Stanley's camp through the darkness.'

'If you are sure, Richard?'

The King nodded.

With a final glance at Murrey, settled again at my feet, her head on her paws, Lord Lovell ducked out through the curtain back into the night.

The King sat back in his chair and swallowed a mouthful of wine, his face thoughtful.

I found my voice, heedless of whether I should speak.

'Hugh Soulsby is here?'

'As you heard – at least for the present.'

He watched me as I struggled to keep my feelings from showing on my face. But the light cast by the torches and the candles on the table was enough for his sharp eyes.

'You have not forgiven him?'

'Should I have?'

My question in reply was impertinent, but as so often, he did not notice – or chose not to.

'Perhaps. It is a long time ago. And maybe it was for the best. '

'That I should be sent away?'

'You have made a good life for yourself in London. You will learn a great deal with Master Ashley, have many opportunities other young men would give much to have.'

'If you say so, Your Grace.' Thinking back over all that I had missed these past two years – time with my friends, training as a squire like Roger – and Hugh – a touch of insolence crept into my voice. 'But perhaps not everyone forgives as easily as you.'

'It is not always easy to forgive, Matt. But sometimes it is necessary and repays the effort.'

'Will you forgive any who betray you tomorrow? Will you pardon Henry Tudor? Lord Stanley, if he should prove traitor?'

'Lord Stanley will stand firm. And there will be time enough after the battle to think of forgiveness – if it is needed.'

Did he truly believe his own words? I could not tell. But his calm half-smile made me ashamed of my outburst.

'But in the meantime, Matthew, you must be on your way. Your badge will take you safely back through my army. Find your way south to the old road that is Watling Street – that will take you directly to London. And mind you go straight to Master Ashley – that is most important.'

Once again it occurred to me that this supposedly vital message was no more than a ruse to send me away from the coming battle.

Before I knew what I was doing, I threw myself down on my knees.

'Not tonight, my lord. Let me take Hugh's place – let me be your page again and sleep at your threshold. Murrey and me – as Lord Lovell said. You know you can count on our loyalty.'

At first my plea was met only with silence. Perhaps my earlier words had angered the King? But then he spoke again.

'Very well, Matt. You may act as my page one more time. You and your brave little hound. But you must be away early, at first light – before the camp is fully awake.'

His amused tone reassured me he didn't hold my speech against me. But was he remembering, as I did now, the last time I had been his page? That morning at

Northampton, when he had had to nudge me awake. When his life could have been in danger from the Woodville plotters.

Surely he didn't recall it. But I told myself I must not sleep at all this night, despite my long journey.

'Thank you, Your Grace, I won't fail you.'

The rest of that evening was a blur of busyness. Lord Lovell soon returned, along with Master Ratcliffe and other gentlemen I did not know. Before Murrey could do more than growl, I hauled her over to sit alongside me on a stool beside the campbed. There I shared with her the last of the food I had carried from London, while the King and his men discussed the morrow.

I understood little of what they said in their quiet deliberations. After a while I took up a leather-bound book of hours from the oaken chest and sat turning the pages, until the King should be ready to retire. I marvelled long at an exquisite picture of Our Lady within, kneeling by a golden-haired, gilt-winged angel, a prayerbook open upon her desk, even as this book lay open before me.

But then my eye was caught by one text towards the end, headed by a fabulous capital letter scrolled in the brilliant murrey and blue of the King's colours. The beautiful handwritten Latin beseeched merciful Lord Jesus to free his servant, King Richard, from every sorrow and trouble and from all the plots of his enemies, and to defend him from all evil and all peril, past, present and to come.

I read the prayer over again and again. How much would my lord need such help in just a few hours' time?

From time to time the guards outside snapped to attention, and a soldier bearing a message, or some sly man, sidled through the curtain into the tent. At first I strained to hear the reports, but before long the effort was beyond me. The past days' fatigues took their toll. Despite my resolve to remain awake to protect my King, I must have drifted into sleep, my back leaning against a costly tapestry, my hand still resting on Murrey's head, close against my thigh.

'Matt.' King Richard's voice seeped into my brain as though through fog or from far distant. 'Matthew?'

I stumbled to my feet. Murrey grumbled as my movement disturbed her.

The King stood before me. The tent was empty of his gentlemen, and shadows danced within it as the torches guttered and burned down.

I rubbed my eyes.

'Your Grace?'

'It is time to sleep, Matthew. A mattress has been placed ready for you.' The brand behind me had long ago died, and his face was in darkness. 'Take what rest you may. It will be a long day tomorrow – for both of us.'

His hand was upon my elbow, leading me towards the doorway. There, just within the curtain, lay a palliasse, covered over with the blanket I had carried with me from London. As I lowered myself on to it gratefully and my eyelids likewise drooped, I was too sleepy to protest as I heard the King say,

'Sleep well, Matt. I shall wake you in good time, never fear.'

19

Blood Moon

Tap, tap, tap.

I shake my head. But the sound is still there.

Tap, tap, tap.

In my head.

I turn.

A grey veil of mist parts before me. Tatters drift off to either side, to left, to right. I put up my hand to push them away. Clammy, cold air.

A dark, vaulted space. Ceiling high above. So high. So dark. Mist vanishing like incense into the void. I look back down.

Before me now a great grey slab of stone. A figure hunched over it.

Tap, tap, tap.

I step forward.

The man twists to stare at me, then turns back. Hammer, chisel in his hands.

Tap, tap, tap.

Upon the slab, a boy. Yet not – Cold, grey stone.

Dark shadowed eyes. Sad shadowed eyes.

I know his face.

Tap, tap, tap.

Biting at the stone. Scarring it. Scribing a name.

I step closer to read it.

E – D – W – A – R – D.

Across the cold, stone boy, two faces. Two boys.

Hollow eyed. Kneeling. Dark shadowed eyes.

I know their faces.

Who? Where?

Tap, tap, tap.

Cold, damp, upon my hand. A push. A whimper.

Tap, tap, tap.

I opened my eyes.

Darkness.

Murrey's nose moist against my palm. Whining. Shoving me to wakefulness.

I drew a deep breath, murmured a prayer to drive away the dream. A sad dream, I remembered. But it was vanishing fast. Like mist touched by the sun's early rays.

I stretched out my limbs to waken them.

Tap, tap, tap.

I froze, my body rigid.

But, no, not the chipping of cold stone this time. The faraway clang, clang, clang of hammer on hot metal. The armourer of last night? Or another. Closer this. But still distant.

A man's cough. Nearer. Outside the tent.

The whinny of a horse, a crunch as hoof scraped on dry ground.

Little noises. Night-time noises.

I knelt up, pushed my blanket away. Drawing the curtain aside revealed more darkness. But greyer now.

My eyes adjusting, I dragged myself to my feet and went outside. Two guards shuffled to attention, then relaxed, nodding at me, the mere boy.

Different men now. How often had the guard changed while I had lain there, oblivious?

The moon was setting.

Almost full, it rested a moment on a far-off hill. But it wasn't the great gold coin of other nights. Its gleam was tinged red.

'Blood moon,' muttered one of the guards as it slid down behind the dark bulk of the hill and soon was lost from sight.

I shivered.

He spat on the ground.

'Bad tidings for the traitor.'

A camp fire flared before a nearby tent, then another further off.

'Not long till sunrise, I reckon,' said the second guard.

He grasped my shoulder, turning me around and pointing. A thick grey line sketched the outline of trees on the other horizon. The tentative call of a bird broke the silence, another chirruping in answer. 'Time to wake His Grace?'

Slipping back through the flap, I rolled up my mattress and blanket, then felt my way across the pitch-dark tent. At the table, I fumbled in my pouch for my tinderbox, and struck a light on a candle in its gilded holder.

I shielded the flickering flame with my hand and, with Murrey a lithe shadow at my heel, approached the King's fabric-shrouded bed.

He was sleeping still, his head upon an embroidered linen pillow, an arm outflung across the fine cloth of his coverlet. In the pool of candlelight his face was younger than I had ever seen before, the lines smoothed away by sleep.

For the briefest moment the face of his son, poor Ed – not glimpsed for two years – swam before my eyes. Then my dream came back to me.

My hand shook and the candle flame quivered.

Murrey whined, her dark eyes liquid in the candlelight as they gazed up at me. The fingers of my free hand twined themselves in the tufted fur of her head.

The King's eyes opened, then narrowed at me, bending over him.

'Matthew?'

'My lord, it is time to rise.'

I drew back, pulling Murrey with me.

He eased himself off the bed, then reaching for a thick fur mantle upon a nearby chair, swung it around his shoulders and strode towards the tent's entrance. As he tugged the flap aside, the guards stamped to attention. He bid them a quiet good morning as he passed.

I trailed after him, still clutching Murrey's collar. The metal fleur-de-lys stitched there was cold against my hand. I recalled old King Edward buckling the leather strap around her neck as I stepped forward to stand beside his brother.

We gazed out at the camp as it began to stir.

Before us, grey ranks of tents marched down the dark hillside, swallowed up by the pool of mist gathered on its lower slopes. In the distance only the tips, their pennons limp in the windless air, poked above the milky depths.

Among the nearer tents, ghostly figures glided, their calls, laughs, greetings to their fellows floating to us above the wreathing mist. Here and there the comforting glow of camp fires. I could see cooking pots hung over the hot coals of the closest.

Far to our right, men were busy among rows of horses, feeding and watering. Again the clang, clang, clang of hammer on metal, but this time I did not heed it. Instead I watched King Richard as his gaze swept across the awakening camp.

A chill still cut the air. As the King gathered his fur cloak about him, I longed for my blanket but did not move to retrieve it.

A serving man scurried up and knelt before the King.

'Your Grace? Do you wish me to waken your chaplains?'

'Aye, and my lords Norfolk and Lovell, if they are still abed. Also Lord Strange. We shall take Mass together this morning.'

The man hurried off and we were silent once more.

Rooks cawed in distant trees. Above our heads, the last sparks of the stars were fading as the greyish light grew in the east.

Then the King spoke.

'Well, Matt, what do you think of your first battle camp?'

And without waiting for an answer, he walked towards the horse lines. To left and right men stopped what they were doing to bow and hail him.

''Morning Your Grace.'

'A fine day for a battle – once that mist clears.'

'The traitor will be quaking in his boots at sight of that moon last night!'

How could they be so bold? To speak first to the King before he had spoken to them?

But perhaps it was a privilege of soldiers. King Richard evidently found no fault with them, for he only smiled and greeted them in return.

But when we reached the first of the horses, the man who hastened up to us took no such liberties. As he knelt before King Richard, I recognized him as the horse master from Middleham.

'I bid you a fair morning, Master Reynold,' said the King. 'How are you and your charges today?'

Master Reynold rose to his feet.

'Well enough, Your Grace, though it was an unquiet night. As ever, they sense what is to come.'

The horses, mostly dark shadows, were quiet now, busy with their nosebags while grooms scuttled among them checking legs and hooves. In the first line, a pearly grey stood out in the lingering darkness. Storm, the King's favourite. Last seen by me carrying the King in his triumph.

His Grace ran a hand along his neck, pulled out strands of forelock trapped beneath his halter.

'Well, boy,' he murmured, 'you have served me well in the past, but today your son shall do me the honour.'

As he slapped the stallion's neck, he glanced past him towards the second row of beasts. And there, tossing his head while a groom brushed his gleaming moonlight coat, stood Windfollower.

Almost three years had passed since my eyes had beheld him, but I knew him. His power and the terror of being on his back as he bolted headlong across the water meadows at Middleham rushed back to me now.

The King looked down at me. Whatever he saw in my face caused him to say,

'He has changed since your little adventure, Matt. He's now well trained and a fitting mount for a king about to ride into battle.'

He gave Storm a final pat and turned towards the throng of tents again. As the light in the sky grew, their outlines were becoming more distinct against the veil of mist. To the east a low bank of cloud on the far hills was edged with pink where the sun would soon rise.

The King's face was calm as he surveyed the landscape.

'One last battle, perhaps,' he said quietly. 'With Tudor dead, there will be no more false claims. I shall push the French to a treaty, like the Scots. And Portugal –'

He glanced at me. Though the light was dim, I caught the trace of a smile.

'You will be pleased to know I have followed your advice, Matt – and that of my advisors, of course. About remarriage, I mean. It has helped to hear that Anne – Her Grace the late Queen – had spoken of it. Though I know not why she spoke of it to you...'

'I had been telling her my story, Your Grace. Of my stepmother and my father.'

'Of course. A happy man. And why should I not find happiness again? I have sent ambassadors into Portugal to offer myself in marriage to the Infanta Joana.'

'Infanta, Your Grace?'

'Princess, Matthew. The King's sister. And though she is Portuguese, she is descended from our third King Edward, and so is the senior Lancastrian heir to the English throne. If we marry, it will unite the houses of York and Lancaster for all time. Would that not be a fine thing? To make an end to the reason for all these years of fighting over the crown of England.'

'Aye, my lord. Truly it would.'

'And she is a most beautiful and religious woman – so her ambassadors tell me. I expect to receive a portrait of her soon. I wonder what she will think of mine.'

The flicker of a nearby fire danced in his eyes as they ranged across the now stirring scene.

I remembered that day in Westminster when I had entered the palace to find him fidgeting while the painter took his likeness. How sad his eyes had been then, so soon after his wife's death. Was that the portrait that would be sent – or would another of him in this more buoyant mood be preferred?

Mention of that far-flung land spurred another memory.

'I had heard tell that your niece, the lady Elizabeth, is perhaps also to marry into Portugal.'

'How do you know this?'

'Is it no more than a rumour, Your Grace? I'm sorry if I've spoken out of turn.'

'Do not worry, Matt. It is one rumour that I hope may have some basis in the truth.'

'Alys Langdown told me of it in a letter.' Or had it been Elen? 'That a Portuguese duke was seeking her hand.'

'Manuel, yes. He is Joana's cousin. And is Elizabeth happy with the arrangement?'

'Alys says she can't wait.'

As the words tripped out, I feared that I had again blundered, but the King only laughed.

'That is good – that she is keen to wed. It is a pity that Alys herself is not.'

'I'm sure she will do your bidding in all things, Your Grace. But... but she would perhaps do it more cheerfully if her husband were not to be Ralph Soulsby.'

'Alys always was a headstrong creature. But we will await the outcome of the battle – and Dame

194

Elizabeth's decision.' He turned to face me. 'Or, tell me, Matt, do you have some other husband in mind for her?'

'No, indeed, my lord. Not I.'

His back was towards the lightening east, his face cast in shadow, and I could not tell whether he was in jest. Flustered, I sought to divert him and reached in my pouch for a morsel with which to entice Murrey to dance.

My hand brushed against cold metal.

Closing my fingers around it, I drew it out. It was the coin that Master Ratcliffe had handed me in London. The crowned head and tiny boar stamp were as fresh as when newly minted more than two years ago.

As I lifted my eyes, they were caught by the ghostly tendrils of mist still drifting before us.

'I dreamed last night of your son, my lord.'

'My son? Edward? You saw him?'

A tug in the King's voice made me regret my words.

'I saw a stone cutter. He was carving his name.'

Tap, tap, tap.

'And I saw two other boys. They weren't Ed, but – but they looked like him.'

I glanced up at the King.

He was staring ahead once more, but his eyes didn't see the newly bustling camp.

'Like Ed – but not Ed.'

'I think they were his cousins, Your Grace, your nephews. The princes that were. I rode with Edward, the elder. I knew his face.'

He was silent.

Perhaps I should have said no more, but...

'Your Grace – those rumours...?'

'Rumours?'

'About your nephews, Your Grace. That were whispered during the rebellion.'

'Ah, yes, those rumours.'

He gazed ahead still.

A pause.

'You believed them?'

'No, Your Grace,' I protested.

'But you remember them.'

'It was just my dream, Your Grace.'

'I had hoped they would be forgotten. Out of sight, out of mind, they say. And they have, haven't they?'

I said nothing. Did he mean the rumours – or the boys?

'The men at Merevale will not be fighting for my brother's sons today. No, rather they will fight for a French-backed pretender who they say has already proclaimed himself king. A traitor who has little more claim to the English throne than many here – or others still abed far from here.'

'My lord?'

'They say he plans to marry my niece Elizabeth. A Yorkist bride, to make his claim more secure. No mention of her brothers. And Tudor could not let them live if he were to become king. There, that is their death warrant – unless those rumours are true and I signed it myself long ago.'

He fell silent.

I cursed myself inside. I should not have mentioned the boys, stirred him to such thoughts. Not on this morning.

Did he sigh before he spoke again?

'But, in any case, the deed is done. Two years ago I accepted the crown – and today I must fight for it. If God grants me victory here, I will know I did the right thing. If I should be defeated —'

Before I dared challenge his words, a serving man bustled up to us and bowed.

'Yes?'

'Your Grace, all is ready for Mass. The gentlemen are gathered in your tent.'

The King nodded, then turned back to me.

'Pay no heed to rumours, Matt – and perhaps even less to dreams. My brother Edward once told me of a terrible dream he had – full of demons and the shades of executed traitors come back to haunt him. Later that day, he won a glorious victory. Have you heard of the battle of Barnet? Myself – I had slept hardly at all that night. I was just eighteen. It was my first battle...'

He placed his hand on my shoulder.

'But this will not be yours, Matthew. You must soon be on your way. Attend Mass, then be off.'

'But, Your Grace, I —'

'Do not be mutinous. You must not await the outcome of this battle – your message is too important. Your master should already know what he must do, but it will do no harm to remind him. Come.'

He swung round. At last the sun broke free above the hill and its crowning bank of cloud, and King Richard's face was flooded with a wash of morning light like liquid gold.

He squinted and raised a hand to shield against its suddenness, then laughed.

'The sun in splendour indeed. It shines upon this day's endeavour.'

And he strode towards the royal tent, the servant in his wake.

But I hung back.

I was angry at myself for revealing my dream, ashamed at provoking the King to speak of – of a matter I had not even thought of for almost two years. Who was I – a mere subject – to question a king – whatever he might have done?

Murrey nuzzled my hand as I watched the sun rise above a copse of trees atop the far ridge. Among them, the spire of a distant church was stark black against the golden sky. As I set off slowly after the King, an idea nudged at my mind.

Inside the tent priests in full vestments were preparing for the Mass. The towering crucifix I had seen the night before stood ready on a cloth-of-gold-covered altar, a silver chalice and a salver for the bread alongside.

Several gentlemen, known and unknown to me, came to greet the King as we entered. Lord Lovell, his fair face solemn as he bowed, then embraced his old friend. Sir Richard Ratcliffe, Master Kendall. Three or four others. One, a young man with a thatch of whitish-blond hair and the palest of brows, hung back until nudged forward into a bow by Master Ratcliffe. Then came His Grace the Duke of Norfolk whom I recalled from my glimpses of him long ago in London.

Tall and lean, his face tanned and lined by long years of soldiering, he inclined his head, then clasped the King's hand in a firm grip.

'Dickon. I trust you've slept soundly.'

'Aye, Jack. Well enough.'

'My lords Stanley and Northumberland are not attending Mass?'

'I did not summon them, though Lord Strange here stands for his father.' The fair young man bent his head towards the King again, his face expressionless. 'Their lordships will have enough to do this morning without trailing here from their camps. Each must take care of his own soul today.'

The King's companions joined him in his smile, but as he stepped across to the campbed to throw off his mantle, their smiles dropped away.

I hastened to pour water into a basin for the King to wash, then helped him on with a loose morning robe. As I fastened it about him, I asked quietly,

'Do you wish me to sing at the Mass, Your Grace?'

No candles lit this corner of the tent and his face was shadowed as he answered,

'Nay, lad, not this morning, though I believe my lord of Norfolk there would like to hear you. Perhaps I will send for you for our thanksgiving Mass on our return to London. But not today. Save your strength – and your voice.'

It was with relief that for once I took no more part in the Mass than the other worshippers. Not only had I been afraid my voice would let me down, but my dream still weighed heavily on me, despite the King's words. The prickling in my eyes came as no surprise as the priest intoned the familiar words of the prayer from last night: 'most gentle Lord Jesus Christ, keep thy servant King Richard, and defend him from all evil and from all peril past, present and to come...'

Before long, we had tasted the bread and the wine, and had risen from our knees, and the candles on the altar were snuffed, and the gilded crucifix was being lifted and affixed to a long pole of beechwood. The priests held it aloft and led the way out into the noise and bustle of the sunlit camp.

A trestle table had been set up outside, loaded with sweet-smelling fresh bread and cheeses and jugs of wine. Beyond it squires stood ready with a suit of magnificent armour, every piece shining like polished silver in the early sunlight.

I swallowed hard. Of a sudden, the coming battle was very close.

As if sensing my fear, King Richard came over to me. He had shed his morning robe and begun to don the garments he would wear beneath his armour.

'Now it is time for you to leave, Matt. There is food for your journey. John tells me you will find your pony in the horse lines. Remember, go straight to Master Ashley and deliver my message.'

'Of course, Your Grace. No – no deceptions. And... Your Grace...'

'Yes?'

'I hope you find your happiness, Your Grace. God be with you.'

He smiled.

'And you, Matt. Now, go. And don't fail me in this small service.'

I knelt and kissed the great ring upon his hand, my eyes stinging once more. His other hand was heavy upon my head as I said,

'Never, my lord.'

Then I rose and walked away without another glance, not trusting my face not to betray me as I gathered my bundle, whistled to Murrey and hurried towards the strings of horses.

It took me little time to find Bess, the smallest by far among the mounts assembled there, and in a matter of minutes we were trotting past the last rows of tents and wagons and straggling soldiers, and heading away from the camp.

But I did not make my way towards the great highway of Watling Street as I had been told. Instead I circled round to the north, staying upon high ground when I could, always keeping the army's camp in view.

So I saw when it broke up – as companies of soldiers marched towards the south-west, as teams of huge horses were set to hauling black cannon, as parties of horsemen wheeled away after them, their armour catching fire in the sunlight.

And I followed.

May the Lord forgive me, I betrayed my King, and followed as his army marched towards battle.

.

20

View from a Tower

'There's no more room!'

The man's face loomed dark against the square of daylight far above.

'He's only a little 'un.'

'And he's wearing the King's badge.'

'Why's he not fighting then?'

Laughter erupted around me as the question was dropped down on us like a stone. I was thankful we were in darkness as I knew my face was aglow. Why wasn't I fighting? Why was that the only one of King Richard's orders that I had obeyed that day?

Another head joined the first staring down.

'Is he a deserter?'

'No!' I cried.

'He's only a boy – twelve or thirteen,' offered a motherly voice. For once I took no offence at being thought younger than I was – perhaps it could work in my favour. But another of the villagers clustered around me was not so sympathetic.

'Wearing a sallet?'

I slipped my helmet off and thrust it into my bundle.

'He'll have picked it up after some deserter threw it down,' the second head called down. 'Fleeing from the traitor's camp, no doubt, when he caught sight of the King's army.'

'Spoils of war.' The first face laughed. 'We've all done that. Send him up. There's room enough for a little 'un – if he promises not to breathe.'

'Go on, lad. Leave your bundle and hound down here with us. You don't want to miss the fun.'

Hands shoved me from behind and I hauled myself up the steep ladder, past a great bell hanging silent, up to the wide-open trapdoor high above. The two men there reached down to pull me through and I emerged, blinking, into the dazzling sunlight.

More than a dozen men were gathered on the small platform atop the tower, two or three deep against the parapet at the southern side.

The first man who had spoken, stocky, grey-haired and little taller than me, eyed me up and down. A livid scar adorned his cheek, scything it from eye to jaw.

'Small enough, and not from these parts, I reckon, from the making of your jack.'

He took hold of my elbow and forced his way through the small crowd.

'Make way, make way. The lad's come a long way to see the sights.'

Some grumbling greeted his words, but it was good-natured, and the men parted to let us through to the waist-high parapet beyond. My companion rested his hands upon the stout carved stone blocks.

'There, boy. Is the view all you thought it would be?'

I leant forward beside him and my heart jolted within me.

Spread out before us was the rolling countryside I had travelled through that morning. For as long as I could I had kept the royal army in sight, but at last I had had to turn away, seeking this distant vantage point. I had not been sure the ancient church would provide what I wanted. But I could not have wished for better – unless it had been riding on the wings of the hawk I espied hovering in the heavens high above us.

Perhaps a mile or more from us, at the end of a long ridge of land, was a vast gathering. I could barely make out individual figures at this distance, but it was plain what I was seeing.

Huge hosts of men, armies; sunlight glistening on armour, weapons, battle standards. Many, many thousands there must be. Ants against the green landscape.

'Mary, mother of God.'

The words slipped out before I could stop them.

My grizzled companion grunted.

'The King's army has found its position, but Tudor's is still advancing, I think. And what of the others?'

I turned to him. His shrewd dark eyes were watching me.

'My eyesight is not what it was, lad. Not since I took this blow at Barnet.' He pointed to the scar and grinned. 'And age is catching up with me too. I didn't let you up here just out of the goodness of my heart.'

'You fought at Barnet?' I cast my mind back to the stories told of that battle a year or so after I was born.

'Aye, lad. And barely escaped with my life. My lord picked the wrong side. I only survived by playing dead after the Earl of Oxford's array was broken. That was due to the Duke of Gloucester, of course. His Grace the King, now, that is.'

'You fought for the Lancastrians!'

'Don't be so worried, boy. It was a long time ago. And footsoldiers like us don't get a choice who we fight for. Save if we choose to desert, of course.' With his elbow he nudged his neighbour, who laughed along with him. 'But if we were called, we'd be for the King today. We don't want the French meddling in our affairs. Now tell us what you see. You've the youngest eyes here.'

A glance about me showed he told the truth. Most there were older than he. Yet all had the light of excitement in their eyes.

So I turned back to the scene laid out before me like a map unrolled upon a table. My voice sounding strangely distant to my ears, I did my best to report all I saw.

'The largest army – closest to us – near the end of that ridge – that must be the King's. I see a crowd of horses behind, and great banners flying there. I think one is King Richard's white boar, another the royal standard. That must show where the King himself is. In the distance dust is still rising, but that army seems to have halted. At its head is a banner with a great star and a blue... another boar, I think. Is that possible?'

'The blue boar? Aye. Then Tudor's vanguard is led by the Earl of Oxford. Perhaps he's come to make amends for Barnet, eh, lads?' More laughter among the men. 'What else do you see?'

'Far off to the left – that other great band of men. As large as an army – but away from both the King's and Tudor's. Many knights on horseback – I see the sun flash upon their armour. But who —'

I fell silent as King Richard's words came back to me: 'Lord Stanley will stand firm.' And I thought of the 'guest' in the King's camp.

'Who is it, lad? Can you see his standard?'

'Lord Stanley. I cannot see so far, but it will be Lord Stanley and his brother.'

The man turned and spat behind him, away from the crowd of onlookers.

'Of course. The Stanleys ever bide their time. It may be that the King will have to do without them today, but surely he has men enough – so long as Stanley doesn't throw in his lot with Tudor at the start. How are the King's men arrayed?'

I tore my gaze away from the motionless Stanleys.

'The King's banner is in the centre. Ahead are row on row of men, a standard with a rearing lion stitched in silver in their middle.'

'Jack of Norfolk.' The man nodded in approval. 'The best choice for the forward line. The King could have no one better. Then it must be my lord of Northumberland in the rear?'

Some way behind where the King's standards streamed proudly in what breeze there was, stood yet another formation of troops – more thousands of men and horses. The largest of their banners was clear and bright to my eyes – a blue lion on a yellow background. Such a one as had been carried aloft behind the Earl of Northumberland on the streets of London, in happier times more than two years ago. Yet, try as I might, I could not spot among his troops the white rose on blue of my fellow men of York. Had my brother Fred yet arrived to serve his King on the battlefield?

As I described the banners to my avid listeners, upon the wind came the blare of trumpets from the King's army, tinny to my ears at this distance. A tremendous shout went up from the ranks of men, then my senses were assaulted by the most monstrous sound. A deep boom, deeper than ever John Swynbourne had played upon his shawm, closer perhaps to a thunderclap resounding through the narrow streets of York.

I staggered backwards under the force of it, clutching at my fellow watchers.

'In the name of —'

'Rest easy, son,' my companion said, though his face too was drained of colour. ''Tis only —'

Another hellish crack, then its echo, struck us.

''Tis only the cannon. See where they're arrayed. To the left of His Grace's flank – where those clouds of smoke are rising.'

Flame spat, brilliant red, more smoke rose, and again the powerful retort punched my chest.

Another flash, another crash, and dark figures could be spied, scurrying around as if in dense fog. Then an answering thunderclap sounded from far beyond Tudor's army, and another, and soon I could see little beyond the mist drifting across the distant landscape and hear nothing but the booming of the cannon and the ringing within my own head.

'And so the battle begins.' My grizzled friend raised his voice above the uproar. 'See the forward lines closing upon one another?'

My eyes followed where he pointed.

'The archers will be doing their worst as well as the cannon. Just thank the Lord you're not down there among the first rows. The sky above you is black with the arrows, the smoke eats into your eyes and throat. Men, comrades, fall alongside you, in front, clutching at shafts plunged deep into their chests – their heads, faces, torn away by cannon balls.'

His eyes were haunted by shadows from his past as I gaped at him and then back at what was unfolding far ahead of me.

'Still you have to move on, clambering over bodies, slipping in the blood and broken flesh. Until the great crash and clamour as the armies meet – pikes, maces, swords – hacking, cutting, stabbing, slicing. The clang and clash of steel on armour, the thud of mace on mail, the crunch of axe on bone. Men's groans, the terrified cries of horses, the stamping of boots on earth as you all try to gain purchase, to push, push back at your foes.'

A catch in his voice, then he forced himself on.

'The smell of sweat and iron sparking, the warm splash of blood, the taste of fear. Seeing the faces and eyes of your enemies in the shadows of their helmets, knowing the horror you see there they also see on your face.'

The cannons paused, and so did he.

Then, quieter –

'Can you imagine it, boy?'

I could. I did.

From my eyrie in the church tower, I watched and saw and heard all that he said.

Though distant from the battle, I could hear the screams, the clarions, horses whinnying, the far clashing of steel. See the surging movement like eddies in floodwaters, the sunlight flashing on weapons upraised and striking down, the weaving patterns of vivid liveries and standards as the battle rippled to left and right along the forward lines – for what seemed hours.

Time passed, oh so slowly.

'And still Stanley waits.'

'And Northumberland,' said the second man. 'For what?'

'For want of a backbone?' asked a third. His words were met by grim laughter.

'Or loyalty,' the veteran of Barnet growled.

'He and the King were ever rivals in the north country,' agreed his neighbour. 'Perhaps he thinks Tudor more likely to leave him be to have his way up there.'

'Look, now!' The veteran grabbed my arm, squinting along the line of his outflung finger. 'The King's vanguard is being turned back by Oxford – there to the far right. Do you see it, boy? It looks like Tudor has put most of his men there – he has few enough now in the rear. The weight of them is pushing Norfolk's troops back.'

His scar stood out sharp in the harsh sunlight as his head swung from side to side, scouring the scene.

'There – look! The King has already committed more men to the centre. Now Northumberland must come in – to help shore up that flank.'

But though, in the time we had been there, horsemen had galloped from the King's party back to the Earl's – messenger after urgent messenger – the rearguard did not move.

More waves of soldiers surged forward from the centre into the front line and rippled out to the right edge, but still the line was being pushed back, slowly, slowly, like the tide.

The standard of the Duke of Norfolk was always at the forefront, in the fiercest of the fighting. The silver lion reared proudly above it all. But then, of a sudden, it disappeared from view as though sucked down by a riptide below the surf of battle. It resurfaced for an instant, then was swallowed up once more.

'The banner – the silver lion - where's it gone?' I asked.

'Norfolk's? Is he down? That will be a grievous loss to the King. Why doesn't Northumberland come?'

I willed the Earl to march forward to support his King. Surely he would prove his loyalty by advancing his men into the attack? Twice, thrice, more, I had seen the great white boar banner thrust into different areas of the forward line, held aloft by one of the King's bravest knights as my soldier companion said – and I knew by that sign that King Richard himself had joined his men in their deadly struggle with the enemy.

In my mind's eye I saw him, urging them to greater efforts, leading them by his example, standing four-square alongside them swinging an immense war axe or his bright sword. Once only had I witnessed him brandish that sword, on that fateful day in Stony Stratford, disarming Lord Grey. After my companion's word pictures, I imagined him now, wielding it with deadly intent, striking left, right, at Tudor's footsoldiers, or at any of his knights who ventured so far.

Was Henry Tudor showing such valour on this battlefield?

Now, again, the boar banner pressed into the thick of the fighting, this time to the right near where the Duke of Norfolk's standard had been seen no more.

And another horseman rode back to seek the Earl.

Yet still Northumberland held back.

My fellow watchers were free with their curses on the Earl's head, and more on top for Lord Stanley, whose forces remained unmoving off to the left.

I described for them again the King's withdrawal from the line, as his banner returned to the higher ground. There, they told me, among soldiers kept in reserve and horses waiting to be used, he would have a matchless view of the course of the battle, and be well placed to decide what best to do.

From our vantage point, we saw the fighting spilling further to the right.

'Perhaps Oxford senses a weakness there now Norfolk is gone,' said one man, concern rising in his voice.

'Do you think he's dead?' The image of the man who had greeted the King so warmly this morning sprang up in my mind. Though I knew not why my thoughts should turn on him more than many another man killing and dying on the field before me.

The grizzled man shot me a glance full of pity.

'Aye, lad, no doubt about it – dead or at least badly wounded, with many of his men. Otherwise, another of his knights would have caught up the standard – his men would rally to it in an instant. Now, instead, Oxford is piling his troops there as if he believes the line will break. See them stream along from the centre, and from his reserve far behind?'

My eyes scanned the heaving mass of men as more trumpets sounded. The thin reedy notes hardly rose above the buzz and grumble of all the other battle sounds merging into one.

Then, my gaze raking to the left, I spied something to the rear of Oxford's forward line.

'What banner is that?'

'Where?'

'Among that small knot of men behind the fighting. Its background green and white – upon it a red... a red dragon?'

And in that instant I was no longer on a church tower.

It was as though I was once again at my King's side.

'The red dragon? Where do you see it?' I heard him say.

I pointed without speaking.

'The Dragon of Cadwallader! Tudor's symbol. Well done, lad. Francis? We have Tudor in our sight. There to the left – behind the main force.'

'But, Dickon,' Lord Lovell's voice was weary, 'it is the fourth time today.'

'Aye, but those before were just decoys. Surely this must be him. Out there, he is not aiming to draw us into the forward line.'

'But what good is that to us? The thickest press is on the right flank. And without Northumberland we have few men to spare.'

'Then that is what he will least expect – that we should aim at him direct. See – he has few men himself. Oxford has thrown everything into the forward line and left him scarcely protected and stranded in the rear now the weight of the battle is moving to the right. One swift stroke and the day will be ours. And with it, an end to all this bloodshed.'

'A swift stroke? You would lead cavalry there? But the way runs past the Stanleys!'

'What of it? Lord Stanley has not chosen to strike yet himself, for either side, though he must see that Oxford has the advantage of us on that far flank. And he knows we still have Lord Strange. He may yet be gambling on my forgiveness for himself and his son – think it better perhaps to do nothing and watch our victory, than risk all and throw in his lot with Tudor.'

'It is too great a risk, Dickon.'

'Then what would you have me do? With Norfolk dead and without Northumberland we cannot now hope to break Oxford's line.'

'Perhaps... perhaps withdraw. Regroup in front of London. Live to fight another day. As your brother once did.'

'My brother Edward? The forces against us that day were overwhelming. Cousin Warwick at their head and half the country behind the old King. Not like this. Not a Welsh rebel with a rabble of French mercenaries. We cannot cede him the battle.'

'Yet it would buy more time. Time for more men to rally to your standard. The men of York, for instance.

Your agents say Northumberland delayed mustering them so they have not yet arrived. In how many other towns has that happened?'

'Perhaps too few to chance it, Francis. No, we have our opportunity now to deal Tudor a fatal blow – if we do not debate too long. But, Francis, you –' a heartbeat's silence, then, softly – 'you need not ride with me.'

'You wrong me, Richard, if you think I will desert you now.'

'Nay, old friend, I know you would never do that, whatever the odds.' Then, his voice firm once again, 'To horse, then. And bring me those men who will follow me to finish this battle now.'

King Richard stood staring out across the smoke and screams and stench of the battlefield as Lord Lovell strode off. Alone once more, motionless, his slight figure cased in plates of steel and surcoat of murrey and blue, muddied and bloodied, fleurs-de-lys, sunbursts, lions – once golden, royal symbols – hardly recognizable beneath the grime. A gauntleted hand resting on his sword hilt. A moment of stillness against the deadly backdrop of the battle.

Then, shattering the seeming calm, a squire led up a light grey horse in full shining armour – Windfollower, dancing skittishly upon his hooves at the bustle and noise pressing in again all around. But King Richard stepped up to him, and at a word and a gentle stroke of his nose beneath the faceplate he quietened, remaining like a statue as the King, iron-clad himself, was boosted into the saddle.

Soon the company of household knights was gathered, a sea of glittering armour, bristling lances, dark red and blue livery, snorting stallions sporting toughened steel as fine as that of their masters.

At their head rode Lord Lovell. To one side was the King's standard bearer, his armour and surcoat already befouled with dirt and blood, like his master's, his strong fist grasping the staff of the great white boar banner. To the other were the shadowed faces of Master Kendall and Master Ratcliffe. Then they flipped their visors closed.

Another squire ran up to the King, a circlet of gold encrusted with jewels in his hands. The King reached down for it, then thrust it skywards. The gems sparkled in the brilliant sunlight.

'Gentlemen, this is what Henry Tudor seeks today. The crown of England. But he shall not have it. Not while I live and have breath within me. Are you with me?'

As one, the knights roared, 'Aye! For Richard!' and clashed their lances against their shields.

The King jammed the circlet down upon his helmet, then snapped shut his visor and wheeled Windfollower about. The other horses bunched up behind him in their eagerness to be off as he raised his own lance, then pointed it forward.

'Á York!' he cried.

'For Richard and England!'

Their horses began to pace down the slope, slowly at first, then gathering speed, faster, faster, until they reached full gallop. The sound of their hooves was as loud as cannonfire as they charged across the battlefield. The silver of the armour and colours of the livery blurred to the sight with the speed that swept them past the battle line and ate up the ground towards Tudor. Above it all, the white boar standard flew as I had seen it long ago upon the highest tower at Middleham.

On and on they thundered, King Richard and Windfollower at the very front, until with a nightmare crash the charge broke like a storm-wave on the wall of Tudor's defenders. Those men had barely time to cluster round him in defence before the impact. Surprise was still mingled with growing fear on the faces of those who died first.

The King and his companions flung away the shattered butts of their lances and set about them with mace or battle axe. Unmounted men had little chance against them and they soon cut a swathe through the ring of defenders around the red dragon banner.

Screams of men and horses rent the air, with the ringing of metal on metal, and the sickening crunch of blade on bone. Blood churned the earth to mud under foot and hoof, but sure of foot and hoof, the King and his men were gaining ground.

A lone man in the richest armour could be seen by the dragon standard, thrust now deep into the ground, defended by a giant of a knight with battle axe seeming as tall as he. The goal of the charge was within their grasp. The King spurred Windfollower forward towards the gigantic knight, his own great axe slick with blood.

Then came the shout that all had dreaded.

'Stanley rides!'

The host of horsemen were careering down from their watching, waiting place, their stag's head banner whipping above them in the wind raised by their speed. The brightness of their armour still shone in the August sun, the scarlet of their surcoats as yet undefiled by the filth of battle. Their trumpet call rang in the shimmering air.

'They come to join us at last. Now they see we nearly have Tudor.' The King's voice was hoarse.

'Dickon, no! You know they come to destroy you. We must withdraw.'

'Never! I live or die this day rightful King of England!'

And the charge slammed into the chaos of the fighting.

I saw it though I was not there. I felt the shock of the heavy horses smashing into, overwhelming the King's forces, though I was not there. I heard the crash and the cries carried to me on the battle wind.

I saw the white boar banner go down. It did not rise again.

And a single word resounded in my head.

'Treason!'

21

Milestones

Another milestone. And another. And another.

It was all I could do to stop myself falling asleep – and then falling to the ground.

Another milestone. Another mile closer to London.

Closer to sleep.

I could barely remember the last time I'd slept. Well and long, at least, not in fitful starts. Afraid to close my eyes.

The night before the battle, perhaps.

Before the waking nightmare began.

In truth I had hardly known whether I was sleeping or awake as I stumbled down from the church tower. As calls dropped from above, warning me to take care. As, in the half-light below, a kindly woman handed me my pack and the leash she had tied to Murrey's collar.

Her royal collar.

Should I take it off and hide it?

Murrey had whimpered, her liquid eyes gazing up beseeching, as my hesitant fingers reached out – then grasped the collar to pull her with me. The leather was rough, the gilt fleur-de-lys upon it cool to my touch.

I had to get out of there, had to get on my way. I had a job to do.

Astride Bess, I had ridden away from the village, back the way I had come. Seeking the old road.

Watling Street.

To the south, King Richard had said.

The King —

To the west hung a heat haze – and clouds of crows and rooks, circling.

Everywhere men were hurrying. Mostly north or east, some south as well.

Some were on horseback, most on foot, all rushing as fast as they could – if they could rush – often looking back over their shoulders. All were filthy, sweaty, bloodied – their own or others' blood? Torn clothes, ripped mail, some struggling out of armour even as they ran, tossing it aside.

Once, in the neighbouring field, riders hunted down a man, thrust their lances into him as he lay writhing on the ground. Dismounted to search his body. One cheered as he stripped him of his boots and held them up for his fellows to see.

I turned away, urging Bess on. But I took my sallet from my bundle and threw it down under a hedge.

More stragglers coming towards me, one limping, another clutching a bleeding shoulder, others with dazed eyes.

In those eyes I saw my own.

Then, between them —

'Make way, make way!'

I knew that voice.

A rider on a light grey horse. Armour encasing both – dirt and gore encrusted, but burnished. Murrey and blue livery.

My heart leapt.

The horse was Storm.

Cantering towards me along the lane. Scattering the trudging, defeated soldiers.

I raised my hand and called, 'Your Grace!'

The stallion skittered to a halt.

But —

The knight was too tall.

He snapped up his visor.

'Matthew?'

Lord Lovell's face. Smudged with dirt, dark dried blood, an ooze of fresh red at his temple. He stared down at me.

'Matthew – for the love of God, flee!'

'I thought you were King Richard.'

I could not hide the misery in my voice.

'He's dead, Matthew. Hacked down by the traitor's men in front of me.'

I had known it – of course I had – but to hear the words...

'Where is he, my lord?'

'Back on the battlefield, where he fell. The fighting moved on, till our men could fight no more. And then we broke...'

'But Storm —'

'I found him loose on the field and took him to save my skin.' He grimaced. 'You wonder at it perhaps – loyal Lovell fleeing? But we are all branded traitors by this new "king" – they say he proclaimed himself such as he set foot on Welsh soil. They are butchering all they catch – no quarter given. Not to flee would be self-slaughter. Would that Richard had left the field when he had the chance.'

He told me of those last moments in few words: the charge, the King killing Tudor's giant standard bearer with his own hands, the carnage as Stanley's cavalry ploughed into their rear... the names of men who died. The Duke of Norfolk, Masters Ratcliffe, Brackenbury... Kendall.

'What will happen to him?'

'The King? His body will be despoiled – stripped of all he has, like any common soldier. Then, when Tudor has found him – if they can still recognize him – he will be taken... I know not where. Leicester, London? To be put on display so all know he is dead.'

My stomach turned over. Thank the Saviour I had eaten nothing since early morning.

'But Matthew, did not the King give you a message to take? Why are you here?'

'I could not... go – without knowing.'

'You must take it – and swiftly. It is of utmost importance – especially after... You must not fail Richard, even now. Wait —'

As though uncertain, he paused. Glanced – left, right – over his shoulders.

Few straggling soldiers were to be seen now – and no pursuers. For the moment.

With difficulty, he dismounted and began to unbuckle his armour. It was slow work and he murmured his thanks as I helped. From time to time he winced as a plate brushed against his wounds.

As we worked, he explained.

'You shall take Storm – no, don't protest. Your journey is more urgent than mine. For me, young Lincoln, Richard's nephew, is the new king, not this traitor. I will find him when the time is right. He will need followers. Rally to his cause yourself, Matthew, one day, if you can. But meanwhile, you can carry your message more quickly aboard Storm. See, we can remove his finery too. Throw it into the ditch for some scavenger to find. Switch his saddle and bridle when you have a chance, or muddy these when you reach water. He will always be a fine horse, but it may help you escape notice.'

He broke off, looking around.

'As for me, I have only what I now stand up in. If you will give me your pony and bundle, it may be that I can make my way across country as a simple pedlar.'

'There is food, too, in the pack.'

'Then we will share that if you are willing – we will both need it on our journeys.'

He reached down to pick up his sword and scabbard. Then, hesitating, he kissed it on the hilt before handing it to me.

'Take my sword too. It may be of use to you – and it is a thing that no pedlar would have. Keep it safe, if you can – and return it to me if ever we meet again. Richard himself gave it to me when I was made viscount.'

He watched as I clumsily strapped it on, his mouth curling in a humourless smile at the way it hung loose about my waist. Then he spied something else.

'Is that Richard's boar upon your chest?'

'Aye, my lord. And I will always be proud to wear it.'

'Your loyalty does you credit, boy, but if you value your life, hide it.'

'I'm not afraid —'

'Maybe not, but your task is more important than your pride. Here...'

He deftly unpinned the badge, turned back the collar of my doublet and refastened it within so it was nestled against my undershirt.

'Now, be off with you.'

He boosted me into Storm's saddle and raised his hand to clap him on the hindquarters.

'I thank you for what you are to do. And do not worry, Matthew – I will take care of your pony. You look after yourself – and do your duty to Richard.'

One slap and Storm was cantering again along the lane, Murrey bounding after.

Another milestone. Then another.

My eyes desperate to close, desperate to sleep.

There had been a village. A well.

I had raised the bucket, drunk gratefully.

While Storm bent his head to the water, I mixed mud pies in the soil like a child and smeared them on his fine saddle and bridle. Plastered them over patches of congealed blood on his coat. Took out my knife, scored lines on the leather, rubbed in more filth.

Murrey growled.

Raucous laughter, shouts and catcalls.

Many hooves. Marching feet.

Round a corner, a procession of soldiers. To the front, banners that had flown among Tudor's forces on the battlefield.

Too late to melt away without drawing their notice. No villagers were about, all doors and windows shuttered against the uncertain times.

I pulled Storm into the shadow of a nearby building, threw the sword belt down and kicked dust upon it. I prayed we would not be seen and my attempts at disguise tested.

But these soldiers had no interest in a boy cowering in a corner. Laughs resounded around the empty street, coarse oaths, ribald jests thrown from man to man. They were having fun, perhaps hoped for more.

Their watchful captain, riding at their head, called to remind them.

'No more, lads, no more. You heard what His Grace the new king said.'

At his words, I had to check myself – must not step forward to catch the rest.

But they too were pausing for water on this warm day.

As they clustered around the well, both horsemen and footsoldiers, the leader finished his warning.

'Don't touch his face, lads. They must be able to recognize him when we get to Leicester.'

There among them, as they jostled each other for water, was the body of a man slung over a horse.

Naked, covered only in dirt and dried blood. Hands and feet hanging down, tied with rope under the horse's belly.

But I knew who it was.

I buried my face in Storm's neck to stifle my cry of horror.

Another milestone flashes by.
Can I reach the next?
Thirty-seven more to go.

Can I hold on? Can I make it?

I followed them. Until they came to Leicester. Turned away from my own road, to follow his.

All the long way back to the town that I – we – had left yesterday.

I followed him, leading Storm, as the sorry procession filed over the old stone bridge and through the western gate.

News had reached the town before us. Messengers. Victorious soldiers.

'Tudor has won!'

'King Richard is dead.'

And crowds flocked to see him as they had the day before. As he had ridden, confidently, to battle, his crown, his armour aflame in the morning sun.

Silent crowds. They stood lining the roads and watched.

Some turned away in sadness and disgust. Others thronged to support the victor.

Mingling amongst them, soldiers. Men at arms.

Job done, horrors faced, comrades killed, wounded.

Death escaped.

Wine bottles clutched.

And so the jeers began.

As I trudged, yards behind, I heard them.

The French I knew, though it was not the French of courtly romances or love songs.

The Welsh, Breton, I could guess.

Sometimes English – it hit me like a blow to hear what was said.

Local voices too, now, egged along by the soldiers. After all, what was a King but a man? And one King is much like another to any common person.

Most held back, kept a respectful distance as he passed. But one or two stepped forward – and before the captain's men could push them away, spat at his body.

'That's for those poor little princes,' one man yelled.

The captain's man just laughed as he shoved him back into the crowd with his pikestaff.

My anger rose. But I could do nothing. Not now, not yet.

Then, as I watched, trailing all those yards behind, a single soldier stepped into the road, urged on by those behind him.

Unsullied scarlet surcoat over mail. Open helmet burnished bright.

Unsheathed dagger in upraised hand. Poised to strike. The August sun glinting along its length.

'This is for all those beatings you —'

A moment's hesitation – by both him and me.

A familiar voice and smirk. Then surprise.

'Look, he's a crookback!'

And in the instant before he drove his shining blade into the lifeless body, I knew him.

Hugh Soulsby.

A moment later it was done, to the jeers of the crowd.

A fresh wound. But no spurt of blood now.

Hugh swung away, triumphant, to the acclaim of his companions, his knife held high.

I recognized a flash of blond hair, a white brow, among them, before I flung myself forwards, my hand grasping at the sword hilt hidden under my cloak.

But before I had gone three paces, kind hands pulled me back.

'Don't get yourself killed, lad,' said one man.

'There may be another chance to honour him,' said another.

Another milestone.

Twenty more to go.

Sweet Jesus, let my task be worth this.

They had carried him into a church – a church! – and strung him up by his wrists to put him on display. And encouraged local people to come and gawp at him as he hung among the tombs of Tudor's Lancastrian ancestors. And kept guard in case any thought to cut him down and spirit him away.

I would have done it if I could. Or even just covered his naked body.

But they kept guard outside too. And I could not leave Storm and Murrey alone.

So I hid in alleys and watched and waited. For I knew not what.

For two days and two nights.

For two long days and two long nights he hung there on display.

Another milestone. And another.

So close now.

On the third day, in the grey of the evening, the good friars had come to ask for his corpse.

They cut him down and rolled his battered body in a shroud. No coffin for this King. And they carried him away to his final resting place.

I followed them to their priory.

I had coins for them, and they let me, a boy only, no threat, enter their church.

I held the stoup as they sprinkled holy water.

My voice breaking, I sang his favourite *lauda* as they lowered him into his swift-cut grave. Too short it proved to be. His head twisted awkwardly, the cloth falling away from his bloodied face, his dark shadowed eyes.

They had had little time to prepare, they said. The new King had been impatient. Take him, dispose of him, let him be seen by living eyes no more, be no rallying point for rebels.

They glanced over their shoulders in worry that soldiers would come.

We prayed together, before the earth was thrown in, the floor tiles relaid.

No monument here for this King.

Let the people forget him.

Storm's hooves clattered across the London cobbles. We reached Newgate minutes before sundown, minutes before the gate would be locked for the night.

News of the battle had already come, the gatekeeper said. His voice was heavy with dread. But what would the council do when Tudor himself came? He shook his head.

Everywhere men's, women's faces were full of fear. People wondering what the future held.

But I didn't care. Not now. I only knew I had a message to deliver – at last.

When King Richard handed it to me, I had thought it just a ruse to keep me from the battle. But Lord Lovell's words had made me think again.

Yet still I had delayed...

Strong horse though he was, Storm had given everything to get us here so swiftly. As we turned into Master Ashley's courtyard, he was trembling beneath me, his flanks heaving and lathered.

I slithered down from his back, my knees almost buckling after my long ride, and stood waiting for a groom to come. To take him and rub him down, feed and water him.

But no one came. The courtyard was deserted. No torches blazing by the doorway.

Murrey sniffed around, her tail aquiver.

I called.

Still no one.

I led Storm to the stables.

No one there.

Only rustlings, stamping of hooves, a gentle whicker, another in answer. The horses shifting uneasily in the darkness.

I tied Storm in a stall and found him oats and water. Then, dread rising like searing bile in my throat, I made my way to the main entrance.

I did not need to knock.

The heavy oak door was ajar, and its iron lock had been smashed to pieces.

22

Old Friends

I pushed the door open.

All was darkness. Silence.

I stepped across the threshold and rummaged in my pouch for my tinderbox.

But I didn't strike it. Danger might be waiting and I must not give myself away.

Murrey whined. I quieted her with a finger on her nose.

I listened again.

Still nothing.

Reaching forward with my hands so as not to stumble, I made my way across the dark entrance hall. Still no chink of light anywhere.

Where to go first? Where was my master? I had come all this way to give him my message, only to find no one at home. No servants even.

But why was no one here?

I stepped with care, my hands still before me, towards Master Ashley's study door at the far end. Once there might I find a clue? If there was still no sight or sound of anyone, I would risk striking a light to see by.

The scent of newly snuffed candle drifted into my nostrils.

How? If no one was there?

One hand moved to my sword hilt.

The fingers of the other touched the smooth wood of the door and nudged it softly open. The smell of smoke was stronger here.

A dog whimpered. I moved to quieten Murrey, but...

The noise had come from inside the pitch-dark room. A panicked voice shushed it. A light, female voice.

Murrey yapped once in reply before I could stop her.

'Murrey?' whispered the voice.

A sharp crack as tinder was struck, and the sudden flare of a candle lit up two pale faces.

'Alys! Elen!' My own voice emerged as a strangled squeak.

'Matthew!'

Alys thrust the candle into Elen's hand and threw herself across the room to fling her arms around me.

'What are you doing here? I mean, why were you *not* here? We heard the horse, the calls. We were afraid – we doused the lights. Was it you?'

Her whispered questions tumbled out as we held each other. Then she broke away and stepped back hurriedly. In the glow of the other candles that Elen was now kindling, her face was flushed and confused.

I looked away so she could compose herself. At my heel Murrey was touching noses with her sister, Shadow, who was more like a ghost in the dim light. I fondled both hounds' ears.

'How did you know it was Murrey?'

'She sounds just like Shadow, and I knew she hadn't barked.'

Alys sounded more her old self now, though as I turned back, it was clear how much she'd changed since last we'd met. Taller, less boyish, she had grown into a young woman while I had been away. Had I altered as much in her eyes?

Questions for another time, perhaps. For now —

'What's happened here? Where's Master Ashley? All the household?'

A shadow crossed Alys's face despite the candle light. She stepped to one side and waved her hand.

Behind her, on the floor, swathed in a blanket and head propped on a cushion, lay my London master. His face was deathly white and his breathing laboured. Fresh blood oozed from a jagged gash on his temple and was matted in his sandy hair.

Elen was on her knees beside him now, dabbing at the wound with a cloth.

'How... ? Who...?'

More questions racing through my brain, I knelt down too and took his hand. It was cold, but the pulse was regular.

'He was like this when we came,' murmured Elen. 'We couldn't move him so we tried to make him comfortable here. His wife had been beaten too, but not so badly. I've settled her in her chamber with a sleeping draught.'

'Beaten? Mistress Ashley? But —'

'Matt, where have you been?' interrupted Alys, abandoning any attempt at keeping quiet. 'We came here to look for you as soon as we heard about –' she swallowed, 'about the battle. Then we found – this! Where were you?'

'I was there,' I said, barely audible.

'What?'

'I was with the King. And then —' My voice failed me.

Alys's eyes grew larger in the flickering light.

'Is it true? That he's – dead?'

I couldn't speak, just nodded.

Elen turned her face away.

Alys fiercely dashed the tears from her cheeks.

'Then Tudor —'

Anger and sadness jostled for supremacy in her face.

'Then Henry Tudor will be King. Elizabeth will have to marry him, and...'

'He's on his way here now. Tudor. I saw him set off from Leicester before I left. I stayed to see the King—'

'What?'

'Buried.'

I could not tell them of all that I had seen.

'Tudor was marching at the head of his army. They were cheering, many still drunk, driving wagons of spoil stolen from the King. It was easy for me to overtake them.'

The small roads, across country, before – before Watling Street and the milestones.

'But I came here with a message for Master Ashley. From King Richard.'

'A message? What does it say?'

'I have no idea,' I snapped, indignant. 'It's sealed, and for him alone.'

'Well, he's in no state to see it now.'

'He has woken once or twice,' said Elen.

'But he's scarcely been lucid, has he?' Alys retorted. 'The message may be important. We should open it.'

I was shocked. I had forgotten my first suspicion that the message was just about me.

'But it's the King's business. Between him and Master Ashley alone.'

'Matthew, if the King is —' She gulped, as though her tears were choking her, and brushed her hand again across her cheek. 'If that is so, perhaps it's important. Perhaps it would explain this.'

She spread her hands wide. My glance followed hers around the room. In the trembling candlelight, I saw that not only was my master battered and on the floor, but so were all the contents of his study. Chairs were upturned, tables on their sides, papers, quills, books scattered everywhere.

'The whole house is like this. Mistress Ashley, when we could get any sense from her, said that armed men came, broke down the door and attacked her husband. While some shouted questions at him and the steward, others ransacked every room. The servants all fled or were taken away, along with the steward. She said she thinks they believed Master Ashley was dead.'

'Who were they? What did they want?'

'I don't know,' she cried in exasperation. 'Except that I think they must have been Tudor's agents. Perhaps they got word of the battle even before we did. But maybe the message will tell us what it's all about.'

I reached in my pouch for the small square of folded parchment that the King had handed me – oh, so long ago now. He had been smiling as he gave it.

As I turned it in my hands, deep within the memory, Murrey growled. A scraping as of feet on flagstones came from the hallway behind me, then a loud halloo.

Elen scrambled up and lunged towards the candles, while Alys grabbed for Shadow's collar, terror scrawled across her face.

I spun round, my hand clapping to the sword hilt at my hip, my fear crushing at my chest.

Whoever was there was making no attempt at stealth. Another holler, and the glow of a blazing brand approaching across the hall.

Elen stopped quenching the candles – it was too late for that. Out of the corner of my eye I could see the remaining lights glittering on a drawn knife in Alys's free hand.

Still, silent, we waited.

The footsteps, two sets, moved closer.

Another call, softer now.

Then Murrey let out a muted whine of welcome and paced forward, and Shadow, still in Alys's whitening grip, sat down and licked her paw, unconcerned.

And into the doorway, lit now by the flame of the torch he held, stepped —

'Roger!'

His name tripped from my mouth in a laugh of relief. But Alys was less forgiving.

'Roger! You idiot! You scared us half to death. What do you think you're doing?'

Roger's face fell at her assault.

'I've come to help. If I can.'

His gaze scouted around the room, coming to rest on the prone form of Master Ashley.

'What's happened? Simon said the house was in uproar, but…'

He ground to a halt.

'Simon? Where…?'

As I asked, the head of my fellow apprentice peered around the door jamb. Seeing me, his eyes lit up.

'Matt? You've come back. Where's Mistress Ashley? She sent me for aid when those men broke in, but there was none there. Only —'

He caught sight of Master Ashley and the colour bled from his face.

'What…?'

Alys took charge.

'I don't know who you are, but if you are of Mistress Ashley's household, can you tell us who did this? And why?'

But Simon only shook his head, his mouth working as though he might be sick. Elen went to him, drawing him in to the room and turning up a stool for him to sit on. She knelt next to him, stroking his arm as his head hung down towards his knees.

'Simon is an apprentice here,' put in Roger before I could say anything. 'He came to Baynard's Castle for help because Master Ashley is a friend of the King, but of course most of the men at arms are with the King's army, or…' He stumbled to a halt, his face crimson. 'I mean, they were with the King. King Richard, of course.'

Alys's lips tightened.

'He's dead, Roger. King Richard is dead.'

He nodded, his eyes lowered.

'I know. That's what they're saying. When the news came to my parents, I looked for you at the castle. But the servants said you were not to be found. No one could be spared to search for you because the rest of the men at arms had gone to join the defence. Then Simon turned up.'

'You were at Baynard's Castle?' I asked Alys.

'Of course. Where did you think I'd be?'

'But —' I thought back. 'I thought you were at Sheriff Hutton with Princess Elizabeth.'

She shivered, shaking her head.

'No. I was, but I travelled down two or three weeks ago. To stay in the King's mother's household to prepare for my wedding. That's why Roger's here too. He came so he could attend me and visit his family while he was in London.'

'Your wedding! But I thought —'

'You thought what?'

'That King Richard… That the old Queen…'

Her face twisted.

'Dame Grey saw me herself when I arrived. She said that I must prepare myself to be married. That King Richard had asked her to reconsider, but … but that he needed the loyalty of all his subjects. That after the coming battle Lord Soulsby must be rewarded. And that Lord Soulsby…'

She bit her lip, then rushed on,

'That Lord Soulsby would be fighting with Lord Stanley for the King. But then we heard that Lord Stanley and his brother… that they…'

Of a sudden, she rounded on Roger.

'What defence?'

Roger rocked backwards on his heels, startled.

'Defence?'

'You said the men at arms – those who hadn't gone with the King – weren't at Baynard's Castle because they'd gone to join the defence.'

'Oh, that. Yes, word came that men of fighting age were mustering. In case... in case the city council decides to refuse Tudor entry to the city. Like they did with old Queen Margaret. All the men, well most of them, had gone to join the militia.'

My mind went back almost two years to when I had tried to do just that. When the city had held firm for King Richard at the time of the great rebellion.

Tears shone in Alys's eyes.

'They won't refuse him entry. How can they? What would be the point? Matt says Tudor's marching here at the head of his army. He won his victory. King Richard... Well, Lord Lincoln would be his heir and he's far away in the north. There are hardly any knights with him. Even if he... even if he chose to march against Tudor... even if London...'

She shook her head again.

'They cannot change what's happened, what God has willed. Whysoever he has willed it... But what use did you think you could be?'

'I...' Roger was crestfallen. 'I don't know. But a serving woman said that you'd had a letter delivered by one of Master Ashley's servants. She said you'd been worrying about it for days.'

'My letter?' I asked Alys. 'Saying I was going to the King?'

'Of course. I couldn't believe you'd be so daft as to do that.'

'The serving woman said that when news came of the battle, you and Elen disappeared,' Roger went on. 'So, when Simon arrived, asking for help... Well, I thought you might have come here. I thought I should perhaps come – to check that you were safe and find out what help I can offer.'

'Well, I, for one, am pleased to see you,' I said before Alys could respond. 'And of course you will be of help.'

He threw me a grateful glance – although in truth I had said it as much to reassure me as him.

'I don't know how,' Alys shot back. 'Unless he can read that message without opening it.'

'Message?' asked Roger.

'From the King to Master Ashley. Matthew brought it. From the battlefield.'

'What does it say?'

'We don't know. And Matt doesn't want to open it.'

'But it may be important.'

Both of them were staring at me. Alys's eyebrow arched.

'That's what I said.'

The creamy parchment, the thick blob of scarlet wax upon it, was still clutched in my hand.

Alys's quick eyes were watching as my fingers turned it over and over.

'It doesn't bear his signet.'

'No,' I said slowly. 'Perhaps it was to be secret. He said I could travel more easily than one of his men if...'

I hesitated.

Her face was set firm.

'That decides it, then. A secret message, sent when he was thinking – thinking that he might lose the battle. And he did. And now Master Ashley...'

She took the message from my hand, glancing at my face. When I didn't move or speak, she deftly broke the seal and unfolded the parchment.

'It's in code.'

Disappointment tinged her voice.

'Then it isn't just instructions to keep me from the battle.' I tried to smile.

Alys skewered me with a glare.

'What?'

'Nothing. It's just...' It was my turn to bite my lip.

Roger was squinting over her shoulder at the scrap of parchment.

'If it's in code, surely you can break it? You made it seem so easy when we were at Middleham.'

'That was different, Roger. We had a book to help us.'

'As the King wrote it, he was consulting a book,' I said. 'I think it was the cipher book Ed found at Middleham.'

'The same book? There were code tables written in it. Perhaps he used one of them. It's in proper letters.'

'It didn't take him long to write.'

'Then maybe it's a substitution code like ours was.'

Roger and I placed Master Ashley's desk back upon its feet while Alys fetched a candle. By its light the three of us pored over the message.

It was just four lines long.

Clyayvbdkl cypluk, Hsz hsslz nvlk nhha zsljoa, olypuuly
tl ola wshu. Ullt kl qvunluz hhu tpqu gbz vw Tljolslu.
Hsz ql uvkpn olia vu, b rbua clyayvbdlu Thaaold gvukly
adpqmls.

    Kpjrvu

'Do you think that's a signature, there at the bottom?'

'He'd usually sign letters Ricardus Rex – King Richard in Latin – but this is just one word.'

'Could it be "Richard"?'

'The two Rs would be a useful clue... but no, it's six letters, not seven.'

'So not "Gloucester" either then.' I remembered the single word he had signed on the paper on the day of my beating,

'He was King, Matthew, not just Duke any longer. I wonder if it could be "England" in Latin – "Anglia"... No – the first and last letters are different. Perhaps it isn't a signature after all...'

Tiredness was stealing back over me now after my ride, but a name wormed its way back into my brain.

'How about "Dickon"?'

'Maybe. I remember the Queen and Lord Lovell calling him that...'

Alys fished some parchment, a pen and a pot of ink up from the floor and scribbled letters on it.

'You know, it might be. If the K is a D, and the P an I, and it is a simple substitution code... then, counting back... Matt, I think you're right. D – I – C – K – O – N. There. But how strange that it is so straightforward. If I've broken it so quickly, how long would it take one of Tudor's spies if they'd got hold of it?'

As she traced out the rest of the cipher and then started to decode the message, dread clutched at me. If it were so easy, perhaps it was just a note to keep me safe away from the battlefield. Had all my horror at betraying King Richard's instructions and the terror of my ride from Leicester been in vain?

'But it's nonsense.' Alys broke through my thoughts.

'What?'

'It means nothing. Unless it's a code within a code.'

I peered at what she'd written. Two words only. '*Vertrouwde vriend.*'

'It's not nonsense,' I said. 'It's Flemish.'

'Really?' said Roger, craning his neck to see.

'I picked up some in Bruges. Master Ashley is fluent in it. That means "Trusted friend".'

'And the King was exiled there when he was young,' recalled Alys. 'Perhaps he knows – knew it as well.'

'And how many of Tudor's spies would? Most Flemish merchants switch to French or English when abroad – they don't expect anyone to learn their language.'

Excited now, Alys worked on, deciphering the rest of the message and soon laid before me the words –

Vertrouwde vriend, Als alles goed gaat slecht, herinner me het plan. Neem de jongens aan mijn zus

op Mechelen. Als je nodig hebt on, u kunt vertrouwen Matthew zonder twijfel.
Dickon

With the little Flemish I knew, it was a struggle to translate it, but eventually, with some guesswork, I had it.

Trusted friend, If all goes wrong, remember the plan. Take the boys to my sister at Mechelen. If you need to, you can trust Matthew without question.
Dickon.

'The boys?' asked Roger.

'His nephews,' I said. The pale faces from my dream swam before my eyes. 'The princes that were.'

'Edward and little Richard? Then they're —'

'Alive.'

Tap, tap, tap.

'Of course they are,' snapped Alys. 'Did you ever doubt it?'

'But the rumours. During the rebellion.'

'About King Richard? Matt, surely you can't have believed them!'

'No, of course not,' I protested. 'But —'

'But what?' She stared at me, exasperated. 'Matt, those rumours were put about by Henry Tudor and his mother – to turn unthinking people against the King.'

I ransacked my memory. Where had I first heard them? Of course – from Hugh. And he from his uncle. And his uncle had fought for... Lord Stanley.

What a fool I'd been to even think twice about them.

To my relief, Alys had moved on.

'But where are they? Still in England?'

A groan from behind us. We turned.

While we had been talking and working on the code, Elen and Simon had been sitting next to Master Ashley, and it struck me now that for some minutes Elen had been making small soothing noises. The patient's eyes were open and he was struggling to sit up. Elen propped another cushion behind his shoulders.

'Bring me the message,' he croaked out.

My cheeks were warm with guilt as Alys took him the unfolded parchment, its seal broken in two.

He squinted at it, then waved it away.

'Not that – the other. Matthew?'

He coughed and pain racked him. Elen held the cloth against his head until the spasm ended, then dribbled water from a flask into his mouth.

'What other?' asked Alys.

'Did they find it?'

She gestured about the room. 'How can we tell?'

'Not here. Matthew? I didn't tell them.'

My master was seized by a fit of coughing again, but this time was able to reach for the flask himself.

Alys glanced at me, her eyebrows raised.

I stepped forward.

'I can find it, sir, if you can tell me where.'

Master Ashley nodded with effort.

'He said I could trust you, boy. That day he first brought you here. And now again. Was he right?'

'Aye, sir.'

'Richard wasn't always a good judge of men. But sometimes I think he saw in them something of himself. Something he could place his trust in. I have failed him in this, but will you serve him one more time, Matthew?'

'Of course, sir. If I can.'

'Then go to the print house. The upper case. The box of letter Rs. Behind there. If they didn't find it...'

They hadn't. In minutes I was back bearing a morsel of parchment, scarce bigger than the plain seal it carried. But I also brought ill tidings.

'Master, the printing press.'

'What of it?'

'They've wrecked it. Torn it apart.'

His eyes closed an instant, as though immensely weary. Then they blinked open again.

'No matter, boy. A press may be mended – or bought anew in Flanders. People, however... The message, Matthew. Open it.'

It contained one word, in King Richard's own hand.

'Gipping.'

'So,' said Master Ashley, 'You must ride into Suffolk.'

23

'Ever My Uncle's Man'

They allowed me two hours to snatch some sleep while they prepared for the journey. That was all we could spare – more perhaps than we should.

Master Ashley, regaining some of his strength with a mouthful or two of wine that Simon brought for him, had spent it on worrying that Tudor's men would return. Or that Master Lyndsey would break down under questioning and talk of people and places connected with his business.

'It seems Tudor has spies everywhere, maybe the Stanleys too. Perhaps more even than Richard suspected, for all the many agents he had himself. Those agents may all be targeted. That may help us if it spreads their men too thinly. Though they may of course be more concerned with finding out how the city will receive Tudor.'

Alys shot a look at Roger and me, a faint shake of the head, a warning in her eyes.

Master Ashley took another sip of wine from the cup Simon held to his lips, before continuing.

'But if they still suspect me, they may keep watch on all my contacts too in case they will lead them to the boys.'

'Why would they be so desperate to find them?' Roger asked.

'Tudor cannot afford to let the boys live. They say he will overturn the law on young Elizabeth's illegitimacy so that he can marry her and make her his queen.'

'If he does that, then surely Edward would be the real King,' said Alys. 'Both he and Prince Richard have a better claim to the crown.'

'Aye,' agreed Master Ashley. 'And he will not stand for that. From all I've heard, he intends to rule, not place young Edward back on the throne. He will not offer the boy his oath of lifelong loyalty, for all his declarations against his bastardy. Tudor is an ambitious man – he will not put aside his desire to be king. If he finds them, he will kill them.'

His words stunned us all into silence. Alys, of course, was the first to speak again.

'If the boys are in such danger, why did King Richard not send them out of the country before?'

'I imagine he remembered his own time of exile, and perhaps not fondly, though it was then that we met, in his moments of respite with his brother in Bruges. And with the shifting politics on the continent, the boys might fall into the hands of his enemies, like Tudor himself – one moment in friendly Brittany, the next in France.'

He paused a moment, thoughts scudding across his weary eyes like clouds in a storm-filled sky.

'I think perhaps he hoped they could live anonymous lives out in the country until they were old enough to move to loyal households as squires like any other noble lad – when the rumours and threat of rebellion had withered and died away. Like old Henry Bolingbroke did with the Mortimer heirs many years ago. And it was working. After Buckingham, what talk had there been of them? And once Tudor was gone...'

He shook his head, his face pale and drawn, showing his age for the first time since I'd known him.

'Now no more talking. Sleep, boys, while the girls make things ready for you. You have a long dangerous ride ahead of you.'

Another one, I thought morosely as I settled myself in a borrowed blanket.

To my surprise, when Elen shook me awake, I found not only Roger, as agreed before I slept, but also Alys kitted out ready for the journey.

'You're not leaving me here,' she said when I tried to object. 'Ralph Soulsby will be coming to claim me in marriage. Nothing will make me forget that he and his father rode with the Stanleys. Princess Elizabeth may have to resign herself to marrying Tudor, but no duty to Dame Grey could ever make me wed a traitor.'

'We spoke of it while you slept,' said Elen. 'Master Ashley agrees it will be for the best.'

'I offered to give up my place to her,' said Roger, smiling more broadly than he had a right to do at that time of night. 'But your good master said I might be useful to you both on the road. Though for the life of me, I cannot think how.'

'Safety in numbers, perhaps,' muttered Alys darkly. 'What other use you may have escapes me too.'

He bowed his agreement.

Unsure though I was that the plan was a good one, I knew there was no point in arguing with Alys if she had made up her mind. And in truth, I would be grateful for her company as well as Roger's. Perhaps it would be almost like those days long ago in Middleham when the three of us had often ridden out together on the moors as the Order of the White Boar. Although one other member of the Order would always now be missing...

Shaking away the memory, I turned to Elen.

'What about you? What will you do?'

'Oh, I'll stay here and help Master Ashley and his wife. I'd only slow you down if I came too – I'm not so good a horsewoman.'

'You will be careful? It may be dangerous here. With Tudor on his way...'

She placed a hand on my arm to quiet me.

'Don't worry, Matthew – of course I will be careful. And Simon will be here with us. He tells me he has been training with you all summer in case of emergency.'

To my surprise, Simon blushed to the roots of his hair at her words and hurried off into the hallway, murmuring something about fetching our bundles.

It was well after midnight when the three of us set out. Sometime while I slept, Roger and Simon had helped

Master Ashley at last to his chamber, but Mistress Ashley had emerged from hers – to find out what was happening, then to make sure we had all we needed for the journey.

Her eye was blackened and her cheeks cut and bruised where she had been struck during the attack. She embraced me as I stood dumb in shock at her appearance, then leant on both Simon's and Elen's arms on the entrance steps to see us off.

Master Ashley had insisted we take fresh horses from his stable and Simon and Elen had swathed their hooves in cloth to muffle the noise as we rode out of the courtyard into the dark deserted streets. At our heels slunk the two hounds, mirror images of dark and light against the cobbled roadway.

The moon, just past full and sinking towards the west, cast crazy shadows from all the buildings nearby. If there were any spies lurking in those shadows, we did not see them.

How, then, we came to be pursued we didn't know.

*

It took many hours of hard riding to reach our destination. But as I had hoped, King Richard's boar badge still commanded loyalty in these early days after the battle. The country was waiting, watching, hardly breathing in this twilight between the golden sun of Yorkist rule and the dark unknown of the Tudor future. We trusted that the dragon symbol of the victorious usurper would not be welcomed so readily – if we were pursued.

Some had not had news of the battle and questioned us before we could leave them and hasten on our way. Others waved us on with a good will and long faces.

As Master Ashley had advised, we made our way north from London first using the system of post-horses that King Richard had put in place when he was still Duke, to send his brother news of his wars in Scotland. In this way, at every post-house we had fresh horses. When we turned off that route, the final pair had to take us far further – to Gipping Hall itself. Though fine horses, we had pushed them so hard that they were dripping with sweat and lather as we clattered on to the cobbles of a wide stable yard.

The sun had long since retired, and darkness pressed upon us, as, dazed with exhaustion and filthy from the journey, and following a few words of explanation, the three of us were ushered towards the nearby mansion, as the grooms came to lead our mounts away.

With the uproar of our arrival in the stable yard, a messenger must have been sent to the house. Lady Tyrell herself was at the main door to greet us, surrounded by serving men holding torches aloft. Several were armed, and all rather elderly.

'Alys! Alys Langdown! What are you doing here?

A formidably tall woman, Lady Tyrell pushed her way past the servants and rushed forward to embrace Alys. As she took her arm and led her into the house, she said,

'You mustn't worry about the men, my dear. Since we heard the terrible news, we're having to be extra careful. But of course all the younger men went to fight for the King. Most of them haven't yet returned.'

She glanced askance at Roger and me, but said nothing to us so we simply followed them into the great hall. A fire was blazing there despite the warm evening, and Lady Tyrell ushered Alys to a seat beside it.

'Sit down, my dear, take some wine. Some bread and cheese, perhaps – or I can ask the cooks to bring something hot, though it is so late? You look fit to drop, my dear. Tell me why you are here. I haven't seen you since we were last at court together. After poor Queen Anne...'

Her busy words ran to a halt as Alys accepted the proffered wine-glass and gulped gratefully. Shadow sidled up and sat down, alert, at her side, as Alys replaced the glass on a nearby table.

'Thank you, my lady. It has been a long day, and a long ride. We have come all the way from London.'

'London! But —' Lady Tyrell drew back a fraction. 'But isn't Tudor...?'

'He had not arrived before we left. We have been sent with a message.'

'Then I'm only sorry that Sir James is not here to greet you. He is on the continent in service for...' She hesitated, her eyes again flickering over Roger and me, 'for King Richard.'

'That is why we are here, Lady Tyrell,' said Alys. 'On the King's service. The true King.'

'Indeed? And who are "we"?'

Alys shrank back from a sudden sharpness in Lady Tyrell's words and her own voice wavered.

'This – this is Matthew Wansford, my lady, and perhaps you remember Roger de Kynton?'

My lady inclined her head as both Roger and I bowed our most courteous bows, but her face was still suspicious. When she didn't speak, Alys stammered on.

'Matthew was sent by... by King Richard from the battlefield with a message to Master Ashley.' A flutter of recognition in Lady Tyrell's eyes, but it was blinked away in a moment. 'Master Ashley – he has been prevented from coming here himself by agents of Henry Tudor. So... so we have come instead.'

'Why?'

The force of the word finally bludgeoned Alys into silence. She took another gulp of wine, her free hand reaching across to fondle Shadow's ears.

Her ladyship's glance darted from her to me and back again.

Roger stepped forward into the breach and bent his knee in a flouncing, ceremonious fashion, whisking off his cap and sweeping it to his heart as he was used to do in dancing classes at Middleham.

'My lady, we have travelled far to bring you greetings from —'

But Lady Tyrell cut him off.

'Not you – the other boy. Speak! Why are you here?'

As Roger retreated, I seized my courage in my hands and took a pace forwards, sensing Murrey hugging close to my thigh and drawing strength from her presence.

Now was a moment for plain speaking – and our task was urgent.

'To take Edward and Richard, the – the princes to safety, my lady. If it will help you trust us, I have this.' I thrust my boar badge, outside my doublet once more, towards her, and then reached inside my pouch. 'And also this.'

She took the scrap of parchment I held out, that I had hoarded since the road to St Albans.

After peering at it, she said,

'That is indeed his signature – the King's I mean. And,' she looked again at the parchment and up at me, 'And Edward's too. Do you know him?'

'Yes, my lady. At least – we have met. I – I was his page once – when he was newly King. On his journey to London. Before...'

'When he was King?'

'Aye, my lady.'

'And yet you are King Richard's man?'

'Yes, my lady.' My voice sounded firm, though my insides roiled. 'More recently I was apprentice to Master Ashley. It was he who sent us.'

'And what do you intend to do with the – boys?'

'King Richard said they were to be taken to his sister in Flanders. Master Ashley told us we should go by boat from Lowestoft – that would be the nearest seaport and the safest crossing to the continent.'

Much of the tension in Lady Tyrell's features seeped away, but doubt still shaded her eyes.

'And you say you know young Edward?'

'Aye, my lady. We rode together one Christmas-tide, and then again towards London. We became friends – almost.'

For so I had believed.

She motioned to one of the old servants, all of whom were standing silently nearby, and in a few moments two figures appeared in the doorway.

Alys and Roger exchanged glances, and for the first time it occurred to me that my friends had perhaps never met these boys.

But I knew them of course.

Edward and Richard. The boys who had been princes.

They advanced a pace or two into the hall, their faces pale, fear in their dark shadowed eyes. I smiled, hoping Edward and I could pick up our friendship across the distance of those two long years. But of a sudden my dream on the morning of the battle burst into my mind – with a shock as powerful as the blast of one of those monstrous cannons that had bombarded the armies facing each other that day.

I quavered inside at the memory, but I stood my ground. It was just a dream after all, nothing solid, nothing that would sway Edward's reception of me. Surely, if he recollected me at all, he would recall our closeness during those days at Northampton and St Albans, how we chatted, joked, laughed together amidst the cares of his uncles' business – how he had clasped hands with me warmly as we took our farewells and urged me to visit him in his royal apartments at the tower. Yet so much had changed in the days and weeks that followed. And now, as though I was being put to a test, the boys and I stared at one another across the cold grey width of the hall.

Would I pass? Would they remember me and know they could place their trust in me and my friends?

After an eternity waiting, to my surprise Edward dropped to one knee, dipping his hand into his pouch.

'Murrey?'

My hound's eyes beseeched me and I gestured to her to go. She bounded across the stone-slabbed floor and, as Edward drew out his hand, performed her usual perfect pirouette for the scrap he held. He threw it to her, waited till she had wolfed it down, then clapped his hands. She fell to the ground, unmoving, as though she had been shot, and stirred again only when he whistled.

Laughing, he slipped her another morsel, ruffling the fur on her head.

Then he glanced over to me and his expression changed. He drew himself up, looking very much like my memory of his father, the old King Edward.

'Matthew? Murrey has not changed, but you – you look – older.'

So he had recognized me – if only through the antics of my hound. Would it be enough to persuade him to trust me?

Crossing the expanse of cold stone flags, I knelt before him.

What should I call him? Two years ago he had insisted on 'Edward'. But now...?

I lowered my head.

'Your Grace, it has been more than two years since last we met.'

'Oh, yes, it has. And a great deal has happened in that time. Then I was King. Now...' He paused. 'And you were ever my uncle's man.'

What was that emotion in his voice? Was it fear, scorn – or anger?

Whatever it was, the greeting I had hoped for would not be mine. Perhaps I should not be surprised after all that had passed. I brushed away the stab of disappointment. The matter at hand was too important to dwell on my own emotions.

I got back to my feet and looked him in the eye – though he was still taller than me.

'Aye, Your Grace, I was and ever will be. And now I have come to take you to safety with his sister, your aunt.'

'Safety!' He spat out the word as though it brought evil tidings. 'And I'm to believe you? After what my uncle did? And now that Henry Tudor has come to restore us? When I was lodged at the Tower, Lady Stanley said he —'

I raised my hand. Whatever he saw in my face caused his words to fade away.

'Listen to me, Edward.' Now was no time for niceties. 'No matter what you may think of your uncle, of what he did, Henry Tudor is the more to be feared. He wants the crown for himself – he won't restore it to you or your brother. The moment he stepped ashore in Wales he called himself King. He has issued proclamations from Leicester in the name of King Henry. He swore to marry your sister and if he makes her legitimate, it will mean you are too – and therefore the rightful King. But he will not bend his knee to you. He won't rest until you are dead.'

Little Richard gasped and his hand crept to clutch his brother's. Edward was silent, but shock was scored across his eyes. Yet I had to go on, to tell them the truth.

'No matter what she said to you, Lady Stanley is Tudor's mother. And her husband, Lord Stanley, betrayed his anointed King on the battlefield. Who would you rather trust?'

I fell quiet myself at last, amazed at the words that had forced their way out. I had perhaps never uttered so many all at once before.

Then, as the boys remained motionless, I drew cool air deep into my lungs and, releasing it slowly, bowed my head to them both.

'We will take you to your aunt Margaret and your friends in Flanders. They will keep you safe. One day, if you wish it, maybe they will help restore you to the throne.'

·

24

A New Morning

'Matt. Wake up.'

Tap, tap, tap.

Someone knocking.

'Matt? Did you hear me? Wake up. We must be off.'

Alys.

Groggy from sleep – the first sound, dreamless sleep for days – I grunted without words. Her quick footsteps faded away along the passage.

I swung my legs off the feather bed, splashed myself awake with the basinful of water placed ready and, dragging on my doublet, went to the window.

Outside a grey dawn was breaking. Threads of mist were floating across the flat fields beyond the stables, the wide fishponds, the chapel, its cut-flint walls lustrous in the half-light.

Something tugged inside me. The sun would be rising soon over the familiar moors high above Middleham, clothed now in the purple velvet of heather. Dew would form chains of sparkling diamonds on cobwebs adorning the golden bracken. The mist would linger in the dale perhaps for hours yet.

I turned away.

Upon a chair were my cloak, my new bundle of things for our journey, and Lord Lovell's sword. I had kept it closely hidden since that first day at Leicester, had not even unsheathed it.

I drew it from its scabbard now. It was a fine-wrought weapon, well balanced, its hilt a simple cross bound with lightly worn leather.

I weighed it in my hand, then skipped to one side, whirling it about me as I had learnt, to parry the blow of an invisible enemy and turn the defence into my own attack. It felt comfortable in my hands, though I had never wielded a true sword before.

As I slid it back into its leather sheath, my eye was caught by some dark red specks where burnished blade met hilt. Lord Lovell had cleaned his weapon after the battle, but in a hurry. I rubbed the stain away with a corner of my cloak.

Downstairs, in the main entranceway, a slender figure was silhouetted against the growing daylight. It was Alys, staring out across the countryside, with Shadow a pale statue at her side.

Hearing the clicking of Murrey's claws and the hesitant scrape of my footsteps on the stone flags, she swung to face me.

Something about her had changed.

'Alys – your hair!'

She threw me a quick smile as her hand crept up to her head.

'Lady Tyrell cut it for me. She says, if I must go, it may be safer if I travel as a boy. In case we are followed. They will be searching for two boys and a girl, not three – or five – boys.'

She gazed back out over the waving fields of corn and barley, touched to gold now by the first shafts of sunlight.

'And if I'm not to be married soon, no one will notice if I don't have long hair just now.'

We stood side by side in silence for a few moments. Then she said quietly,

'Matt, will you tell me all that happened? There was no time to ask at Master Ashley's. All we heard was that Lord Stanley...'

I turned to her, as she stood upright in the pinkish twilight, her ragged hair sticking out all-ways out from under her boy's cap, her eyes catching the rays of the sun and melting into liquid emeralds.

But my heart seemed to force its way into my throat. All I could croak out was 'No – not today', before I buried my face in the shoulder of her doublet, and let out all the sobs I had held in for days, and all the tears.

She embraced me for some minutes, wordless herself, her arms tight around me as my body shook in distress. Then, as the sobbing died away, she loosened her hold and pushed me a little away from her.

'We must carry on. We must finish this.'

Her voice, though broken, was fierce, determined.

I nodded and, wiping my face with my sleeve, followed as she led the way back into the great hall, the two hounds trailing behind.

Roger hailed us from where he was helping himself to bread, cheese and ale at a long trestle table, cheerful as ever, despite all our troubles and the early hour of the morning.

Sitting a little way along from him, and similarly dressed in rough travelling clothes, Edward and Richard were also breaking their fast. They didn't speak as we joined them, but again in Edward's face was that mixture of anger, fear and defiance I'd seen last night. But also perhaps a new respect. Richard, as I discovered, followed his brother in most things, though there was still more of fear in his younger eyes. I neither knew nor cared what they could read in mine.

I had hardly time to chew a first mouthful of bread and cheese, and drop some down to Murrey, before Lady Tyrell came hurrying in.

'You must leave at once. Strangers have been seen in Stowmarket asking questions. There's no time to waste. Horses are being saddled in the yard.'

As we each swallowed a last draught of ale and snatched up our bundles, she carried on, addressing me apparently as the leader of the party.

'Remember what I said last night. Cut across country until you reach the River Waveney. It may be slow going, but safer than the roads. Follow it until you come to the sea. The town there is Lowestoft. You should be able to buy your passage in the harbour there.'

She ushered us out to the stable yard where five lean ponies were waiting patiently while grooms finished harnessing them. As Alys and the boys went to sling their packs across the ponies' withers, Lady Tyrell's hand on my shoulder held me back.

'Be careful who you show your badge to, and don't tell anyone who you really are. The ships' captains are fiercely independent like all men of the sea. They may not want to become entangled in affairs of the English crown.'

I nodded, but she didn't release her grip on my arm.

'And, Matthew, my husband does not know the boys were here. He is so often away on business. To him they were just two new pages – he was never at court with them and they have been sworn to secrecy. It was thought safest. If you should meet him abroad...'

'Of course, my lady. I understand.'

At last she let me go. A minute later the five of us and two hounds were trotting along the lane away from the hall, turning east towards the rising sun.

25

Lowestoft

Our journey that day might have been a pleasure in less troubled times. For all my yearning to be home in Yorkshire, even I could have found beauty in the slow-moving, meandering river, fringed by gracious willows and warm sunlit water meadows. As herons leisurely took to flight on their great grey wings at our approach and flocks of geese paddled honking away from the river bank.

But as we drew nearer to the sea, the trees thinned and the lush grassland became scrub, and the feeling crept through me that we could be seen for miles across this flat, almost featureless landscape.

Lady Tyrell had assured us that she and her people would tell any pursuers that we had headed north-west, as though towards King Richard's northern strongholds. But how long would that keep them from our trail?

Darkness was falling as our ponies' hoofbeats echoed along the main street of Lowestoft. There was little more than this one paved way, with scatters of houses along alleys climbing on our left-hand side and tumbling downhill towards the harbour to our right. The swell of the sea reached my ears from far below and lights twinkled on the masts of ships and from lanterns on the quayside – a black mass now against the dark grey of the water. A mist was rising in the cool of the evening, carrying the salt tang of the sea to my nostrils.

Roger and I left Alys and the boys with the horses and made our way to the tavern on the corner where Lady Tyrell had said sea captains might be found. I glanced up at its swinging sign as we entered and nudged Roger. The sign of the silver lion. We were in the country of the Dukes of Norfolk and I took it to be a good omen.

The first two or three captains only laughed at the sight of us, despite the coins we offered, but within minutes we had made a down payment on a passage across to Friesland, the rest to be paid on our safe arrival.

'It's a boat called the Falcon, though its master is Friesian,' Roger told the others on our return to the dark, misty corner where they had waited. 'It sails just after midnight on the ebb tide.'

'Can we go aboard now?' asked Richard.

Of all of us, he had found the day most tiring, though his complaints had been few. I was sorry to have to shake my head.

'Not until an hour or so before. The crew are still loading their cargo of wool and we'd just be in the way.'

'Let's get some hot food,' suggested Alys. 'Shall we try that tavern?'

'We passed a quieter one on the way back – the Fleece. It might suit us better and there was stabling.'

The Fleece laid on a fine stew of lamb and aromatic herbs and mugs of good ale, and we arranged to leave the ponies there until Lady Tyrell's people could claim them. At last we were closing in on our goal. I almost began to relax.

Richard was nodding in the corner of the settle and the rest of us were in the middle of a spirited debate about the latest French romances when I realized Alys had fallen quiet.

'What's wrong?' I asked.

Her usually clear eyes were troubled.

'I'm not sure anything is. But... a few minutes ago a man came in, talked to the serving man and left again almost straight away. I noticed him because he seemed familiar. He's just come back in and I think... I'm not sure, but I think he's watching us. No!' The word came out as a squeak as Roger began to turn round. 'Don't look his way. That will just alert him – if it is anything to worry about.'

'Everything is something to worry about,' I said grimly.

'What do you think we should do?' asked Roger.

Alys shook her head. 'I don't know.'

'Perhaps,' I said, thinking quickly, 'perhaps if we go out separately – maybe you two and Richard through the main door, Edward and I through the stables, as though we're checking on the ponies. He's only one man – he can't follow all of us.'

Roger looked doubtful.

'But if there are more watching outside?'

I shrugged.

Edward said, 'I think we should try it. What if he's the only one now? He may be keeping an eye on us in here while waiting for others to join him.'

'That's possible,' said Roger. 'Well, you're the—' I kicked him under the table; he smiled, 'the one who's used to giving orders.'

'Not any more,' Edward said, darting a look at me, but Roger forged on.

'Are we to go, then? Shall I wake Richard?'

As Richard rubbed the sleep from his eyes, I reminded them all what had been arranged.

'Captain Hans said his boat is the first tied up along the quay – it has a hawk as a figurehead. Also he said any of the alleyways opposite, back along the road we came along – he called them "scores" – they lead down to the harbour. You three head for one of them. We'll wait two minutes after you've gone, then leave through the back door.'

Alys, Roger and Richard, his eyes more haunted than ever, took up their bundles and, with Roger making much of calling his farewells to Edward and me, made their exit through the front door, Shadow hugging close. A second later, a fair-haired young man in dark travel-stained riding gear set down his mug, cast a hurried glance at the two of us, then stood up, threw coins upon his table, and followed them out.

I cursed under my breath.

'Richard and I have our swords,' said Edward. He half-unsheathed his – I caught a glimpse of curlicued words inscribed darkly on the well-honed blade.

'I hope it won't come to that.'

We didn't need to wait any longer. Without another word, we rose, gathered our things, and soon we were out on the main street, Murrey a silent shadow at our heels.

At first the place appeared deserted. The sea-fret was coiling everywhere, grey and ghostly in the darkness. It deadened our footsteps on the cobbles as we trailed first one way, then another, squinting to see where our three friends or the strange man had gone. From a few house-fronts lanterns were hung, but they shed pools of light that hardly penetrated the murk. There was no sign of anybody.

Edward opened his mouth as if to speak, but then the silence was shattered.

A shout, then another. A man's voice, urgent.

Thirty, forty yards away, maybe more – it was hard to tell in the fog.

Edward and I exchanged glances, then began to run, he drawing his sword as he did.

In a moment, in the light of a single house lantern piercing the fog and the dark, we spotted who had called.

The man from the tavern.

His back against the house wall, his face turned away from us, he was cursing quietly now. Then he raised his voice again.

'Put down your sword or I'll cut his throat.'

A few yards in front of him stood Richard, his sword in his hand. He was panting heavily, staring wide-eyed at the man. Another sword was lying on the cobbles between them, three bundles abandoned nearby. Roger was crouching off to one side, his face glimmering white with terror in the swirling mist, his arms wrapped round a squirming, whimpering Shadow.

And then I saw who else was there.

The man held someone close against his body with one arm, while his other hand pressed the glittering blade of a dagger to their neck.

It was Alys.

She was rigid in his hold, her head forced back against him, fingers clutching his arm, eyelids fluttering, her throat curving back as though straining away from the sharp steel.

Edward darted to his brother's side, all the while keeping his gaze fixed on the young man and his captive, and his sword at the ready.

'What happened?'

The man twitched round a little at his movement. The point of the knife was dark now against Alys's pale skin. Her hands tightened convulsively on his wrist.

My fist clenched Murrey's collar, as Roger inched towards me, tugging the other wriggling hound with him.

'He came at us with his sword,' Richard said hoarsely, his eyes not leaving the man's face for a second. 'I disarmed him with that trick Father taught us – remember? But then he drew his knife and grabbed her.'

'Her?' the man cried in surprise. 'What do you mean?'

'Let her go!' I yelled.

His head snapped towards me. Knowing Alys would hate me for it, I shouted again, 'She's a girl, not a boy!'

His grip must have faltered in his astonishment. Sensing the blade no longer so close to her neck, Alys took her chance to drive one elbow into his stomach while tearing his knife-hand from her throat, then stamped on his foot and flung herself away from his flailing grasp. Her stumbling strides cannoned her into Roger and Shadow, spilling all three into a sprawling mess at my feet.

But as the man buckled under her onslaught and himself staggered forward, his hand snatched at his sword and, rolling over to the side, he was back on his feet in an instant. There he faced Edward and Richard, standing now shoulder to shoulder, their swords upraised before them.

His eyes flicked sideways to where I was hauling Alys and Roger to their feet, the hounds milling about us, whining. He clearly saw that we were nothing to worry about and turned back to the two armed brothers.

'Two against one,' he said, a mirthless grin unfurling across his handsome face. 'But two little ones. I've had worse odds.'

And he attacked, throwing himself towards the boys, both his sword and knife slicing and stabbing through the greyish eddies of mist.

Alys gasped, catching at my arm at the ferocity of the onslaught. But if the man had thought he'd have an easy time of it with boys, he was wrong.

For all his superior height and weight, he was matched against brothers who, as sons of a King, must once have had the finest weapons masters available. Perhaps they had never fought in earnest before, but an onlooker could not have guessed. Had my fellow pages at Middleham displayed such footwork, Master Fleete would have burst with pride, and their anticipation and skill in attack and counterattack was as good as I'd ever seen.

Stroke for stroke they began to get the better of their adversary. The sea-fret muffled the clang of swords on sword and dagger as, between them, step by gruelling step, they battled him back to the wall again.

But still they could not overmaster him.

Tiredness and despair were creeping on to young Richard's face, and Edward's frustration was likewise written in his eyes. Though on the defensive, did the man also see it – or feel a waning of their attack? Or was he simply desperate, like an animal forced into a corner, with nowhere to go? Whichever was the case, he both redoubled his efforts and sought for a way out.

And found it.

In a moment of respite from Richard's attack, the man flung his dagger at him. Though Richard parried it with his blade, knocking it away, the man, with his free hand, caught up Alys's pack from where it lay abandoned on the ground and swung it at both boys. Richard took the brunt of the impact, his sword spinning out of his hand, but the move also took Edward by surprise.

His opponent saw his advantage and leapt at him, landing a blow that the boy could barely parry. His sword glanced off Edward's blade and struck the boy deep in his shoulder. Edward staggered back, blood spurting from the wound, while the man, also tipped off balance by the force of his deflected blow, fought to keep his footing.

As, twisting about, he regained it and started to raise his sword for the killing thrust, Roger and I threw a terrified glance at one another. Then, he drawing his knife and I my sword, we rushed forward yelling, Murrey and Shadow bounding barking at our side.

We caught the man unawares, so focused was he on Edward. And, with Richard also recovering his sword and his balance, somehow, between us – three boys and two hounds – we charged him to the floor, Roger and I toppling upon him in our onrush.

He fell beneath us like a sack of grain tossed from a wagon, heavy and awkward. With a sickening thud, his head hit the timbers of the house-front, knocking him cold. His eyes were sightless as Richard's sword point swung down to his throat and his own sword fell from his unconscious hand. It lay on the ground, dark blood seeping from it into the dust.

Roger and I dragged one another to our feet and while he scurried to catch hold of the gambolling hounds, I hurried across to Alys. Crouched down beside Edward, she was busy tearing her cloak into strips.

'How is he?'

'Not good,' she said, starting to bind his wound. 'It's deep. I may be able to stem the bleeding for a while, but he'll need a surgeon.'

Richard shoved the fallen man with his toe and when his head lolled to one side, he sheathed his sword and ran over to his elder brother.

'Ned? Can you walk?'

Edward's face was pale with shock and pain, but he nodded.

'I think so, Dickon. Once I've caught my breath.'

Alys finished tying her makeshift bandage, then relinquished her place to Richard. He knelt down and, propping Edward against himself, stroked his head, murmuring to him all the time in gentle tones.

Alys came over to where I now stood, my sword pointing at the unconscious man's chest – just in case.

She said quietly, 'Matt, I – I think he's Ralph Soulsby.'

'What?'

'I thought I recognized him in the tavern, but it's been so long since I saw him. He was just thirteen or fourteen then. It was only when he grabbed me and called out that I realized.'

'You knew his voice?'

'Yes.' She hesitated. 'No. The name he called. It was Hugh.'

All my insides turned to ice.

The shining blade, the cowardly stab.

The jeers.

The horror. The shame I'd felt at doing nothing.

The anger. The desire for revenge. Now more than ever.

But not for me. For my King.

And the ice melted to fire.

Alys caught at my hand as my sword tip wavered closer to the prone man's chest.

'Matt, we have to get out of here. If Hugh is in the town somewhere, there may be others too. We can't afford another fight. Now is not the time.'

She was right, of course. I knew it. I could no more hope to fight Hugh and gain my revenge now than at any time when we had met before. Even with Roger or young Richard alongside me.

And I had my duty still to do. And perhaps all of this could have been avoided if I had done that on the day of the battle...

My betrayal of my master vivid in my mind, the flames died down.

Roger was hovering close by, a hound grasped in each hand. The expression on his face told me that he had heard Alys's whispered words.

'What should we do?' he asked. Alys only stared at me.

Not for the first time since the evening at Master Ashley's, they were looking to me to decide.

I resheathed my sword.

'You three take Edward to the boat. I'll tie this one up so he can't make more trouble and then I'll join you once I'm done. Go carefully. If Hugh is out there...'

Alys hissed through her teeth.

'I'll stay with you, Matt. Shadow and I can —'

'No,' I said, firm, though my stomach was churning now at the thought of Hugh perhaps nearby. 'Go with the others.

'Then Roger —'

'Richard will need his help with Edward. And Captain Hans knows him.'

Relief flooded across Roger's face, though he tried to hide it, turning away towards Richard and Edward.

'Take a couple of the bundles if you are able, Alys. And tell Richard to carry his sword ready if he can.'

I peered back the way Edward and I had come, through the confusion of mist, darkness and glimmers of occasional lanterns.

'I think the third score back was the widest and best paved. There was a lantern at its entrance and I think I saw another further down. That may be the safest way to go.'

She nodded, then glanced up at the lantern flaring in the seething mist above our heads.

'Lady Tyrell was right about local people not wanting to become involved. You'd think that with all this racket going on in the street...' She shook her head. 'Come after us quickly, Matt – and take care.'

I watched as Roger and Richard helped Edward to his feet, then half-supported, half-carried him as they walked slowly away. Alys hefted two of our packs and followed after with Shadow. They all soon disappeared into the mist like wraiths at the tail end of a dream, leaving me alone with Murrey – and the man lying senseless before me on the ground.

Pushing to one side my thoughts of him and his cousin, I set about my task, gathering the rest of the strips Alys had torn from her cloak and tying his wrists and ankles with them. He groaned as I wrenched one binding tight and his eyelids flickered. Duly warned, I wound the final strips of cloth into a thick gag and somehow forced it between his teeth.

Sticky blood darkened my hands as I drew them from beneath his head. Gulping back a retch, I wiped them clean on his doublet, then stood, keen to escape from the scene and the memory of what had happened here.

Picking up the remaining bundles, I whistled to Murrey, who was sniffing about among the shadows of the still-empty street, and together we headed off back into the veil of mist, clammy and chill against my skin.

Had I miscounted the alleys as I passed them, or had Alys? Or, despite Edward's injury, had my friends travelled faster than I thought possible?

Whatever the reason, when I reached the entrance of the wide, paved score, I could see and hear no one ahead of me in the darkness.

True, the lantern at its mouth threw little light into its black throat, and the sea-fret gathered closer here. It was seeping and creeping all around, spectres crowding close upon me from the shadowy depths of the passage.

Even the familiar clicking of Murrey's claws upon the cobbles sounded damp and heavy under its weight.

I paused a moment. But I had to go on, I knew. Time was passing and soon we had to be aboard the ship. The tide and captain would not wait. And I had promised to help the others find their way.

I patted Murrey's head and said, 'Good girl.' The words were more to comfort me than her and their sound was deadened by the fog. She gazed up at me, letting out the slightest whine, her eyes small sparks in the gloom. Then, side by side, we plunged into the alley.

In the instant it took to cross the pool of lantern light, strange details imprinted on my mind.

Our shadows stretching thin before us.

Crumbling brick walls curving in and out before my eyes.

Pebbles of every colour pressed into pale bands of mortar.

Cut faces of flint gleaming, glassy dark.

Tiny blooms of purple toadflax clinging on for grim death.

Then we passed into darkness and the grey swirl of the mist.

Black branches of trees, overhanging, looming out of the fog.

Beyond the wavy walls, the mewing of a cat, the rattle of a chain and whine of a tethered dog.

The sweet smell of rotting vegetables wafting. Woodsmoke from a high chimney.

I glanced back. The glow of the lantern still shone, reassuring, through the tendrils of sea-fret, through the murk.

We walked on.

A plaintive hooting. A swoosh of air as the owl swooped over and was gone.

The dull clump of my boots on the ground.

The walls – rippling spans of brick – closing in on us. The alley was narrowing. Ahead, veering to the right.

And there through the drifting strands of mist was the faintest glimmer. That second lantern I had seen? At the corner of the alley?

But something warned me to stop, forced my hand to my sword hilt. What was it?

The light.

It was moving. Moving towards the corner. Towards us.

A grumble deep in Murrey's throat.

The scrape of boots on cobbles.

The swish of my blade being drawn. The thud of three bundles being dropped.

The reek of sweat – and of fear. Was it mine?

Around the corner came the lantern, held high in someone's hand. A tall, broad figure. A burnished open helmet above a familiar face.

Hugh.

26

The Score

The lantern crashed to the ground as Hugh reached for his sword.

Glass shattered, oil spilt. Flames flashed across its surface.

Flaring, they lit up the narrow alleyway, casting demonic shadows across my old adversary's face and up the high brick walls. The sharp blade of his sword glittered only inches from mine.

My heart hammered against my ribs, echoed by the fast rise and fall of his chest. But he recovered more swiftly.

'I should have known it would be you,' he spat.

Yet he hadn't attacked.

Relief swept through me. For all that I had grown and filled out in recent months, he would always overmatch me in size. But I was also bemused at his words. Playing for time, I said, 'What do you mean?'

A sneer spread across his broad face.

'When we called for Alys and found she'd gone to that man's house. That merchant. I remember Roger telling us when he became your master.'

'What of it?'

'He thought you'd done so well for yourself,' he scoffed. 'Going to London, becoming an apprentice.'

'Better than you have,' I shot back. 'Son of a traitor, riding with a traitor.'

His smirk slipped, twisting into a darker expression.

'What do you know of my father? And my uncle is no traitor!'

'He fought with Lord Stanley.'

'Who will be right-hand man to the new King.' He rallied, his face smug once more.

'Only because he betrayed the old one.'

'Old Dick had no right to be King. Everyone knew it.'

'That's not true,' I retorted. 'King Richard had more right than Tudor ever will. Even he knows he must marry Princess Elizabeth before the people will accept him.'

'He's doing it to unite the houses of Lancaster and York and put an end to all these wars.'

'Is that what you truly believe?' I asked. 'What war has there been in our lifetimes – until Tudor came?'

He was silent, his eyes hooded, the flickering shadows from the lantern playing across his stony features.

How strange was this talk, in a dark alley, between two such enemies? But I forced myself to speak on, to gain time to decide what to do.

'Why are you here anyway? Why did you follow us?'

'We have our orders. They come from King Henry himself.' Pride was blazoned across his face and voice.

'Which are?'

'I don't have to tell you.'

I pushed on again, thinking desperately.

'Why did your cousin try to kill us?'

'What? Where is he?'

He flicked his gaze from side to side, chary of taking it away from my sword, but seeking into every shadowy, mist-shrouded corner of the score.

'Don't worry, he's still alive,' I said. 'But he won't be coming to help you. He shouldn't have tangled with Alys.'

'Alys? What's she doing here?'

'She rode with us, of course.'

'We thought she'd stayed at Tyrell's place. Our informants said five boys. That her companions had ridden on just with the princes and a guide.'

My insides lurched at his words.

'So you know who they are.'

'The princes? Of course. Why do you think we're here? To hunt you down and kill you? You're not worth the effort!'

Despite all I'd heard from King Richard and Master Ashley, and repeated to Edward and Richard at Gipping, until that moment I had perhaps only half believed it myself – that Tudor really would seek to murder Elizabeth's brothers in cold blood. But Hugh's mocking face didn't lie.

I forced myself to carry on.

'And you knew they were at Gipping?'

'Not until we got there. Then we put two and two together. As Ralph said, what other two boys would Yorkists go to so much trouble to hide – and then smuggle away when Henry Tudor came.'

'And it's just you and Ralph here then?'

He didn't answer with words, but his expression as he realized that he was now alone was reply enough for me. My decision was made.

I hurled myself at him so suddenly that he could do no more than roughly parry my blade, and then I had a chance to pivot and land a blow on his body before he had recovered.

But my heart sank at the crunch as my sword struck him. He was wearing mail beneath his doublet. I had hoped to take him by surprise, that it might give me an edge. But instead he had the edge – of being armoured while I wore only a jack.

Yet my blow had at least winded and bruised him, if it had done no more damage. It gave me a little time to think again as we circled each other warily in the narrow score, he grimacing with the pain.

'You wretch!' he snapped. 'Think you can best me, eh? You never have before.'

That I knew well. But my mind had to stay in the present, not the past, if I were to have any chance at all.

267

He flung himself at me with a snarl, but I skipped out of the way, at the last moment twisting and striking out as he passed. The flat of my blade caught him hard on his upper arm. His flinch told me he wore no mail there.

He was stronger than me, more skilled, better armed. But was I more agile, lighter, quicker? Might his greater height and weight work against him – however unlikely that seemed?

These thoughts flitted through my brain as we circled once more, slowly, carefully, watching one another, each with heaving chest, catching our breath. All talking was now over. Silent again, Hugh fixed his eyes on me, no longer scouting for his cousin, for help, focused only on me, searching for any warning sign, for any movement, any action. And I did the same – quietening my breathing, ignoring the pounding of blood in my ears, praying I would be ready for his next move – forgetting who else was there in the score with us.

With a flurry of deep red, glinting in the lamp's glow, Murrey darted in to snap at Hugh's ankles, then danced away, yapping sharply as he lashed out with his boot. A growl, a twirl around, then another swift, scarlet rush into the fray.

As Hugh kicked again at my hound and she spun away, I took the chance she gave me. I catapulted myself at him, lunging with my sword and aiming this time for his unprotected, bull-like neck.

He roared in anger as he drove his own blade up in response and our swords clashed and sparked. My blade snagged on his hilt and, with a fierce twist of his wrist, he forced it down and then away, wrenching it from my hand. It clanged as it hit the wall while I, thrown off balance, sprawled to the floor.

As my hand flailed in a grab at my sword – too far! – he whipped round and followed through, and I rolled to the side just in time for his sword to smash down on the cobbles instead of my head. I tried to scramble to my feet, but wasn't quick enough. He kicked me back to the ground, winding me, and before I could rally, his heavy boot was on my chest, pinning me down.

I struggled for breath, and writhed to left, to right, but he only stamped down harder until I could not move for the crushing pains in my ribs. And as I stared up at him, helpless, he brought his sword down, down, until the tip almost touched my nose.

Motionless now, but for my straining chest, I gazed along the shining blade, its point unwavering between my eyes, its polished length reflecting flickers from the lantern flames on to the dark, looming walls of the score. Into my terrified mind crept unbidden a memory from our time at Middleham. Weapons training, two years or more ago. When Hugh had beaten me like this before. Then the sword had been wooden, not tempered, sharpened steel – but the hate in his eyes was the same.

Those eyes narrowed now, black slits in the devilish red of the flaring lamplight.

'Runt!' he taunted. 'Upstart!'

I had never felt so alone, so defenceless. A gaping hollow yawned inside me like the mouth of hell, a pit of sheer terror so deep I would never fall to its end. The faces of my friends, my family – my long-dead mother – images of my short life, all chased through my head as the cool sword point traced across my chin and down the length of my neck.

It rested there a moment, its razor edge against my skin, then he lifted it and delicately tapped it on my throat – once, twice, three times – as though playing with me.

Then his eyes and mouth tightened, and he clasped both his hands upon the hilt, raising his sword high to plunge the point deep into my neck.

But before he could ram it down, a ferocious snarl rang out, and Murrey, in a flash of red, launched herself at his sword arm, sinking her teeth deep into the flesh.

Hugh screamed, dropped his sword and thrashed at her with his other hand. But she would not let go and hung there, teeth clamped on his upper arm as he hit her and hit her to no avail.

His falling sword missed my head by no more than an inch and I plucked it up and flung it to the far side of the score before I rolled over and over, out of the way of his now tramping boots. I grasped the wall and hauled myself back to my feet, gasping one pain-filled stabbing breath after another. How many ribs had Hugh's boot broken?

One hand pressed to my side against the pain, I bent to reclaim my own sword. Hugh's curses were echoing round the alley together with the clatter of his boots, and my only thought now was to dash back to help my loyal hound.

But as I swung round, Hugh's left hand dragged the dagger from his belt. The lamplight flashed on its upraised blade, then he jabbed it sharply down, thrusting it deep into Murrey's flank.

I heard her strangled yelp, saw bright blood gush from the wound, saw her grip loosen. Though Hugh's face was contorted by pain, a smirk lurched across it. He shook her from him before slumping to his knees, his hand clutching his arm.

A howl of rage smote my ears and before I realized it came from me, I had charged the half-dozen paces to where Hugh knelt and dealt him such a blow on his jaw with my sword hilt that he toppled to the ground.

In an instant, all was reversed.

He lay sprawled on his back on the cobbles, gulping in great gasps of air, staring at my sword point lined up unwavering between his eyes.

Such hate had never seized me before, or such fury. As I stood there, enraged, with Hugh at my mercy, Murrey whimpered once, twice, a gurgling breath, then she was silent. And I knew my loyal, royal hound would never dance again, or come back to life at a whistle.

My eyes stung, but I dared not tear them away from Hugh. A moment's distraction, a split second's indecision, and for all his bites and bruising, he would throw me off him and finish what he had begun.

Yet, staring down at him now, I sensed fear in him for the first time – fear of me, of what I, a runt and an upstart, would do. And power surged through me, the power of life or death over a fellow human being.

'Traitor!' I hissed at him. I saw again the stab. First one, then another. 'Coward!'

And in that instant I wanted to hurt. To hurt that cringing cur at my feet.

Murrey had never cringed, never once in all her life. In all her oh-so-short life. My loyal, courageous hound. What had King Richard called her? A brave little thing? Little she may have been, a runt even, but she had always been brave. Never a coward like this creature before me, pleading for his life.

For out of his mouth came choking sounds, barely words, entreating.

'Please, Matthew... please... I beg you... My uncle... Lord Stanley... They will...'

But those words were not the ones to help him. He must have seen it in my face. His voice faltered, died away.

For again into my mind came the sights and sounds of that fateful day, the banners whipping in the wind as the traitors charged, the screams, the horror, the stench of blood – in my nostrils again now. The jeers, the insults – the stab.

And I wanted to inflict pain on him as he had on Murrey, on me. To stab him as he had her – as he had my King.

And my sword point edged closer to his throat.

'Matthew!'

Alys's voice broke into my thoughts.

'Matt! What —'

Roger's too.

Hugh's eyes darted to the sound, but mine didn't move, didn't dare leave his.

271

Into the darkness on the fringe of my vision, the pale ghost of a hound trotted, bent its head, nudged the unmoving dark shape that lay there. Shadow.

Roger, raising a ship's lantern above his head – casting light upon the whole scene.

Alys, her cropped hair stark in the harsh light. Clutching – what? A sword. Glinting. A glimpse of scrollwork inscription on the blade. Edward's.

'Matthew. What happened?'

Her voice was soft, softer than I'd heard it before. Before...

'He stabbed...' A croak. Me? 'He killed...'

Roger peeled away, moved further up the score.

'I'll go check the main street. See what —'

He disappeared into the murk, the swirling mist.

Alys's hands clasped mine, still clenched upon the sword hilt. Warm fingers on my cold.

My eyes didn't waver. The sword point inched closer.

'He —'

'I know, Matt, I know.' Her words were barely a murmur, so close to my ear. 'I see her. I see what he did.

'I have to —'

'No, Matt – no, you mustn't.'

'But – but he would...'

He would do it, wouldn't he? Finish it. He wouldn't flinch from it – wouldn't stay his hand – if this were reversed.

'But, Matt – you're not him. You never will be.'

Her hands pressed tighter, closed over mine. Her voice as firm.

'Matt... Matt, tell me. What – what would King Richard do?'

And I knew then. That was all it took.

Those words. Those memories.

Of all those times when I had watched, listened, learnt.

All that the Duke, the King, had ever said to me, done for me. His half-smile, his gentle mockery, his firm handshake in farewell, the final promise I had made. And when I had betrayed his trust and his memory. Once. But not now. Never again.

I knew then that I wouldn't kill Hugh – wouldn't thrust the sword home. Wouldn't do to him what he would have done to me without a second's thought. I couldn't. No matter what he had done.

And Hugh saw it.

His eyes narrowed, his lip curled, his face relaxed. The fear had fled. Now only contempt remained.

But the tip of my sword pressed still against the soft base of his throat. As I unbuckled my sword belt with my other hand and passed it to Alys. As she slipped it out of the scabbard and threaded it beneath his booted legs, strapping it round them as tight as she could. As I ordered him to turn on to his face and raise his wrists behind him.

Next Alys held her sword to his neck while I unfastened his own belt and, ramming my knee into the small of his back – ignoring his cry of pain – I pulled his injured arms up to tie them fast. Then Alys's deft hands tore a strip of cloth from his cloak, fashioning a gag.

Soon we had finished, and Hugh lay trussed and helpless on the cobbles in the guttering light cast by his smashed lantern. He struggled and strained against his bonds, but he could scarcely move, and not so much as a whimper escaped from his stopped-up mouth.

I brushed the dust and grime from my doublet as best I could, before slipping my own old belt through Lord Lovell's scabbard and resheathing his sword. I silently offered up my thanks to his lordship for his gift on that dread day that now seemed so long ago.

Footsteps pounded down the alley towards us. Shadow crouched low, a small growl in her throat. Alys stood ready, her sword raised, though I had no heart to draw my own again.

The glow of a lantern approached the corner and rounded it. It was Roger, of course. Out of breath,

'They've found Ralph. The villagers. They're untying him. We must go.'

Hugh recommenced his writhing with renewed hope. But a swift kick in his ear from Alys's booted foot quietened him.

She leant down close to his face.

'Count your blessings, Hugh,' she whispered. 'You're still alive. Next time you may not be so lucky. We all had a good master, a good teacher. Not everyone is so ready to forgive. And lessons don't always last.'

She stood back up and collected one of the discarded bundles, while Roger scooped up the other two.

'Come, we must be off. We'll be safely away long before they find him. All of us. Long before – and far away.'

I gathered up Murrey's lifeless body. She weighed heavy in my hands as she had never done in life, and her bloodied head lolled against my chest.

Alys, calling Shadow, slipped her free arm through mine. And, with Roger raising his lantern to light our way, together we three walked down the score towards the midnight harbour, to where the ship awaited us and the tide had begun to ebb.

Here ends THE KING'S MAN, the second book in the sequence called THE ORDER OF THE WHITE BOAR. The third book will continue Matthew and his friends' adventures in the years that follow.

Author's note

Within days of the battle at which King Richard III died (which came to be known as the Battle of Bosworth), members of the council in Matthew's home city of York wrote that 'King Richard late mercifully reigning upon us was through great treason . . . piteously slain and murdered to the great heaviness of this city' and called him 'the most famous prince of blessed memory'. Two years earlier on his coronation tour of England, the Bishop of St David's had said of him: 'He contents the people where he goes best that ever did prince' and a Scottish ambassador remarked that 'Never has so much spirit or greater virtue reigned in such a small body.' Dominic Mancini, reporting back to his French master on events in England in 1483, said of the new King, 'The good reputation of his private life and public activities powerfully attracted the esteem of strangers.'

But more than a hundred years later, in a play by the great playwright William Shakespeare, King Richard was described as 'deform'd, unfinished, sent... Into this breathing world, scarce half made up... that bottled spider, that foul bunch-backed toad... determined to prove a villain... the bloody king', being portrayed as a tyrant with a hunchback and withered arm.

It's often said that history is written by the winners. This is perhaps particularly true in the case of the history that was created during the Tudor dynasty after the first Henry Tudor was victorious in battle and took the crown from King Richard. He reigned for twenty-four years as Henry VII, his son for more than thirty as Henry VIII, his grand-daughter for more than forty as Elizabeth I. And it was under her rule than Master Shakespeare provided the most famous condemnation of King Richard – and the one that sticks in most people's minds more than four hundred years later.

This book is one of an increasing number seeking to roll back those centuries of misinformation by going back before the creation of the Tudor myths about King Richard, to the records of his time, and considering them with an open mind. The first to do so was written by Sir George Buck in the early 1600s, almost as soon as the last Tudor monarch was dead – and no longer had to be reassured of her rightful place on the throne by slandering her dynasty's predecessor.

I've tried to stay as close as possible to the scant information we do have from the months of turmoil after the death of King Edward IV – the period from April to June 1483 that is covered in the first chapters of this book. Scant information, but major events and conflicting views on them. These first few chapters may be confusing to some readers – but no more confusing than they must have been to the people living at the time. Some of this confusion I've tried to communicate through Matthew and his friends in the Order of the White Boar, themselves trying to make sense of it all, perhaps without much success. If you've reached as far as this note, I hope that means you've read all the way through that – and beyond – to where I was able to focus again on the relative simplicity of Matt's own story – and how it touches and weaves more closely again about that of 'his' Duke – now 'his' King.

All history is interpretation, and historical fiction too. And where reliable evidence isn't available – as for much of the period covered here – gaps have to be filled in. One of the most gaping holes in history is perhaps the mystery of what happened to the two sons of Edward IV, who have become known as the 'Princes in the Tower'. No matter what Shakespeare says – or many historians down to the present day – no one alive now actually knows for certain. All that can be said is that they weren't officially seen in public again after the summer of 1483.

Tudor-era propagandists proclaimed that the boys were murdered in the Tower on the orders of their uncle, by then King Richard III. Interestingly, Henry Tudor himself, their mother Elizabeth Woodville and their sister Elizabeth of York never made such an accusation. No one did during Henry Tudor's reign as Henry VII – almost twenty-five years; at least we don't have evidence of any accusation – and records are relatively numerous and complete from that period. The story only grew and became widespread over the following decades – until, repeated and embellished often enough, it became accepted as 'true history'. This of course suited Elizabeth I, only England's second crowned queen (a woman on the throne?!), and a Protestant one at that, in a period of religious turmoil. She didn't want there to be any doubt that she was on that throne by right, and that her grandfather, Henry Tudor, had won that right to rule

– and from a ruthless, usurping, child-murdering tyrant, as Richard was now made out to be.

History is written by the winner… even, or perhaps particularly, when they themselves usurp the throne illegally…

So what did happen to the 'Princes', Edward and Richard? Today we can only speculate, which is what I have done in the latter part of this book – and also all that any historian can do, given the lack of evidence. Rumours, hearsay – it's all we have. And as Duke Richard says to Matthew, rumours are 'dangerous beasts'.

However, it is possible that a project underway since 2015 may one day find the answers. Philippa Langley, who led the search for King Richard's grave with the Looking for Richard Project, has turned her efforts to the 'Missing Princes Project', seeking evidence from anywhere in Britain and Europe that may shed some light on the mystery. If you can offer help in any way, for example investigating local archives, please contact http://philippalangley.co.uk/missing-princes-project.php.

Many others aim to look again at the real Richard III. In 1924, the Fellowship of the White Boar (which of course influenced the title of my books) was set up to do just that, and was subsequently renamed the Richard III Society, which can be found at www.richardiii.net. More recently another international society has been founded, the Richard III Loyal Supporters, www.r3loyalsupporters.org. Memberships of these groups run into the thousands, and there are many more 'Ricardians' worldwide who may be members of neither.

I have had help and support from, and valuable discussions with, many of them – too many to name individually here without risk of missing any out – but I hope they know I am grateful for their contribution. One or two may even spot themselves somewhere in these pages. I would, however, particularly like to mention historian Matthew Lewis, whose meticulous research and rational blogs have been an excellent guide along the way, and to thank him for one especially apt metaphor! And also Deborah Willemen @MamaMoose_Be for her help with the Flemish. Whatever its faults, social media does a wonderful job of bringing likeminded people together!

Is it strange that a man who has been dead more than five hundred years stirs such interest, even passion in some? For me, it's the continuing injustice of the smears against him, when he's unable to respond or fight back – and when indeed he had few friends and family left to do it for him – that spurred my interest and sympathy.

By what seemed an incredible coincidence, 12 September 2012, the day of the first press conference at which it was announced that King Richard's grave had possibly been discovered, was also the day on which was published the long-awaited report into the tragic deaths of 96 football supporters at Hillsborough in April 1989. The false stories about what happened that day in Sheffield began immediately, with modern tabloid media swinging into action, and they were made 'official' by repetition in the UK Parliament and by apparently 'upstanding' police officers. Those stories sought to place the blame for the tragedy on the Liverpool supporters, to shift the focus away from the failings of those who were really at fault – the authorities, the police themselves. The ones who had control – the ones who could get the 'official' story out there to the public.

Those supporters had family and friends to fight for their good name – and fight they did. Tirelessly, for almost twenty-five years – the time it took for the 'official' story to be overturned and shown to be the lie it was. Such injustices can be reversed – by people with extraordinary courage and determination such as they showed.

This book is dedicated to those people – the families of the 96.

About the author

A Ricardian since a teenager, and following stints as an archaeologist and in publishing, Alex now lives and works in King Richard's own country, not far from his beloved York and Middleham. Much of this book was 'seen' and 'heard' while striding over the nearby heather-clad moors with a loyal hound, 'rescued' in the golden summer of 2012 and named, indecisively but Olympically, Milli Mo Ennis Ohuruogu Murray – Milli for short.

Follow Alex on WordPress @AlexMarchantBlog and on social media – on Facebook at Alex Marchant Author and on Twitter @AlexMarchant84.

Translations of coded text

Qcas og gccb og dcggwpzs – Ozmg
[trans.] Come as soon as possible – Alys

Qb eia ijwcb epmbpmz bpm jwga apwctl . . .
[trans.] It was about whether the boys should be moved from the Tower. I thought it was to stop them being a focus for rebellion, like they have been – but maybe it was about their safety. And with the Duke of Buckingham as Constable of the Tower . . .

Nyrk r nzkty!
[trans.] What a witch!

Fqp'v vgnn Oqvjgt!
[trans.] Don't tell Mother!

Qtdfqyd gnsix rj!
[trans.] Loyalty binds me

Made in the USA
Middletown, DE
15 January 2019